THE DOCTOR AND THE DUCHESS

The Duke's Bastards
Book 3

by

Karyn Gerrard

ARE YOU SIGNED UP FOR DRAGONBLADE'S BLOG?

You'll get the latest news and information on exclusive giveaways, exclusive excerpts, coming releases, sales, free books, cover reveals and more.

Check out our complete list of authors, too!

No spam, no junk. That's a promise!

Sign Up Here

www.dragonbladepublishing.com

Dearest Reader;

Thank you for your support of a small press. At Dragonblade Publishing, we strive to bring you the highest quality Historical Romance from some of the best authors in the business. Without your support, there is no 'us', so we sincerely hope you adore these stories and find some new favorite authors along the way.

Happy Reading!

CEO, Dragonblade Publishing

Additional Dragonblade books by Author Karyn Gerrard

The Duke's Bastards Series
The Detective and the Baroness (Book 1)
The Chef and the Countess (Book 2)
The Doctor and the Duchess (Book 3)

PROLOGUE

Early April, 1898
London, England

DOCTOR DREW HORNSBY wasn't often called to peerage residences since most of his medical practice was spread across various free clinics for the underprivileged. So he was a bit surprised to be summoned to 10 Chapel Street in Belgravia this afternoon. The residence's appearance matched most town houses in the better neighborhoods of London, with marble, stucco, and the accompanying wrought iron terraces. The door opened to reveal a middle-aged man wearing a livery: the butler, no doubt.

"I am Doctor Hornsby. I'm to see the Duke and Duchess of Barnsdale."

The butler showed Drew into the grand hallway replete with crystal chandeliers and marble floors. "I will let His Grace know you are here."

An older man stepped out of a nearby room. Drew immediately disliked the look of him as he possessed an arrogant stance and glared at Drew as if he were horse dung clinging to his boot. The man was of medium height, and his receding hairline showed threads of silver intermingled with the brown shade. Considering the expensive day suit and neatly tied cravat, Drew surmised that this must be the duke.

"No need, Yarrow. Doctor, come with me. You are to attend the duchess."

Drew was led into a plush sitting room decorated with gold

and various hues of blue. He glanced about. "Where is the patient?"

"I want to speak to you before escorting you to the duchess. I have grave concerns about her health and mental state. She—" The duke coughed for several minutes, pulling a silk handkerchief from his pocket to cover his mouth. His face turned red from the force of the coughing.

"Perhaps you also need a doctor's care, Your Grace," Drew offered politely.

"It is nothing, a slight congestion of the chest. I feel fine." The duke waved the handkerchief dismissively before tucking it away in his pocket. "As I was saying, the duchess has been suffering from a prolonged period of melancholy."

"For how long, Your Grace? And do you know why?"

"You are the doctor. It's the reason you were sent for!" the duke snapped. "And how long? A few years, more or less. Anyway, she fell down the stairs, you see."

Drew's inner alarm started to ring. He had attended to enough female patients across the social spectrum to know what 'falling down the stairs' signified. "What about the dukedom physician, Your Grace?"

"I have no need for one."

Drew did not like the sound of that, either. Since when had anyone in the peerage not kept a physician on retainer? Some even had more than one, especially dukes. In his experience, it meant there was something to hide, like bodily and emotional harm. Drew stared into the duke's eyes, seeing a decided aloofness mixed with haughty cruelty. How old was the man, fifty? More? Regardless of the dismissal of his health, Drew observed the dark circles under those cold eyes and a certain pallor to the duke's skin.

With the tip of his finger, Drew pushed his spectacles up the bridge of his nose. "That will be five pounds, Your Grace."

"What? You have not even examined her yet!" the duke barked, clearly annoyed.

"If you wish me to examine the duchess, I require a payment up front. It is my standard practice with new or unknown patients." Who knew how the duke had come across Drew's medical credentials and decided to contact him? Drew was not about to ask.

"Yarrow!" the duke yelled.

The butler stepped into the room. "Yes, Your Grace?"

"Fetch this sawbones five pounds. Be quick about it."

The butler disappeared into the hall, and the duke turned to face Drew. "My wife has not been herself for some time. I believe that an extended stay in a private institution might do her the world of good. The duchess acts like a screeching harpy one moment, or mopes about the place doing nothing but reading books the next. She has also become extremely clumsy. I mean, falling down the stairs. How undignified."

Drew fought to keep his expression neutral. This man was reprehensible, and Drew wished he had asked for ten pounds instead. It was blatantly obvious he required Drew's signature on a report to start the wheels in motion to send the duchess to an asylum. He pulled a notebook from his pocket. "The patient's full name, Your Grace? For my records."

"Selena Seaton Woodhouse, Duchess of Barnsdale. Speaking of the duchess, I believe hysteria is a good summation of her behavior," the duke concluded smugly.

"I would never sign a report on such a short acquaintance or by one examination alone, Your Grace. Besides, with the Lunacy Act of 1890, you need more than two signatures from medical doctors. A legal certification from a magistrate is required, and several clauses must be met, as a patient has the right to appeal." Drew tucked his notebook and pencil in the inside pocket of his coat.

The duke's eyes narrowed, giving Drew a look of pure venom. "You appear to know all about it, but I suppose you would, since you have an insane uncle. You *are* related to the Duke of Gransford; is that not so? If I recall, you're a street urchin adopted by the duke's viscount middle brother. I never understood how a duke's brother could become a viscount, able to sit in the House of Lords. But then, I never cared enough to discover the reason. Equally questionable is how the duke's youngest brother has managed to escape being institutionalized all these years. Or has he finally been carted away to the insane asylum? Spencer Hornsby is his name. Correct?" The duke started coughing violently again, then brought the handkerchief from his pocket, and wiped his mouth.

Drew was not quick to anger. As a medical professional, he had to keep his emotions in check in all situations. This was the first time he was tempted to pummel someone unconscious. "The Duke of Gransford *is* my uncle. My father, Tremain Hornsby, became Viscount Hawkestone through letters patent. The queen bestowed his title on him for his service in the army during the Anglo-Zulu War. As far as my Uncle Spencer, he is happily married and a professor of ancient civilizations."

The butler entered the room and handed Drew a five-pound note. Drew quickly stuffed it in his pocket. The sooner he was gone, the better. He sensed misery in this fancy residence, a deep-seated gloom that permeated the very walls.

"Regardless of the laws, you may be called upon to testify about the duchess's overall health and state of mind," the duke said with a sniff.

"I can hardly make such an assessment on one fleeting examination, Your Grace."

The duke's mouth pulled into a taut line of annoyance. "Well, you have been paid. You might as well have a look at her, at any rate. I daresay this is why I do not have a physician on retainer. Regardless of their training or lack thereof, doctors act too lofty for their station. Come with me, Hornsby." It was a blatant attempt at an insult that Drew chose to ignore.

Drew was taken into another sitting room farther along the hallway. When he entered the room, Drew stopped short. The duchess was one of the most beautiful women he had ever seen.

The way she sat, with her hands resting on her lap and her chin held high, made her look like a portrait painting. With golden-red hair and bright-blue eyes, Selena Seaton Woodhouse possessed the features often attributed to an 'English rose.' She had flawless, fair skin, reddish lips, and a delicate attractiveness that most men desire. Drew had never counted himself among them. Yet, the sight of this lady took his breath away. She was also much younger than her duke husband, by twenty years or more, Drew guessed. The duchess was unequivocally stunning.

Keeping his features as impartial as possible, he came to stand before the duchess. "Your Grace." Drew inclined his head slightly. "I'm Doctor Drew Hornsby. Your husband tells me you had an accident."

There was a slight twitch of her lips, but she did not reply.

"I will need to examine you." Drew turned toward the duke. "We need privacy, Your Grace."

"I think not, Hornsby. Get on with it," the duke snapped.

"I insist. You may return in five minutes. By then, Your Grace, I will have completed the physical exam."

The duke gave the duchess a warning look, then stepped outside and closed the door.

Drew sat beside the duchess on the sofa. "Did you fall down the stairs?" he murmured as he opened his physician's bag.

No reply. The duchess stared straight ahead.

"If your husband has hurt you," he continued hurriedly, "tell me. I can help."

"You cannot, legally or otherwise." The duchess turned and gazed at him. They were sitting close enough that he could detect an enticing odor of vanilla and almonds. "He's never laid a hand on me until today. His abuse was always verbal, when we spoke at all. In this instance, he took it too far. It will never happen again." The duchess's steely tone made it plain that she was not a delicate hothouse flower.

"How did he injure you?" Drew whispered, in case they were overheard.

"He knocked me to the floor and kicked me—once," the duchess replied in an equally low voice. "And, as I said, it will never happen again. I will see to it."

God above. "Can I call the police for you or contact a family member?"

"No," she hissed through clenched teeth. Then the duchess sighed. "Thank you for offering, but no. I will handle this *my* way."

As Drew was fully aware, the police never interfered with a "domestic dispute" until it had gone too far, which was usually too late for the victim. The laws were not fair to women and children, despite slight improvements and protections.

Barnsdale paced outside the door like a restless tiger. Drew leaned in and whispered, "Your Grace, your husband claims you suffer from melancholia. A warning. The duke mentioned placing you in an asylum. Beware."

Her perfectly shaped eyebrows arched in surprise. "Did he? Thank you for telling me."

More loudly, Drew said, "Can you remove your gown, Your Grace?"

"You will have to assist me," she replied.

He leaned in again, his mouth inches from her ear. "Listen, if you ever need my assistance, come see me at 4—"

"No," she replied emphatically in the same low tone as his. "Do *not* give your address. You do not want to be involved with this. Make your examination, then depart, and do not look back."

After she unbuttoned the tea gown, Drew assisted her in pulling it off her shoulders. She grimaced as he peeled the clothing and undergarments away further. The duchess held her corset close to her chest. Drew could already see the reddish marks indicating blood collected under the skin. The discolorations were evident on her right arm, where the duke had grabbed her. There was also a large welt on her right side, no doubt from the kick. Drew's blood boiled. There was nothing that turned his bile more than the mistreatment of women and children.

Unfortunately, he'd witnessed more than his share in the past few years of his practice.

At that moment, the duke entered the room with such force that the door banged against the wall. "Finish your examination, Hornsby."

"You have taken quite the tumble, Your Grace," Drew said in a normal tone. "These red marks will turn to purplish-black bruises. In five days, they will turn greenish yellow. In ten days, a yellow-brown color, until they fade altogether. I detect no swelling. Are you having trouble breathing or experiencing pain when you cough?"

"No," she murmured. Then she coughed. "No pain."

Drew pulled his stethoscope from his bag, breathed onto the chest piece to warm it, and placed it against her skin, to listen to her lungs. "Please breathe in and out." She did it several times, and her lungs sounded normal. He set aside his stethoscope, leaned forward, and felt all around her ribs.

Drew was not used to having physical reactions to patients. The duchess was the first. He admonished himself for it, for he was a professional and had to act as such. But each time the tips of his fingers trailed across her ribcage, touching her silky skin, his heart rate sped up. No woman had caused this reaction before, patient or not. At least, not to this extent. Drew immediately sat upright and tucked his stethoscope into his bag. "You have no broken bones, Your Grace, but you will be sore for several days. I recommend bed rest for the next week with plenty of willow bark tea and a light dinner of boiled chicken and vegetables. I can return in three days to—"

"That will not be necessary, Hornsby. Your work here is done for all the good it is to me. Yarrow will see you out," the duke stated. He snapped his fingers, and the butler entered the room.

"A maid should assist Her Grace to her room," Drew instructed.

"It will be done. Goodbye, Doctor," the duke replied contemptuously.

It was a firm dismissal if he had ever heard one. Drew stood, gathered his bag, and turned toward the duchess. Taking her hand, he palmed his business card to her along with a small packet of willow bark powder, hopefully without the duke seeing it. Even that slight brush of skin against skin made his heart pound double time. Drew released her, and she trailed the tips of her fingers across his palm, which nearly made him moan aloud from the contact. The duchess then closed her hand into a fist, hiding the card.

"Willow bark for any pain, add ten grains to a cup of tea when needed. Good afternoon, Your Grace." Drew turned and exited the room. It was not like him to go against a patient's express wishes, such as giving her his address when she'd firmly said no, but the duchess had his card in case she needed to contact him.

But she never did.

Over the following months, he often thought of the lovely duchess, with her determined, courageous tone, and wondered how she had fared. He had worried about her well-being. Ultimately, what did it matter if he found her attractive and she stirred his heart?

A married duchess was not for him.

Drew was unlikely to ever see her again. Or so he thought…

CHAPTER ONE

Early February, 1899
London, England

SELENA SEATON WOODHOUSE, her tattered wool skirt fluttering, sprinted as fast as her booted feet could carry her. She was less than a mile away from her rented rooms on Victoria Street, but with Lucian Sharpe's criminal lackeys hot on her trail, she was doing her best to outwit them among the labyrinth of alleys and courtyards that made up Devil's Acre, a slum area nestled behind Westminster Abbey.

"Bloody do-gooder," one of the men yelled. "We'll catch ya!"

They hadn't captured her yet. For over two months, Selena had defied the rookery boss, Lucian Sharpe, and his felonious minions to administer her charity work. She had never met the man, but had heard enough about him from those she assisted. Many had told her Sharpe was angry about her meddling in his business. And how had she done that, exactly?

Selena ran across a courtyard onto Duck Lane. The path was narrow, only wide enough for one carriage. The place seemed all the more perilous with the buildings so crowded together. Swiftly, she removed her second-hand winter cloak, hid it behind a pile of crates, then lifted the sizeable woolly shawl from her shoulders, and covered her head before ducking into Finnian's Chop House. Selena had heard Lucian Sharpe himself owned this grubby tavern. What better way to hide than under the villain's very nose?

Selena sat at a small table near the door. A young man with

fair hair and wearing an apron approached her. "What can I get you?" he asked politely. "The special today is beef stew. It costs five pence or six if you want bread."

"I'll have me a bowl of beef brown and a crust," she murmured, mimicking the accents and slang she had often heard these past two months. "Do ye serve tea, lad?"

"Aye. Two pennies."

Selena reached into her skirt pocket and dropped a handful of pennies on the table. "'Tis enuff?"

"Aye. I'll bring the stew and the rest."

Selena looked around the crowded tavern. She had only been here once when she first arrived in Devil's Acre. It appeared cleaner and brighter, though any slight improvement would have made the grimy pub more welcoming. It had been a little over two months since she had left her ailing duke husband, sneaking away under the cover of night. Selena knew her mental state was deteriorating the longer she stayed with that horrid man. And so she'd left, feeling that the only way to repair the damage done within was to cleanse the dark places in her soul by doing what she could to help others and learning to stand up for herself when warranted.

Keeping in character, she wiped her nose with her sleeve and swung her gaze to the far corner near the massive stone fireplace. There was Sharpe, holding court, as always. She had heard that was his habit, and he certainly fit the description she had been given. This slum rookery was his kingdom. And though she wasn't sure why, Selena had angered Sharpe to such an extent that he wanted her gone from the area. But she wasn't ready to leave. Not quite yet.

Devil's Acre was close to the River Thames, built along the River Tyburn, which was more of a stream than an actual river. Devil's Acre was a labyrinth of lanes, courts, and alleys laden with squalor and disease, and Sharpe was the head of it. He sat with his back to the wall to observe the tavern's doings and to watch everyone who came in and out of the pub. The criminal was partly hidden in shadow, but Selena felt his malevolent presence from across the room.

A man wearing a patched coat stumbled toward her. "Buy me a drink, love," he slurred. "Spare a penny for a thirsty old man. Even a ha'penny."

The waiter returned, holding a tray. "Charlie, hie off and leave the paying customers alone. Sit in the back, and I'll bring you bread and cheese, yeah?"

"Cheers, young Teddy." The man touched his forelock and disappeared into the shadows. "Yer kindness itself."

"He doesn't mean any harm, miss," Teddy said as he laid the food before her. "Eight coppers for the meal." His kindness was a welcome contrast to the unlawful elements that surrounded her. He must be a new employee.

Selena waved her hand toward the small pile of coins on the table. She watched as Teddy counted and slipped the money into his apron pocket. He was honest, at least, and younger than she first supposed. She took a spoonful of stew. It was warm, laden with juicy cuts of beef. "'Tis excellent," she murmured.

"Thank you, miss. I made it. I'm the new chef at Finnian's. Good, hearty food at reasonable prices. Tell your friends." Teddy touched his forelock and moved to wait on other customers.

Selena greeted the warmth that spread through her. The generous bowl of stew was delicious, brimming with celery, onion, carrots, peas, and potatoes. The cold outside had settled deep in her bones, so anything heated and hearty was welcome. What an enhancement, indeed, for the tea was also hot, and the thickly sliced bread was fresh and tasty with a golden crust.

Three men entered Finnian's and headed toward Sharpe's table. The din of voices quieted enough that she could make out the conversation.

"We lost her. Again."

"You bloody incompetent plonkers. How hard is it to find one fool woman wearing a cape?" Sharpe yelled. That silenced the customers.

One of the men said, "Well, I don't think she always wears a cape, guv. Maybe she's in disguise."

The man wasn't wrong. Selena often wore disguises when on the streets. She only wore a cape to stand out and remind those who didn't want her around that she was, indeed—here. Selena kept her head down and continued eating the stew.

"I came to tell you that Nigel Graham is gone," the man continued. "His rooms are empty. Wife and kiddies gone as well. Neighbors said the Angel's been to Nigel's more than once. Just like with Charlie Bonner. I know you'd want to hear about this, as Nigel ran your best buzz crew."

Buzz? Oh, no. Nigel was a cutpurse, a pickpocket. And he had worked for Sharpe. Nigel never said. And Bonner, too? No wonder Sharpe had his men looking for her.

Sharpe banged his fist on the table. "That's two gone, along with Hannah Clark. I want this angel found."

"I offered rewards to anyone willing to give her up," the man continued. "But they ain't willing. 'The angel does good works,' one said to me. Others say they never heard of her."

Most people never heard of her because Selena kept a small, tight group of individuals she assisted—those who welcomed the help and promised not to snitch to the criminals. So far, the strategy had worked. Even if some of those she helped worked— or *used* to work—for Sharpe.

Sharpe pushed the table aside and stood. He was rather good-looking with his tall, lean but muscular frame, flawless features, and golden hair. The chilling effect of his presence was palpable, and his handsome appearance a stark contrast to his true nature. Under that glossy outer exterior lay a black soul and a pile of cinders where his heart should be, or so she assumed. And that sent shivers down Selena's spine.

"Let's go upstairs. We'll discuss what to do next," Sharpe grumbled.

As they exited through the rear, Selena let out a breath she didn't realize she'd been holding. She continued eating, the tension slowly dissipating. Seeing Sharpe full-on reminded her of another tall, muscular, good-looking man with a similar shade of golden hair.

Doctor Drew Hornsby.

The good doctor wore gold spectacles, had kind blue eyes, and a deep, sympathetic voice. When she first met him, she was in no condition to notice a man's enticing features, but how could he not make an impression? Beyond his empathetic nature, he possessed a boyish handsomeness, the kind that he would carry his entire life, always looking younger than he was. How many times had Selena looked at his card these past months? How often had she been tempted to contact him and take him up on his offer of support?

There were reasons why she hadn't. For one, she didn't know the doctor well enough to entirely trust him. But more importantly, she believed that she had to do this herself, find her path to redemption. Draining the last of the tea and placing the enamel mug on the table, Selena slipped outside, still holding the shawl over her head. When she returned to the place she'd hidden her cloak, it was gone. But she wasn't concerned. She had other capes. Hopefully, the cloak would be useful to someone.

Whistling under her breath, Selena slowly ambled toward nearby Victoria Street.

⟫⟫⟫⟪⟪⟪

THE BALLROOM AT the Langham Hotel, a grand and opulent space with high ceilings and ornate chandeliers, was not a high-society social situation Drew Hornsby would purposely seek. Still, he was here with his father, Viscount Hawkestone, who had returned to London six days ago to convene a meeting of his progressive caucus even though Parliament was still in recess. The room was filled with political and social elites, at least those who had not retired to their country estates for the winter months. It was also Drew's first society appearance as Baronet Hornsby. That honor had been bestowed upon him by Queen Victoria last month. He could still not believe such an important recognition had come to a—what had the Duke of Barnsdale called him?—an orphaned street urchin.

His past was something Drew often tried not to think about. The first ten years of his life, he had lived in wretched poverty with his mother, always moving about, with each new place worse than the last. Living in filth, starving, begging for scraps from merchants…Drew inwardly shuddered at the memories.

"ANY EXCUSE FOR a party, what? Jolly good revelry!" The slurred words of a stranger tore him from his tortured thoughts. The man downed a glass of scotch before shuffling toward the bar for another.

Drew nodded politely, then glanced about the crowded room until he located his father.

Tremain Hornsby, Viscount Hawkestone, walked toward Drew carefully, using his cane to guide him. His father's war injury had not improved over the years, making traversing increasingly tricky. If he felt any pain, he never complained. If it weren't for this generous man adopting him, Drew shuddered to think what might have happened to him.

"I forgot to mention, the new beard suits you," his father stated as he came to stand beside him.

Drew subconsciously stroked his close-cropped beard. "Most doctors have them. I wanted to add a little age to my appearance instead of looking like I am barely out of short trousers."

His father chuckled. "So it does, Doctor. How are you holding up? Has the party annoyed you as yet?"

"I am not sure why I agreed to attend," Drew murmured.

"Because London wishes to see the queen's freshly minted baronet," his father teased. "You needed to make an appearance in society, and now was as good a time as any."

"I attended the queen at your recommendation. Why, I am not certain, as she has numerous physicians, apothecaries, and other medical staff to care for her." He did not want to inform his father that the rumors were true and that the queen was quite ill. Drew guessed she might live a year or two, but no longer. Drew wouldn't be surprised if she soon ceased all public appearances, not that she made that many in past years. The queen had always held the Hornsbys in high regard.

"The queen has close to two dozen people on her medical staff. Queen Victoria has often knighted or made her physicians baronets through the years," his father added.

"But *I* am not on retainer," Drew replied.

"I sing your praises every time I am in the queen's company, which unfortunately, isn't as often as late. She is well aware of your charity medical work. *That* is why you were granted a baronetcy and why she asked to see you. The queen wanted to give you a thorough inspection. I am proud of you, son. Or shall I say, 'Sir Drew?'"

Drew winced inwardly. Never in his wildest dreams as a young child living in wretched poverty with his dear mother had he imagined such a scenario. Becoming a doctor, meeting the queen, and her royal highness deeming him worthy of being a baronet. *Unimaginable.*

"And it is a hereditary title," his father continued. "When you marry, any son you may have will also become a baronet when you pass on. You deserve the honor. And although a baronet is not part of the peerage, you are now firmly part of London society, like it or not. There are advantages to having powerful connections, which will further aid your charity work. I would like you to join my progressive group. I know I asked you before, but circumstances have changed. There is no need to answer now, but think about it."

"I shall."

"Now, come meet a few key people. The Duke of Chellenham is here."

Drew perked up and glanced about the crowded room. "Is he? Where?"

"I will seek him out momentarily. Have you had any chance to talk with him since you discovered your mutual blood ties?"

Damon Cranston, the new duke, was the only legitimate offspring of the previous duke, Edward Cranston. Drew had only recently discovered he was part of a vast group of progeny from the late Duke of Chellenham. Drew was still coming to terms with the revelation. His mother had never told him who his father was, but she revealed the secret to Tremain Hornsby when he was a vicar attending her deathbed. Should Drew be angry and resentful that his father had kept this secret from him since adopting him at age ten? He only told Drew a few months ago, after Edward Cranston had passed. Once Drew discovered what a contemptible, loathsome man the old duke was, he was glad his father had never broached the subject earlier.

"Drew?" his father questioned, pulling him from his thoughts.

"Yes, on a few occasions. I was at Chellenham's for dinner two weeks ago. He and the duchess were gracious and welcoming."

"I am glad to hear it." His father caught Chellenham's eye and waved at him. Damon made his way through the crowd toward them. They all shook hands.

"Good to see you, Drew. My lord," Damon offered.

"Call me Tremain, please. We are related through Drew."

"That we are, Tremain. And how are you, Sir Drew?" Damon winked.

"Overwhelmed, but adjusting—on a number of fronts."

"I understand completely," Damon replied soberly. "There have been many revelations lately, including newly discovered blood ties. How is Liam Hallahan settling into married life?"

Yet another newly discovered half brother. "All is well. He and Celia have great plans for their restaurant and the Hallahan Initiative, their charity." Drew turned toward his father and said, "Liam is making a presentation for the Rakes of St. Regent's Park's monthly meeting on the 17th. I introduced Liam to Damon three days ago at Liam's restaurant."

"Bloody good food, I daresay," Damon interjected.

"Drew took me there four days ago to meet Liam Hallahan, and I concur about the food. Since many members of the Rakes are part of my progressive group, perhaps that charity initiative should be something we look at," his father ventured.

"As the chief medical officer of the initiative, I concur," Drew replied.

"And as chief member of the Rakes, I also agree," Damon added.

"Then let us do all we can to further such worthy plans. Look about the room, Drew," his father instructed. "Money and influence are needed to make those well-intentioned strategies a reality."

Drew frowned. "I am neither a politician nor a dealmaker nor wish to become one—or both."

"But while moving about society, a person must *think* like one," his father stated. "Do what I do: smile, no matter how inane the conversation is, be polite but distant, shake hands, and remember everyone's name. Do all that, and you will find some like-minded men and women who wish to do their part to assist the unfortunate. Do you not agree, Damon?"

"Absolutely. Believe it or not, there are a few in the aristocracy and upper class who have a genuine desire to help. You just have to find them."

His father and half brother had a point. *Play the game.* It galled Drew to no end, but thanks to the queen, he had been pulled further into London society's greedy and arrogant clutches, whether he liked it or not.

Damon leaned in and whispered, "However, there are those that are to be avoided at all costs. See that cluster of garish and bejeweled standing by the ferns? Stay well clear. The older woman with the garish red wig is Viscountess Chesley, and the short, slender man standing obediently at her elbow is her viscount husband. The older couple next to them? Viscount and Viscountess Weybridge. All of them are shameless gossipers and generally unpleasant."

Weybridge and his wife looked to be in their mid- to late-seventies, and both used canes. "They keep glancing over here," Drew murmured.

"They no doubt wish to find out about you and your acquaintances and their recent marriages while slipping in veiled insults. They will not come over as long as I am here. The whiff of notoriety still hangs about me," Damon smiled.

His father chuckled. "The same was said of me back in the day."

This is precisely why Drew never wanted to be involved with society, even though he became a member of the Hornsby family and could hardly avoid it, try as he might. Thank God his family seldom came to London, so he had been spared most of these stuffy social situations. The incessant gossiping and backstabbing were enough to turn his bile.

"The prevailing gossip concerns the Duke and Duchess of Barnsdale, the duke's illness, and the duchess's sudden disappearance," Damon stated.

Drew started at the mention of the duchess, whose beauty and courage instantly came to mind. His heart skipped a beat at the thought of her. When Drew had traveled to Devil's Acre with Liam Hallahan a few weeks ago, Drew could have sworn he saw the Duchess of Barnsdale running about the grimy alleys. It was only a fleeting glimpse—probably a figment of his exhausted mind. But the belief that it *might* have been her had nagged at him so much that he recently revisited the area. Again, he thought he saw the duchess, but he lost sight of her before approaching her.

"I was called to the duke's residence to provide medical assistance last month," Drew murmured. "It is true he is ill." *Perhaps even fatally ill.* "I should make another visit to follow up." But the duke had waved away any closer examination, irritated that the butler, Yarrow, had sent for Drew in the first place. Drew had instructed Yarrow to find the duke a physician or at least a nurse to offer around-the-clock care. Since he hadn't heard anything further, Drew assumed a doctor had been found.

"I do not know Barnsdale all that well," his father said. "Not the sort that carries on any friendly conversation."

That was an understatement.

"Come," Damon said, pointing toward the bar. "Let us have a drink and avoid the gossips. I want to hear more about the charity work and our ever-expanding family. I say here and now that my door is always open. Neither of you should ever wait for an invitation. My home is yours."

"Dashed generous, Damon," his father replied. "And the same for the Hornsbys. We must plan for a get-together when everyone returns to town."

His father and Damon continued conversing, but it faded to the background as Drew's thoughts slid to Selena Woodhouse, the Duchess of Barnsdale. As they strolled toward the bar, Drew couldn't help wondering how she was faring. And where could she be? In a few days, he would return again to Devil's Acre and make a more thorough inspection, perhaps even making inquiries among the populace.

Drew was determined to get to the bottom of this mystery. For as much as he tried to dispel her, the lovely duchess was never far from his mind.

CHAPTER TWO

"**Y**OUR GRACE!"

Penny Holdsworth, Selena's trusted lady's maid and companion, guided the duchess to the upholstered chair before the fire. Selena sat, trembling from the cold.

"What happened to your wool cape?" Penny asked. "Don't tell me it was stolen!"

"I had to toss it. Those horrid men were hot on my heels." Selena tore off her gloves and blew into her hands in a vain attempt to warm them. Her gloves were too thin, and the bitter cold had seeped through the material.

Penny grabbed a blanket from the sofa and draped it over Selena's shoulders. "Mark my words, those miscreants will catch you sooner rather than later, Your Grace."

"Penny, please don't call me that. Someone will overhear. I am Mrs. Beecham, widow of a sea captain."

Penny smiled wryly, pointing to the book on the end table. "Did you get the name from another of your romantic adventure stories?"

"Perhaps. *The Buccaneer and the Lady* is quite a rollicking read. You should try it," Selena replied. She pulled the blanket about her more securely. "I should not be feeling a chill. I had a lovely bowl of stew and a warm mug of tea at Finnian's."

Penny gasped. "You ate in that crook's pub?"

Selena smiled slyly. "Lucian Sharpe was there, too, irritated that his men couldn't find the Golden Angel."

Penny pulled a wooden chair next to Selena and sat on it. "You've angered that criminal in some way."

"It seems I've inadvertently diverted some of his best pickpockets toward a legitimate path. I assume that interfered with his making money."

"Right. We're going to have a serious talk. It's past time. You haven't been yourself for quite a while. Not since the—you cannot deny the incident is the reason for your melancholy state these past few years," Penny said softly.

"I don't deny it. That heartbreak, along with my intolerable situation with Barnsdale, affected me deeply."

"I understand why you ran away from the duke. He's a detestable old git who never treated you kindly or respectfully. I didn't blame you for taking money from his safe, your jewels, and other bits and bobs because you deserved it for what you had to put up with."

"But?"

"I don't understand why you're here, one street away from the slum known as Devil's Acre, acting like some fairy godmother. We are only three miles away from the duke! I think we should have traveled farther. It's not too late. We could find decent rooms in North London, or in a nearby village or town. Why here? You've never explained it properly. You know I'd follow you to the end of the earth. But I deserve to understand your reasons."

Selena shivered from the cold. The fire was doing little to warm her up. "I am not sure myself."

"Try. Please."

"Fairy godmother?" Selena chuckled softly. Then she sobered. "I understand I can only assist a few people, as I do not have enough money to aid everyone. I've selected a few dozen deserving families, and they are grateful for my help. A sack of pennies, some bread, vegetables, and cheese. They will not give me up to the rookery boss, Sharpe."

Penny shook her head. "You're far too trusting. When threatened with bodily harm, they will give up anything. Poverty will cause the most trustworthy people to do terrible things. Remember that. It's smart to wear disguises, but how long can you keep up this ruse? And what does all this have to do with the duke?"

Selena sighed. "Ah, yes. Barnsdale. I never wanted the marriage; my parents hounded me until I gave in. I was unhappy from the day of our wedding. You know that, because you have been with me since that first day. Barnsdale hiring you was the only decent thing he ever did for me."

Penny smiled warmly. "Thank you for that, Mrs. B. You've been kind to me despite your misery."

"And I was miserable. From the moment he came to my bed. And a-a-after—" Selena faltered. Recalling all this tore her heart in two. Speaking this openly showed how much she trusted and respected Penny. Selena carried a sizeable emotional weight on her shoulders. Talking about it lessened the burden to a point.

"After losing the baby?" Penny offered gently.

"Yes. I never told you this, but the doctor in attendance said he wasn't sure if I could have any more children and that I needed time to heal. I'm sorry to speak about such personal things. You are all I have."

"You know you can talk to me about anything. I know there are days you cannot bear to discuss that time, but talking about such upset helps to heal. Now, the doctor?"

"Because of the physician's vague diagnosis, Barnsdale got frustrated. He wanted an heir, and when it appeared that wasn't likely, the verbal abuse started in earnest. We never talked about what happened; perhaps some of that was on me."

"Aye, I witnessed some of his nasty disposition aimed toward you," Penny observed sadly.

"I never told you this either, it's so personal. When Barnsdale returned to my room, I became physically ill. Who wants to bed a woman who casts up her accounts all over the sheets? Eventually, he stopped coming to my bedchamber. I had won that battle, at least."

"It was a bad time, Mrs. B," Penny said, tsking. "Did he hurt you physically beyond that time last year?"

"No. Just the once. But once is more than enough."

Penny shook her head. "We should've departed long ago."

"I was not ready, emotionally and otherwise." Selena pulled the blanket to her chin. "I had to make plans, first and foremost. When he wasn't looking, I watched as he opened his safe numerous times until I learned the combination. I also saw that he never counted the pound notes; he just tossed them in. His 'mad money,' he called it. Over several months, I started stashing away my jewels and expensive bric-a-brac to sell." She sighed. "Remember the young doctor who came to examine me last spring?"

"Oh, yes. Handsome he was, with caring eyes. The young man wore spectacles, if I recall. It made him look even more appealing in my book," Penny said, chuckling.

Yes, he was *very* appealing—the first man to ever elicit any reaction from her. Her heart stuttered to life—albeit briefly. "Doctor Hornsby told me in confidence that Barnsdale wanted to place me in a private asylum. I knew then that I had to accelerate my plan to leave. Barnsdale must have come across a legal impediment to mental incarceration because he never followed through on his evil scheme, thank goodness. And when Barnsdale became ill, and kept mostly to his bed, I saw my chance to escape. Thankfully, you came with me."

Penny clasped her hands and rested them on her lap. "You never said a word about that. How disturbing it is that the duke wanted to place you in an asylum. What a miserable man. Anyway, I couldn't let you leave all by yourself."

Selena exhaled. "What does it say about me that I abandoned an invalid? What about in sickness and in health? I can't help feeling guilty about it when I give it some thought."

"None of that, now," Penny said decisively. "Don't you forget he shoved you to the floor and kicked you—hard. It would have occurred again. You know it. He never apologized, did he?"

"No, but then we never shared any conversation of consequence. That is when he called in Doctor Hornsby and mentioned putting me away."

Selena had recognized the Hornsby name and, looking it up later in *Debrett's Peerage*, discovered he was related to the Duke of Gransford and Viscount Hawkestone. *That* was the main reason why she'd never contacted him for assistance. In her experience, peers tended to stick together.

And what did she know about the doctor? Nothing at all. *If* she confided in him, he could tattle to her husband or innocently let something slip to his aristocratic relatives, and they might contact Barnsdale. Regardless, she'd kept Hornsby's card. Why, she was not sure. Perhaps it was his generous offer of support and the slim possibility that he could be trusted if the situation warranted it. This was all rather vexing.

"Then you did right. But it still doesn't answer why *here*? Why assist those in need?"

"There are plenty in London in dire straits, Penny—especially the children. As a young girl, I read about Devil's Acre in the newspaper. Granted, the area is not as large as it used to be, but I never forgot the horrifying stories of poverty. I want to make a difference. I want to feel alive, even just a tiny amount. Also, using Barnsdale's money gives me a fragment of satisfaction. I have lived too long as a porcelain doll, stored in a dusty cupboard, only to be brought out to show off in front of Barnsdale's wealthy contemporaries."

Penny clucked sympathetically. "And what do we do when the duke's money runs out? You have me checking the papers every day to see if his death notice is there. He lingers, and for how long? Do we know for sure he is even dying? What if he isn't as ill as you suppose? What if he sets the police on you or hires one of those private investigators to track you down? Some of them are very talented. If you return to Belgravia *after* his death, what is your explanation for disappearing? Does that old bugger have an heir?"

Selena's head spun from the multitude of questions. "I have no idea if there's an heir. He never said, and I never cared enough to ask. I assume not, since he tried his best to get an heir off me. As for why I departed, I will say I had a breakdown and needed time to recover." *Which is not far from the truth.* It was a large part of why she left. She felt herself slipping away, not physically, but mentally. To Selena's thinking, the only way to save her soul was to escape.

Penny shook her head. "They will ask for proof. A letter from a doctor or a private sanctuary. What then?"

"Oh, Penny. I will cross that particular bridge when I come to it. As for the reason I assist those in need… Beyond the fact that those unfortunate people are in need of aid, it is therapeutic to *me*. A balm to my damaged soul. Helping others assists *me* in recovery. Do you understand?"

"Aye," Penny whispered. "I do understand. What you're doing is commendable. Perhaps assisting children specifically helps you deal with the loss of your baby."

Selena nodded. Penny had the right of it. "Regarding that assistance, I will need you to buy me a pair of men's trousers. I cannot run in skirts. I will need a man's oversized coat and one of those caps with the peak. Oh, and better gloves, preferably with a fur lining."

Penny's eyebrows shot skyward. "Men's clothes? Oh, my giddy aunt!"

"Moving about in long skirts, petticoats, and capes is difficult, particularly in snow. I think I am five inches over five feet—"

"You're *seven* inches over five feet, Mrs. B," Penny replied.

"That is as tall as some men."

"Very well. I'll take your measurements later. Let's pull the sofa closer to the fire, and you can have a bit of a lie-down. You're still shivering. I'll fetch the quilt from your bed."

"But the sofa is where you sleep," Selena said.

"I don't mind if you use it for a few hours. Besides, look—"

Penny pointed to the window at the opposite end of the room, where the small kitchen was located. "The sun will set soon, and it's snowing. You don't want to go back out in that."

Penny again made a valid point. What would Selena have done without her companion? At times, the middle-aged woman was her only link to the outside world and her only friend. Social events in these past years had been few and far between. When she reconnected with her school chums, Corrine and Celia, this past November, it had given her that final piece of courage to leave Barnsdale. How strange it was that the three of them were in unhappy, arranged marriages to older men. Selena thought those types of marriages went out of fashion during the Napoleonic Wars. *Apparently not.*

However, before she left, she had read in the paper about Corrine's baron husband being murdered. Selena hadn't looked at a newspaper since. She must write to Celia soon and send a note to Corrine. She could visit Corrine, but Barnsdale knew of her baroness friend and where she lived. What if Selena's cruel husband threatened her friends? No, they must be protected. Corrine and Celia had their own problems. Besides, Selena had to do this alone.

Once they slid the sofa closer to the fire, Penny assisted Selena out of her coat, wool dress, and undergarments and into her flannel nightgown.

"There now. Get under the covers," Penny soothed as she tucked Selena in. "And you get some rest."

Selena drifted into the twilight of slumber. Her last thoughts were of Doctor Hornsby and his long, elegant fingers brushing across her waist as he examined her. And how his gentle touch had elicited a reaction. It did not mean anything—the last twitching of her near-dead heart. Or did it?

Hard as she tried to put the handsome doctor out of her mind, he kept popping back in—at least in her dreams.

CHAPTER THREE

The next morning…

BEFORE DREW VENTURED to Devil's Acre, he decided it would be wise to visit the ailing Duke of Barnsdale. He did not know why he felt the need, because he was not the duke's physician. But Drew was also curious. Had the duchess returned home? He rang the bell, and the butler, Yarrow, opened the door.

"Doctor Hornsby. Do come in. How nice to see you again."

"How does the duke fare?" Drew asked as he removed his hat and handed it to the butler.

"There has been no improvement. Perhaps it is a little worse. Nurse Gretchen is upstairs with His Grace."

"Good, you hired a nurse, then. What about a doctor?"

Yarrow shook his head. "The duke would only agree to the nurse. May I congratulate you on becoming a baronet, Sir Drew?"

The announcement had just been published in the newspapers, much to Drew's chagrin. "Thank you. But since I'm here in a medical capacity, please call me Doctor Hornsby."

"As you wish, Doctor," Yarrow replied as he hung Drew's wool coat on the hook of the hallway tree.

"When last we spoke, you mentioned your intent to contact the duke's solicitor. Have you done so?" Drew asked.

"I have, Doctor. Mr. Mecklenberg released funds to pay the nurse and asked me to engage a doctor. Would you take on the position? Since the duke hired you before, perhaps he will not object."

It would mean checking in more often, even daily, Drew

realized. But as much as he disliked the duke, he would never refuse medical treatment and care, though, at this stage, there was not much Drew could do. "I accept, Yarrow. Has Mr. Mecklenberg come by?"

"No, he has not, Doctor."

"I would send a message to him today and strongly suggest he visit to get the duke's affairs in order. Are there moments when the duke is lucid?"

"On and off, Doctor. More so in the late morning."

"The solicitor should visit at that time. And soon. Has anyone heard from the duchess?"

Yarrow sadly shook his head. "Nothing, Doctor, and it has been over two months now. The solicitor has not heard from her, either. I had hoped Penny Holdsworth, the duchess's lady's maid, would contact me, but she has not."

Drew whirled about to face Yarrow. "The duchess did not leave alone?"

"No, Doctor. Penny departed with the duchess. I am glad Her Grace has someone to look after her."

So was Drew. It eased his mind somewhat. "I will examine the duke now."

"I know it is in bad taste to discuss money, but the solicitor said to mention he will pay any doctor forty pounds for the next two months. He said to let him know if more is needed beyond that."

"The price is more than fair, and between you and me, Yarrow, I doubt the duke will live past that timeline. I will seek you out before I leave."

"Very good, Doctor."

Drew climbed the stairs and entered the duke's bedchamber. As soon as Drew crossed the threshold, Nurse Gretchen stood. She had a pleasant countenance and looked to be in her early forties.

"Good morning, Doctor Hornsby."

"Nurse. How is the duke?"

"He's asleep at the moment," she said in a low voice. "He has been in considerable pain. I went to the apothecary's shop to fill the last laudanum prescription. It's losing its effectiveness. Also, he's spitting up blood more often now when he coughs. As for nourishment, he manages beef broth and not much else."

Drew glanced at the duke. The man wheezed with each expelled breath and had lost at least two stone, yet his face was swollen. *That* was not a good sign. "Nausea?"

"Yes, Doctor. He has frequent bouts. He finds it hard to swallow, so I give him broth more than anything."

Drew took the duke's hand. It was clammy to the touch. "Clubbed fingers," Drew murmured, which indicated a condition of the heart or lungs, particularly lung cancer. Drew gently laid the duke's hand against the quilt, then felt the lymph nodes in his neck. They weren't swollen. Perhaps the cancer hadn't spread elsewhere. Regardless, it was likely the duke would soon die of lung metastasis.

"I listened to his heart. The beat has grown weaker these past few weeks," the nurse said gravely.

The duke was probably suffering from the beginnings of heart failure, as well, which would hasten his demise more than the cancer. "I will examine him when he awakens." Looking around the room, Drew was impressed by the cleanliness and the fresh air. "You have cared for the duke well, Nurse. I hope they're compensating you satisfactorily for your dedication."

"They are, Doctor. I'm in the connecting room, and they bring up my meals on a tray. The staff is also very efficient in responding to my requests regarding the duke. The maids help me change his sheets daily and tidy the room when I ask. We keep the fire going but also open the window fifteen minutes every hour, just as you instructed in your written notes."

"Well done." Drew pointed to the doorway that led to the connecting room, and Nurse Gretchen followed him inside, closing the door behind her. The room was pleasant, with lilac-and-gold wallpaper, and white provincial furniture. "The duchess's room?"

"Yes, Doctor. The servants moved her possessions into storage. Do you know if she will return before the duke worsens further? Yarrow tells me that he has heard nothing."

"Alas, I have no news, either. As for the duke, I will be coming every day or every other day from now on. We will start with morphine injections soon. Yarrow is contacting the duke's solicitor. It's time to make arrangements."

"Bitch!" a hoarse voice called out from the next room.

Drew's eyebrows arched. "Is he calling for you?"

The nurse shook her head. "No. He is calling for his wife. He says that every time he awakens from a nap."

"Selena, you dozy mare!"

Even on his deathbed, the duke continued to be a miserable bastard. Why he used cockney slang was puzzling. *The mind acts in bizarre ways when a person is sick and dying.* "We had best attend him."

They entered the room. The duke was propped up with several pillows. As soon as he made eye contact with Drew, his lips curled. "What the hell are you doing here?" he rasped. "Glorying in my downfall?"

"Mr. Mecklenberg has retained me to be your attending physician. And it's more than a downfall, Your Grace. I regret to say that you are dying."

"How long?" the duke asked, his voice no more than a whisper.

"A matter of weeks."

"I figured. One doesn't spit up blood unless it is dire. Attend to me, then. One sawbones is as good as another."

"Since you are awake, I want to listen to your heart." Drew did not wait for a reply. Instead, he set his bag on the bed and located his stethoscope. He placed the chest piece on the duke's breast and listened, hearing a decided whooshing sound which indicated that blood was not flowing correctly through the valves. Drew slid the stethoscope to the left lung, then the right. The duke's breathing was ragged and raspy, all signs of cancer. But it also indicated the beginnings of heart failure. This would bear watching. Drew stood upright. "We shall attempt to serve you scrambled eggs with melted cheese. You need the protein. It may lessen the pain." It was a slight fib, but it couldn't hurt.

"I want bacon," the duke said, pouting.

"That is also a good choice for protein. I will instruct your staff to prepare your breakfast right away. Are you in pain, Your Grace?"

"Of course, I am in fucking pain, you idiot!" the duke screamed.

Drew could see he was about to earn those forty pounds. "Nurse, please inform the staff about breakfast." Nurse Gretchen nodded and left the room.

Drew leaned in close so the duke could hear him. "I will do all I can to keep you comfortable until the end," he said calmly. "But speak to Nurse Gretchen or me like that again, and we will both leave you to die, writhing in pain and coughing up what's left of your lungs. Do we understand each other?" Drew never spoke to patients in such a way, but Barnsdale's past and present behavior was more than Drew was prepared to put up with.

Sweat beaded on the duke's hairline as his mouth stretched into a downward frown. Drew could see pain radiating in his eyes. The duke nodded, then turned his head toward the wall.

"On a scale of one to ten, what is the pain?" Drew asked gently.

"An eight," the duke muttered, still looking away.

Eight. And that was after a hefty dose of laudanum. "Your Grace, I will start with injections of morphine tomorrow. That should give temporary relief for a short while. I can only increase it so far until it stops having an effect. Do you understand?"

"Completely. I am to experience a horrible death. Writhing in pain as you said, losing control of my bodily functions until darkness takes me," he rasped.

The duke was not wrong about any of it. "We shall try to

avoid such an outcome. I'm here to assist and treat you and will do so to the best of my abilities."

"Right. You will give me more and more morphine until I am insensible and unconscious. Correct?" the duke asked, his voice hoarse.

Drew nodded. "If you prefer, Your Grace, I can admit you to the London Cancer Hospital. There is a Doctor Herbert Snow there who is an advocate of using morphine and other opiates not only to relieve the pain but also to treat cancer." Drew had doubts about that last part, but who was he to say? Advances in medicine were occurring so frequently that keeping up with them all remained a challenge.

"What is the point? There is no treatment. I'm too far gone. Consult with this Snow if you must. I will agree to whatever drugs you say. Anything to relieve this pain!" The duke pounded his fist against the bedcovers, clearly agitated.

"Very well, Your Grace. I will not lie to you. The cancer has advanced to the point of no return. If you wish to die at home, I will see it done. I will consult with Doctor Snow this afternoon and come up with a plan for your opiate treatment."

The duke exhaled in relief, his breath rattling.

"Now, relax. Your breakfast will be here soon, and I want you to eat as much as possible. You must remain calm. No more shouting at the nurse. She is here to treat you and keep you comfortable." Drew patted the duke's shoulder.

Drew headed toward the door.

"Thank you," the duke said gruffly.

"You are most welcome, Your Grace."

AFTER CONSULTING WITH Doctor Snow, they agreed that moving the duke to the hospital at this stage would be fruitless, as nothing further could be done. However, Doctor Snow had given Drew instructions for a concoction he had developed for pain—the Brompton Cocktail. The elixir consisted of morphine, cocaine, ethyl alcohol, chlorpromazine (for nausea), and cherry syrup to mask the bitter taste. In the later stages, adding distilled water and chloroform along with heroin to replace the morphine was recommended by Snow.

With his medicinal notes tucked into his bag, Drew hired a hansom cab. He might as well have another look around Devil's Acre, even though it was late afternoon. Hearing that the duchess was being spoken of amongst the gossips brought her to the forefront of his mind again. And he was still very worried about her safety.

The remaining area of Devil's Acre, a shadow of its mid-century self, consisted of six streets of unfathomable poverty built on a murky swamp. These marchlands were never considered prime real estate, regardless of their proximity to Westminster Abbey, Parliament, and Buckingham Palace. In '51, the construction of Victoria Street removed over three thousand homes, effectively cutting the slum in half. The new road, however, had not eliminated the poverty. It just crammed people into a smaller area.

Drew glanced at the passing streets. Many old tenements were being pulled down, and the Peabody Trust Housing Association was building new brick flats to replace them. They had started the project over a decade ago, but the progress was slow. Nothing would remain of Devil's Acre in a year or two, and all the criminal types—Lucian Sharpe included—would have to find another place to dwell. Many barefoot children dressed in rags often stood at the head of the dirt alleys, but now that there were a few inches of snow, many had dirty strips of cloth or blankets tied around their feet.

When the cab approached Duck Lane, Drew banged the roof, and the trap door opened. "You can drop me here," Drew instructed the driver. After he paid the fare, Drew stood on the walkway, pulling his wool scarf tighter about his neck. There were not many businesses on this street besides Sharpe's grubby pub. There were two pawn shops, handy for the many thieves and pickpockets to sell their ill-gotten gains, as well as a small grocery that did not appear prosperous. The many row houses had broken windows with rags stuffed in them in a futile attempt to keep out the cold. Some of these tenements housed over one hundred people.

Where to start his search for the duchess? Drew tucked his doctor's bag under his arm, holding it snug with his other hand. He never carried much money, but his few coins were safely tucked away in a secret compartment in the bag, with keys, a handkerchief, and anything else that a gentleman usually kept with him. Any thieves would be sorely disappointed if they tried to pick his pocket. Exhaling, Drew stepped into a dark alley and soon regretted the decision. He had studied maps of the area, but they did not show the maze of alleys and courtyards. Stopping short, he realized he had come to a dead end. As Drew turned, he saw three men standing at the head of the alley, holding clubs.

Trapped. He clutched his bag tighter, regretting coming here without dropping his doctor's bag at home. Drew should have planned this brief excursion more carefully, but this alley was definitely not on the map. His equipment, medicines, and other remedial items, along with the quality leather case, would be pawned. It had taken him a great deal of time to collect and purchase only the best apparatus, and now they would be taken, perhaps, as well as his life. Drew stood his ground as the men walked closer. His mind raced, trying to remember if he had a scalpel in his medical bag. It would make a handy weapon. Alas, he did not. He rarely carried surgical tools when making house visits; they were at home in his study. *Blast it.*

"Give it up, guv," one man growled menacingly. "And mebbe you'll live."

The other men stood in shadow. They were taller and more heavily muscled than the man who spoke. They slapped the clubs against their hands, and the sound of the wood making contact with the skin of their palms in a threatening and rhythmic fashion sent a feeling of dread along his spine. Three against one? Drew did not like those odds.

About to swing his case at the first man who rushed him, someone grabbed his arm through the alley's darkness and pulled him through a hidden gap between two buildings. Drew barely fit through it.

"This way," the muffled voice urged.

Drew hardly needed any convincing. They ran through a courtyard, where the overcast sky above cast barely any light. They entered a decrepit building that appeared ready to collapse. The man grabbed what looked like an iron bar and pried open a trap door.

"Down there," he hissed through clenched teeth.

Drew hesitated. What if this was a trap? What if this man worked with the others, and this was where they brought their victims to be robbed—or worse? The thought of being physically violated and beaten caused Drew's stomach to churn.

"Hurry, you pillock!" the man whispered.

The distant voices of the men chasing them grew closer. There was nothing else for it. Drew hurried down the few steps to the cellar. The other man followed, quietly closing the door. In a smooth but swift motion, Drew dropped his bag, grabbed the man's arm, and brought him about, slamming him against the stone wall.

The slight man grunted and tried to escape, but Drew had a firm grip. There was enough space between the planks of the rickety wood floor above that muted daylight from a nearby window shone through. The man stopped struggling as the thieves entered the dilapidated house.

Their boots thumped against the floor, and dust and snow trickled down on them from between the wooden slats. After several agonizing minutes, the men departed, swearing under their breaths.

Drew pulled the scarf down from the man's face, and, in the slight illumination, he could see that it wasn't a man who had come to his rescue. The features were decidedly feminine, and the face quite beautiful. His heart slammed against his ribcage.

"Your Grace?" Drew whispered incredulously.

CHAPTER FOUR

*B*LAST IT! SELENA could not believe this. She had just delivered the last of her bread, cheese, and sacks of pennies when she saw a man run into an alley that Selena knew, at first sight, was a dead end. She could not leave the man to be beaten and robbed. She had hidden her basket, and slid between the shacks to grab the man from behind. In the bright moonlight, she had observed that the man was tall, had blond hair, and carried a doctor's bag.

Her heart had nearly skittered out of control when she recognized Doctor Hornsby. How could she not? His handsome image was seared into her brain: Tall, broad-shouldered, gold spectacles, and blond hair a little longer than she remembered—and it suited him. So did the new beard. His nearness sent her senses into a jumble, much more intense than when they'd first met. The doctor possessed an enticing scent of bergamot and lime, probably from his soap. What was he doing here, of all places? There was no time to contemplate the reasons. She had to escape.

"Give over," Selena growled in a low voice. "You're barmy."

Before the doctor could reply, Selena snatched the doctor's bag from the dirt floor and tried to swing it toward Hornsby. The blasted thing was too heavy, and instead of knocking him senseless, she only managed to hit him in the chest. The doctor grumbled and cursed, and without hesitation, Selena swung for a more vulnerable area of the male anatomy. She made contact enough that Hornsby dropped to his knees. That gave her sufficient time to escape.

Or so she thought.

Selena scrambled up the few stairs to the trap door but hesitated. In the distance, she could hear the men still lingering about.

"Wait!" Hornsby croaked.

Turning, she saw him struggling to reach his feet, and a pang of guilt arrowed through her. What a terrible thing to do to a man, but Selena had had no choice. When he had said, "Your Grace," she had felt trapped and reacted as such. Honestly, she didn't think she had it in her.

How to play this? Deny that she was the Duchess of Barnsdale? Highly improbable, considering he had examined her all those months ago and sat on the sofa practically eye-to-eye with her. Could she trust him? There was no time to explore the pros and cons.

"I'm goin' above," she ground out, using her street voice. "If I'm not back in five minutes, that means 'tis safe to leave. Don't go back in the blasted alley. Slip between the huts and turn right. Aye?"

Selena did not wait for a reply. Once above ground, she cautiously closed the trap door and silently stepped outside. Deeming it safe enough, Selena stuck her hands in her oversized coat's pockets and nonchalantly sauntered toward where she hid the basket. *Still there.*

She slipped it on her arm and continued her journey toward Victoria Street. Selena frowned. She would have to wear disguises all the time now. What if Hornsby came back to this area? *How annoying.* Perhaps she should move elsewhere, as there were pockets of poverty all over London.

Still, she couldn't help wondering why the good doctor was in Devil's Acre. He was not looking for her, surely. That seemed outrageous and rather arrogant on her part. Perhaps he'd just come from one of those free clinics and had patients in this area. Could there be one nearby?

Regardless, Selena had the uneasy suspicion that their paths would cross again.

DREW GROANED AND sank to the dirt floor, his stomach roiling. As a doctor, he was well aware that male genitals were packed with numerous nerve endings, more concentrated than in any other part of the body. He was also aware he could and should not stand up right away. Honestly, he felt like vomiting, and he would have to stay still until the nausea passed. Once he returned home, he'd need to take some aspirin powder and apply a cold compress. He doubted there was any permanent damage, as thankfully, he did not receive the full brunt of the attack.

And damn it all, it was an attack. And it had caught him completely off guard. For a moment, he doubted his eyes. If his attacker were a man, he was one of the most beautiful men he had ever seen. No wonder he wore a scarf over his face. The slight glimpse in muted daylight shining through gaps in the floor had the words "Your Grace" tumbling from his lips before he was even sure it was her. Did he ache to see her so much that he imagined her distinctive and lovely facial features? Obviously, in these past several months since he treated her, the beautiful duchess was never far from his mind. Why else had he come here, for the third time, no less, unless he yearned to see her? Had he imagined he saw her because she had set his heart racing? Was he doing it again, here and now?

Drew closed his eyes and recreated the scene in his mind. The person who grabbed him had certainly saved him from a beating—or worse. But it wasn't the face that had such an impact on him. It was the scent. There was no mistaking the faint odor of vanilla and almonds, the same scent he had detected when he examined the duchess months ago. A young man of the streets would not be wearing such a decidedly luxurious aroma. They had stood close, face-to-face. His rescuer-attacker had blue eyes, just like the duchess. It was too bad he did not get a good look at the person's hair, for there was no mistaking the duchess's glorious golden-red mane. Unfortunately, his rescuer's hair had been tucked under another scarf with a peaked cap holding it in place.

Blast it, it was her! There was no doubt in his mind.

Why is she in Devil's Acre? And wearing a disguise?

With no forthcoming answer, Drew slowly stood, reached for his doctor's bag, and followed Selena's directions. Yes, he was thinking of her by her first name. Once on Duck Lane, he headed toward Orchard Street, where he could hail a hansom cab. At least there were a few businesses there, shoddy though they may be, which meant more of a police presence. From what he observed, there were no officers anywhere near Devil's Acre proper.

"Doc! My mum needs help!"

Drew turned to find a dirty-faced child staring up at him. Was this another trap? It was a sad state of humanity that such a thought even crossed his mind, but he stood within the bowels of hell. But one look at the frantic child's face told him this wasn't a play. All thoughts of his own discomfort and pain disappeared. "Where is she, lad?"

"Just there. In that door. She's breathing queer-like." The boy then gave a wheezing imitation.

Drew followed the youth into a dilapidated rooming house. The place was noisy, with people shouting, doors slamming, and babies crying. Multiple families often shared a few rooms. The boy led him into a bottom-floor room only large enough for two small beds, a table, and two chairs. The woman, who looked to be in her thirties, lay on one of the beds, laboring for every breath. Nearby stood two young girls dressed in ragged pinafore dresses.

A basket on the table held fresh bread, cheese, apples, two candles, and a small sack stood out in this misery. The only saving grace was that the room was not all that cold, thanks to the number of people crammed into these flats. But the odor of dampness, mold, and dubious cooking smells hung heavy in the air, as the conditions in this area were appalling.

Drew placed his case on the table and turned toward the woman. "Describe your symptoms, please." As he stepped closer to the bed, the odor of feces slammed his senses.

"Lad, go and empty the chamber pot. How old are you?"

"Twelve."

The boy looked to be nine or ten. Malnutrition often stunted or delayed growth in those living in poverty.

"What is your name?"

"Jimmy, sir."

"Where is your father?"

"Gone. He did a runner months ago."

"Jimmy, you're the man of the family now. That comes with a good deal of responsibility. You must do all you can to look after your mum and sisters, and you can start by keeping human waste away from your living area. Is there an outhouse or bog nearby?" The boy nodded. "Then go and empty it there. Rinse it out with the outside water tap. Then come right back."

"Aye, sir."

When the boy departed, Drew pulled the rag from the window, and a blast of air filled the room, masking the human waste odor. The air was not exactly fresh, but cool and crisp nonetheless.

"Can you sit up?" Drew asked the woman.

She nodded and, with great effort, sat upright.

"Your name?" Drew asked as he pulled his stethoscope from his bag.

"Annie Critch," she gasped, then coughed.

"Annie, what are your symptoms? Tell me how you're feeling, and when did you take a turn for the worse?"

"'Bout three days past. Coughin' and the like. 'Tis hard to breathe. Then I grew weak-like, not able to get up."

He listened to her chest. "Annie, you have an infection. It's most likely bronchitis, which means your lungs are affected."

"So, 'tis not consumption?"

"No."

Annie burst into tears, then wiped them from her cheeks. "I thought I were going to die and leave me young ones."

"Bronchitis is an infection of the airways in your lungs that causes excessive mucus. Luckily, you do not have a serious case of it." Drew handed Annie several cotton handkerchiefs. "But you do not want your condition to get any worse, for that *could* prove to be fatal. Do you smoke?" Annie shook her head. "Good. Stay away from smoke, and do not burn coal in your room. It will make your condition worse. Allow air into this area every hour for several minutes, but not when it's foggy, understand?" Annie nodded. "Stay warm." Drew pulled the threadbare blanket over Annie's legs. "Also, try to sit upright as much as possible, as you do not want the mucus to accumulate and hamper your breathing. Your son must take charge of your care, which means keeping this room clean and tidy." Drew reached into his bag and placed a cake of lye soap in Annie's trembling hands. "Scrub everything, including yourselves. Understand?"

"Aye, Doctor. Thank you."

Jimmy entered the room and placed the chamber pot under his mother's bed.

Drew took the boy aside. "Your mum is sick. Follow my directions, and she will get better. If you don't, she may worsen and die. You're in charge now, the man of the family. Do you accept this duty?"

The lad's eyes grew wide, but he nodded. Drew hadn't meant to frighten the boy, but he must understand the seriousness of the illness and that it could be fatal in some cases. He told Jimmy everything he had told Annie. "First. Do you have salt?"

Jimmy shook his head. "No, sir."

"I will bring some next I come. Add it to warm water then give it to your mother so she can gargle. It will help a sore throat.

I will also bring castor oil to help with the coughing. And finally, you must make mustard plasters. They're to be placed on your mother's chest. Get your sisters to help. Leave one on all night or even for a full day. Can you get hot or warm water?"

"Aye, Mrs. Greenough next door has a fireplace," Jimmy replied. "She boils water for us for tea and the like. She sells pots of stew for two pennies."

"Then have her boil water for the mustard plasters and cleaning purposes. A cup of hot tea would not go amiss. Do you have money? You need to buy ground mustard seeds, and you should buy hot stew from her if you can."

Annie pointed to the basket on the table. "Aye, there's pennies in that sack. I know how to make the plasters. I'll teach the lad."

"The Golden Angel brought us a basket today," the older girl stated.

Drew froze. *Golden Angel?* When he was in Lucian Sharpe's pub with Liam last month, he recalled hearing that Sharpe's men were looking for the Golden Angel. Sharpe had called the woman a do-gooder who was interfering with his business.

"What did this angel look like?"

"Well, sir, she be lookin' different every time she comes here," Annie stated as she wiped her nose with one of the hankies.

Disguises. "What did she look like the first time you saw her?"

"She wore a gray cape with fur trim," Annie said.

"She's so beautiful," the older girl interrupted. "With golden-red hair and lovely, like an angel from above."

"Sally!" Annie admonished.

Apparently, the girl should not have revealed that. *My God. Selena?* It had to be! "How often does she visit?"

"Once a week, but never on the same day. I met her on the street. I were tryin' to find a job takin' in some mendin' and she helped me find work." Annie pointed to a pile of clothes at the foot of the bed. "I'm behind in me work, and I'm that scared I'll lose me job."

"Where is the business located?" Drew asked.

"Just over on Great Peter Street. Jennie's Tailors. And I shouldn't have told you that. The Angel said I were to tell no one about the job or her."

"Do not worry, Annie. Your secret is safe with me. I'll stop at the tailor's and tell them you're sick and need a few days' rest."

"You'd do that for me? Thank you, sir. Doctor—"

"My name is Doctor Drew Hornsby, Annie. I'll come by in two days. Jimmy, follow my directions. When I return, I want this place to look ship-shape and Bristol fashion." His words were not just a command but a promise of his concern. Though he often did not outwardly show it, seeing good people living in such conditions tore at his heart.

Jimmy smiled. "Aye-aye, Doctor."

The youngest girl pointed at Drew's hair. "Mum, he's a golden angel too!"

Drew laughed, and Annie joined in. "You are that, Doctor, I'll grant. A godsend, to be sure. Take a few pennies for your fee."

"No, Annie. No fee. You use it to get well." Drew packed up his bag, then laid four shillings on the table. "Use this, too. Eat some bread and cheese and buy some tea. You need to keep up your strength."

Annie wiped a tear from her cheek. "You're so kind. Thank you."

Drew touched his forelock, stepped outside, and closed the door, but lingered, his ear by the door. Already, he cared about what would happen to this family.

"You heard the doctor, Jimmy. Buy mustard seeds and clean rags for the plasters. Sally, fill the kettle, take it to Mrs. Greenough, and then order a pail of stew. Then, we'll get this place clean. Jane, get the basin. We all need a good scrub, eh? We'll wash some clothes, too."

Drew smiled. His intuition told him this was a decent family, and that was why he'd left them money. Though not as expensive as in decades past, soap was still a luxury to those struggling in poverty. As he stepped onto the street, his thoughts turned to Selena. What in hell was a duchess doing running about these grubby streets assisting the unfortunates of Devil's Acre?

CHAPTER FIVE

EXHAUSTED AND FILLED with regret, Selena trudged back to the flat. The more she wandered the streets, the more she lamented her actions in the cellar. What had come over her? Doctor Hornsby had been nothing but kind and understanding when he'd examined her last April. And yet, she had lashed out at him. It was a stark reminder that she was still grappling with the stressful aftermath of her ill-fated marriage, a battle that seemingly had no end in sight.

Selena slipped the key in the lock and entered the flat. Penny was at her side in an instant.

"Look at you, in such a state! Come, sit by the fire. You look utterly spent." Penny took Selena's arm and guided her to the chair. She then helped her out of her coat and took her hat and gloves. "I'll put the kettle on and make your favorite sandwich. The costermonger's cart had seafood today, so I bought plenty of shrimp. I got a nice piece of haddock, too. I'll bake that later." Penny's considerate gestures were a soothing balm to Selena's weary soul. Penny laid the wool blanket over her knees, and the comforting warmth almost made Selena moan aloud.

"You should get out of those clothes, Mrs. B. I'll fetch your flannel nightgown," Penny chided.

Selena stood and undressed, tossing the cold, damp clothing to the floor, then wrapped the blanket around her until Penny returned with her nightgown. Selena quickly pulled it over her head and then sat in the chair. One thing she hadn't relayed to Penny was that Selena felt overly exhausted, and her throat was scratchy. All this running about in inclement weather was starting to take its toll. At first, she had chalked it up to her previous sedentary lifestyle. Sitting about in drawing rooms reading and drinking tea wasn't recommended for improving a person's constitution.

It was only when Barnsdale had shown the first signs of his illness that she began going out at night. She needed something worthwhile to do, as sitting about the house had become tedious. The relief she felt when she finally took time away from Barnsdale's oppressive presence was almost overwhelming. Because of her husband's deteriorating health, he stayed home more, and didn't seem to notice that she wasn't there. For once, she was grateful for his neglect.

When she read in the newspaper several months ago that a charity group sponsored by the nurses of St. Thomas's Hospital were looking for donations and volunteers, she'd jumped at the chance to help. Besides donating money, she'd assisted the nurses in any way she could, serving soup in the early evenings and even treating minor ailments. That three-month experience had sobered Selena. Seeing such crushing poverty and the courage of those living such a reality spurred her on to do more. But nothing touched her heart more than witnessing so many innocent children suffering in such stark conditions.

Gathering up what remained of her courage, she decided to leave Barnsdale and carry out her plan to assist those in need. She desperately hoped that helping others would heal the damage within herself.

Her experience assisting the nurses was how she guessed Annie Critch was unwell when she delivered the basket, even though the woman had tried to hide it. Selena would check on her in the next day or so. The fire crackled in the hearth, casting a warm glow that enveloped Selena. She closed her eyes, reveling in the comfort. For a moment, her thoughts turned to her estranged family. She hadn't seen or spoken to her parents in over five years. And her older sister, Katherine? It had been well over a decade since her sister ran away, and they'd had no contact since. She could have used Katherine's counsel and friendship these past years. How she missed her. Selena was almost asleep when Penny placed the food before her on the table.

"Hot tea, just how you like, Mrs. B. One teaspoon of sugar with the milk added first. Drink it down."

Selena opened her eyes. On the plate before her were eight perfectly cut sandwich triangles and sliced cheese. "And you cut the crusts off the shrimp sandwiches," Selena whispered. "You take such good care of me."

Penny pulled the wooden chair next to Selena, placed the lunch on the table, and sat. "Always. I bought a paper today, looked it over, and then tossed it in the bin as you instructed."

"Any word on Barnsdale?" Selena asked between bites.

"No. But I did read something interesting. That handsome doctor you mentioned the other day, the one who treated you last spring? Queen Victoria made him a baronet for his dedicated medical duties in treating the unfortunates of London."

Selena started coughing and choking on the sandwich. A baronet? Now, she really felt terrible for attacking him. A man who assisted impoverished people deserved her respect, perhaps even her trust. Swallowing, she grabbed the mug and took great gulps of tea. Finally, the coughing subsided. The surprise concerning Doctor Hornsby's title certainly added a dramatic twist to today's doings.

"What's amiss?" Penny asked, a worried look on her face.

"You *are* speaking of Doctor Drew Hornsby?"

"Yes, that's the one."

"We had a run-in today," Selena said. Then she proceeded to tell Penny everything.

Penny's eyes widened. "Mrs. B. you didn't. You can do serious damage to a man by kicking him down there."

"I didn't *kick* him. I swung his doctor's bag at him. I don't think it was even a direct hit. Blast it. I feel guilty about the entire incident. I don't know what came over me. I acted like a crazed animal caught in a snare." Selena's sense of guilt grew as she regretfully recounted the sorry incident to Penny. What had she done?

"What do we do now?" Penny asked worriedly. "He recognized you. Please don't say we have to leave. We paid a month's rent in advance, and I've learned where to buy the best bread and other foodstuffs. We can't go on the run. Sooner or later, you must return to the Barnsdale residence. You *know* this. There is no escaping the future, let alone escaping the past."

Selena sighed as she reached for her tea and took a sip. Penny was correct. Running away again was not the answer. But what to do? Indeed, she should have left Barnsdale ages ago, as Penny said earlier. The solicitor she had sought out after meeting her friends this past November had told her so. They could have negotiated a permanent separation with a possible divorce further along. Selena had even broached the subject with Barnsdale before she and Penny had departed. He was livid. "No divorce! It is scandalous!" Barnsdale had thundered. Then, he had marched from the room, slamming the door, which was usually how all their feeble attempts at serious conversation had ended.

But legal separations were not as scandalous as they had been in generations past. Divorce, while not common, did occur occasionally within the aristocracy. However, the process was protracted, making the case public for society and newspapers to gossip about. As the solicitor explained, there had to be just cause—adultery on the duke's part *and* one of the following options: incest, rape, bigamy, desertion, or cruelty. Well, cruelty fit, if nothing else, but Selena could not use cruelty alone for the cause; she had to prove adultery as well, so it was a moot point. Barnsdale, on the other hand, only had to prove adultery. That was hardly fair, but as the solicitor said, "Laws are made by men." So, yes, Barnsdale was correct on that score. It would be scandalous.

Realistically speaking, she should have stood her ground and fought for a permanent, legal separation. Selena could admit that, at the time, she was not emotionally strong enough to execute such a plan. But she found the courage to face her fears and make a difficult choice. Running away had seemed the only solution. It was either she do that, or stay and break into shards and never recover.

"You're right, Penny," Selena said softly. "There is no running from the future or the past. All I can control is the present. I know I must return to Chapel Street soon, but I still have loose ends to tie up with the people I am assisting first. In the meantime, I must heal. I *am* healing. And this is the only way I know how."

"A trip to Spain to relax in the sun would have worked just as well." Penny shook her head. "I blame those nurses you worked with when you performed that charity work. They turned your head."

"No, they opened my eyes. I cannot begin to explain how helping others shone a light on my dying soul. Am I acting selfish? Perhaps. I want to get better. This horrid marriage—and everything that occurred within it—have taken a toll, but I genuinely wish to aid those who need help."

"Very well. We stay for now. But you should tie off those loose ends as soon as possible. I will speak up when I see you driving yourself into exhaustion. I suggest you stay home the rest of today and tomorrow." Penny patted her shoulder. "Please. Take my advice."

"I will. Thank you," Selena replied. The truth? She was near collapse. But the day after next, she would be sure to check in with Annie Critch.

As for Doctor Hornsby, Selena was truly sorry for her attack on him today. She respected the young doctor who volunteered at free medical clinics, which were no doubt sponsored by his family. While admirable, it wasn't enough for her to let her guard down and confide in the doctor.

Or was it?

Two days later...

AS PROMISED, DREW traveled by hansom cab to visit Annie Critch and her children. Between attending to other patients, including the Duke of Barnsdale, and stopping at the free Bethnal Green clinic, he thought about what he had discovered from Annie. Why would Lucian Sharpe think the Golden Angel had interfered with his business? The only possibility Drew could think of was that Selena must be encouraging and assisting some of the people in Devil's Acre to find better jobs, instead of thieving for Sharpe. She had located work for Annie, although Drew doubted Annie had ever worked for Sharpe. If Drew was going to poke his nose in Devil's Acre, he should tell Sharpe he would be around to treat patients. Criminal types liked that kind of deference, as they assumed it meant fearful respect, which was far from the truth.

Once he paid the driver, Drew hurried along the walkway toward Finnian's Chop House. Drew stopped short when he entered the pub. A fire roared in the large hearth, and the room was bright and clean, as much as it could look as such. More candles and numerous gas lamps were strategically placed around the pub's interior for maximum illumination. His gaze slid immediately to the dark corner where Sharpe usually held court, but he was not there.

"Doctor Hornsby."

Drew swung about to face a young lad.

"It's me, Teddy Chisholm, from the Crowing Cock. Liam's place."

"Of course, Teddy. How are you?" Teddy had been an apprentice of Liam's but recently returned to Devil's Acre when he finally acknowledged Lucian Sharpe as his father. Teddy had lived on the streets for many years and had been in terrible shape when Liam had taken him in. Because of malnutrition, he had looked far younger than his years. Liam only discovered the lad was sixteen and not twelve when Teddy returned to Sharpe. Under Liam's care, the lad had regained his health and even grew a few inches.

"I'm doing well, Doctor. I go to school in the afternoons, and in the mornings, I work here. I sort of took over. Lucian said I could do what I want with this place."

Drew glanced around the pub. "You've done a fine job. It's quite an improvement from the way things were when I was here last month. And it seems as if you're doing a fair bit of business, as well. Well done, Teddy. Liam would be proud."

Teddy blushed. "He told me so. Liam, Tommy, and Timmy came to see me this past Sunday and stayed for a meal. They brought my things. Liam gave me a recipe for seafood chowder, which is on the menu today. Care for a bowl? It's on the house. I also have eel pie, but I don't think you'd like that."

Drew had tried eel pie once in the East End. To say it was an acquired taste was the only polite way to describe it. Spying an empty table, he sat in the chair. "Chowder would be perfect, Teddy. Thank you."

"I'll bring you a mug of tea, too." Teddy touched his forelock and hurried away.

Loud laughter and conversation filled the air, along with a haze of smoke from pipes and cigarettes. A few servers, both young men, quickly carried trays of food and pints of bitter to the various tables. For Teddy's sake, Drew hoped this building would be spared when the clearances reached Duck Lane, but somehow, he doubted it. To London and the people who ran it, the best way to clear out slum areas was to raze them to the ground. In most instances, it was the only solution. Unfortunately, it also displaced a lot of people living in poverty.

Teddy returned with a tray, placing a large bowl of chowder, fresh bread, and a mug of tea before Drew. "Everything looks delicious, Teddy. Thank you. A quick question: Is Sharpe about?"

"Aye. He's upstairs with his men. He doesn't like to be disturbed when in his office."

"Could you let him know that I will be about Devil's Acre for a while? I have patients that need tending. I want him to be aware of my presence in the area."

"Aye, I'll tell him now. He doesn't mind if I interrupt."

Drew took a spoonful of chowder. "As I said, delicious. Is Sharpe treating you well, Teddy?"

"Aye, as well as Lucian can treat someone. He mostly leaves me alone, which I like. Enjoy your meal." Teddy smiled and headed toward the kitchen.

By the time the crockery bowl was almost empty, Teddy returned to the table. "I spoke to Lucian. He said, 'Be about your doctoring, but don't linger.' He'll put the word out that you're to be left alone."

"I should have come here first," Drew smiled wryly. "I was cornered in an alley the day before yesterday."

"You were attacked?"

"Nearly. Someone came to my aid, pulling me between two buildings. Do you have a few minutes?"

"Aye, I leave for school soon." Teddy removed his apron and sat across from him.

"Are you open to taking on an apprentice?"

Teddy arched an eyebrow. "Like Liam did with me?"

"Yes, similar to that. I have a patient whose twelve-year-old son might be looking for work. I believe he has some schooling, though I am unsure how much."

"I could use a pair of hands in the morning, clearing tables, doing dishes, chopping vegetables, and the like. What's his name?"

"Jimmy Critch."

"Tell him to come see me before noon any day. I can't afford to pay much. A shilling a week to start while he learns. More after."

"That's more than fair. I will mention the position today when I visit his mother. I have one more inquiry. Have you heard of the Golden Angel? I ask because one of my patients mentioned it."

Teddy exhaled. "Oh, aye. Lucian goes on and on about her."

Drew sipped his tea. "Why does he care if someone does charity work here? As far as I can tell, the woman only leaves baskets of food, candles, and a handful of pennies to those in need."

Teddy shrugged. "I asked him that. I told him that I wished someone like that had been around when my mum and I were struggling. He claimed he gave my mum money regularly, but I never saw it. She spent it on gin."

"I'm sorry, Teddy."

"That's why I wanted nothing to do with Lucian. I thought he ignored us and let us starve. Anyway, I knew I had to stop running and face my past. I understand what Lucian Sharpe is, and I watch my back. He doesn't like anyone interfering in his rookery and upsetting the balance. The Golden Angel is stirring up trouble. People are buying less of his cheap opium and gin and they aren't thieving as much for him. His income is dropping. She also encouraged some people to move away. One man who ran a pickpocketing gang just up and left. Lucian was not pleased."

"Besides his income, I imagine Sharpe's influence has dropped as well," Drew murmured. "His income has decreased because the London City Council is pulling down tenements around him, and people are moving elsewhere. Soon, Sharpe will be lording over piles of rubble."

Teddy nodded. "Aye, and he knows it. I think his anger comes from knowing his time is near its end."

"You are very wise, Teddy. Would Lucian harm this angel of mercy?"

Teddy frowned. "He's capable, no mistake. He might make an example of her to keep everyone in line. But who's to know? The man is changeable as the weather."

"Has Sharpe done murder?" Drew asked quietly.

Teddy rubbed his chin. "Well, that I don't know for sure. There are a few rumors, but that's all they are. If you're asking if he'd kill the woman, I can't say. Like I said, he's unpredictable. If you come across her, tell her to get gone."

"I will do that, Teddy. I'll put the word out with my patients, too."

Teddy stood. "You're a good man, Doctor. For your own safety, see to it you get gone, too. Soon." The lad touched his forelock and disappeared through the door leading to the kitchen.

If Drew had not known better, he would have taken Teddy's warning as a threat. But he knew the lad hadn't meant it as such. Still, Drew would heed the caution. He must find Selena and make it clear she was in grave danger, a mission of utmost importance.

London was undergoing a massive change. The surge in population over the past decades meant many people were crammed into run-down dwellings. Thanks to the Houses of the Working Classes Act of 1890, social housing building projects were underway all over the city. It was the reason Sharpe was desperate to hold onto power, as his influence was shrinking along with the size of his domain. And his desperation led to peril for anyone who stood in Sharpe's way, at least until he decided to find another place to conduct his criminal activities, if he could locate one. Most territories were already taken by others of Sharpe's ilk. Finishing his last sip of tea, Drew stood, grabbed his case, and headed outside. He needed to locate the duchess as soon as possible.

CHAPTER SIX

S ELENA, IN HER working-class-bloke attire, headed toward Annie Critch's room. Jimmy let her in, and she was astonished by the change. The first thing Selena noticed was the strong scent of lye soap. Annie sat upright in bed, holding a mug of tea. Selena laid her basket on the table. "I've brought cooked onions, potatoes, carrots, slices of ham, and bread."

"Thank you, you're kindness itself." Annie coughed, bringing a handkerchief to her mouth. "Sally, set the table." The oldest girl jumped from her chair and gathered together the few pieces of mismatched crockery the family possessed.

"You're not well," Selena observed as she unpacked the basket.

"'Tis bronchitis, so the doctor says."

Her insides tumbled in warning. "Doctor?"

"Oh, he was ever so nice," Annie gushed. "He left us four shillings; he did. He put Jimmy in charge, and the lad has been doin' a smashin' job. We cleaned everythin', ourselves included. The doctor told us to let air into the room and order stew from the neighbor. We've never had it so good with that and what you brought." Annie coughed into her handkerchief again.

"Did this doctor mention his name?" Selena asked warily.

"Aye. Hornsby. Tall with golden hair and a beard. He said he's comin' back to check in on me," Annie replied as she wiped her nose. "Could come here anytime today, I warrant."

Heaven above! Selena had to leave—and right this minute. "I have to go. Keep the basket. I'll collect it later—"

A loud knock sounded at the door. Selena frantically looked about the room, but there were no cupboards or closets to hide in, let alone under the beds, for they were merely two pallets with thin straw mattresses on top of each other.

"Listen," she whispered fiercely. "I'm a neighbor who brought you a meal." She pulled her scarf tighter across her face. Thankfully, she was wearing different clothes than the last time she encountered the doctor, if indeed, it was him at the door.

Another knock, firmer this time. "Annie?"

There was no mistaking that deep voice. "My name is Billy Bosley. Got it?" Annie nodded. "Jimmy, open the door."

The lad hurried to the door and swung it open. "'Tis Doctor Hornsby!" Jimmy announced a little too loudly.

Hornsby entered, and his sharp gaze immediately landed on her. His eyes narrowed as he pushed his spectacles up his nose with the tip of his index finger. He closed the door behind him but stood before the entrance, effectively blocking her exit. "You have company."

"Mrs. Bosley, who lives across the way, sent her man over to give us a fine meal," Annie said brightly. "'Tis kind, and I thank you. Tell her so for me."

Selena grunted and nodded, then stepped toward the door. But Hornsby stood his ground, drat him.

"I found a job for Jimmy," Hornsby stated, keeping his gaze firm on Selena. "Working mornings with an acquaintance of mine who manages Finnian's Chop House. He'd be taken on as an apprentice, doing kitchen work. Jimmy will be expected to attend school in the afternoons. The salary is a shilling a week to start. It will increase after training to maybe close to three shillings."

Annie gasped. "A shilling, and three later? Cor, we could use that and all. But Finnian's?"

"Lucian Sharpe owns it, but his son, Teddy Chisholm, is a

decent young man who will treat Jimmy fairly. He is running the pub now and has made many improvements."

Hornsby wasn't wrong there. Selena had witnessed the positive changes for herself.

"Do you have any schooling, Jimmy?" Hornsby asked.

"Aye. Some. I went to the ragged school until last year, but it closed. Then it was torn down."

"You can discuss it with Teddy. He attends Blewcoat School in the afternoon and will undoubtedly suggest you study at the same school as him. Are you interested?"

"What do you think, Mum?"

Annie nodded. "'Tis honest work. We need the money, lad. Just stay clear of Sharpe."

"You can see Teddy before noon anytime in the next few days. I gave him your name."

Jimmy stepped forward and held out his hand. "Thank you, Doctor. I'll do a good job."

Hornsby took the boy's hand and shook it. "I know you will. Look at the thorough work you have done here. The room almost sparkles. Well done! But you must keep it this way if you want to keep sickness at bay."

Sally giggled. "That rhymes!"

Selena stepped forward. "I've got to go to me job. I'm late," she said gruffly.

Hornsby set his doctor's bag on the floor, then took her arm and gripped it tightly. "Allow me to escort you into the hall, Mr. Bosley. Annie, I'll return shortly."

Selena's heart sank. He *knew* it was her. Try as she might to struggle, he held her close. They stepped into the hall, and Hornsby pulled her around the corner into a shadowed alcove, then swung her about until her back pressed against the wall. With his free hand, he pulled the scarf aside. He grasped her upper arms, effectively pinning her.

"Selena Seaton Woodhouse," he whispered.

There was that enticing scent of lime and bergamot. Selena

was tempted to bury her face into his neck, nuzzle it, and revel in his warmth. "Yes. It's me. If it's a conversation you want, it would be better to go outside. I want no one in this tenement to know my identity."

Standing this close to him, Selena felt her breath come in short gasps. That blasted attraction she had felt in the cellar came to the forefront again. Although he had a secure hold on her, he did not hurt her, nor did she feel trapped.

"Then we will converse outside." Hornsby nestled against her. "Vanilla and almonds. The scent is faint, but I recognized it from before. A dead giveaway, *Your Grace.*"

Drat it. "How clever of you to remember," she replied sarcastically.

"You are indeed a puzzle," he murmured. "There is so much to discover. You have piqued my curiosity, which means I have a multitude of questions." Hornsby lingered, his warm breath feathering her neck. Then, with a lightning-swift motion, he clutched her arm and pulled her along the hallway. "And I intend to get answers."

They stood outside, and the cold winter air blasted Selena's lungs. "I am none of your business. Besides, there is nothing to discover, I assure you. I am not all that complicated."

"Right. From what I can tell, there are layers and layers of complexity. Where do you want to talk?" Hornsby barked, clearly growing annoyed with her. In her few encounters with the doctor, he'd always appeared unruffled and in complete control of his emotions. Not so much here, with her.

"Down that alley." Selena pointed.

Hornsby held her in the same position as he had in the hallway. He clasped her upper arms. "Why are you doing this?"

"Doing what?" she replied innocently.

"Running about these treacherous streets, acting like you're an angel of mercy."

Selena sputtered. "I am *not* acting. This is *not* a game to me. I take my charity work very seriously."

Hornsby gave her a dubious look. "There are safer ways to do your part in assisting those who need it."

"Don't say joining a ladies' club where all they do is sit about in a parlor and drink tea while arranging meaningless gestures that have no impact at all."

"Not all such organizations are meaningless. I know of several—"

Selena stopped and cleared her throat. "Before we go any further, allow me to apologize for attacking you in that cellar."

"So, it *was* you. I thought so."

"I feel terrible about it. I felt trapped and lashed out. I wasn't thinking clearly. I *am* sorry," she said contritely. "Are you—all right? No permanent damage?"

"Nothing a cold compress could not cure," Hornsby murmured wryly.

Selena winced. "Again, my apologies."

"Why, Selena? Why lurk about these streets? Are you aware of the danger? The local rookery boss has his minions looking for you. Lucian Sharpe is not to be crossed."

Selena bristled. "I did not give you permission to use my name!"

Hornsby frowned. "And there is the cold duchess I've heard so much about."

Cold? The description stung, but it was one Selena had heard before; honestly, she had fostered the belief for her own protection. And when she was with her husband, it was a more apt description than she cared to admit. Funny, she did not feel the least bit cold standing here so close to the astonishingly attractive doctor. Quite the opposite, in fact.

"Your husband is dying of cancer of the lungs, by the way," Hornsby continued. "I saw him yesterday."

Selena blinked. The news was not shocking, as she had surmised he was seriously ill. She waited a moment before replying to see if she felt anything: relief, joy, regret, or sadness. No, she felt nothing, which meant maybe her heart *had* turned to a cold pile of cinders. "I see," was all she could manage to say.

"The duke's solicitor has placed me on retainer to give medical aid where possible, which is not much, considering how far gone Barnsdale is."

"You?" Selena gasped. "Why?"

"It's a long story, and there is no time to discuss it here." Hornsby sighed. "Allow me to assist you," he said gently. "Please tell me where you're staying, for I have news about your friends. Celia, in particular, is worried sick over your disappearance."

"Celia is in London?" Selena could not believe it. She had only reconciled with her school chums, Corrine and Celia, a few months ago before they went their separate ways. Celia had returned to Northern England with her aged and ill husband. What had happened that she was now in town? Selena was about to ask that very question when a shrill whistle sounded, then another. "The nearby gasworks. It's time for the workers' afternoon break. The men cut through this alley to head toward the pubs."

Hornsby frowned again. "It is why you picked it, yes? So you can get away?"

Selena lifted her chin. "I do not deny it. Let me go, and I promise I will contact you. I still have your card. You live at 46 Gloucester Square, correct?"

The sound of rowdy men and their boots hitting the cobbles grew closer. "Yes. That is my address. You kept the card?"

Selena nodded, then, standing on the tips of her toes, kissed Hornsby's cheek. "Trust me, I will be in contact." Why did she do that? She had no idea. To distract him or for her own pleasure? There was no time to think of it now.

He released her long enough to cup her cheeks and look deep into her eyes, as if to ascertain if he *could* trust her. The raucous laughter and chatter grew closer. Hornsby leaned in and gave her such a tender, barely-there kiss on her lips that she nearly swooned. As the men turned the corner, he released her. "See you soon—Selena," he murmured huskily.

Selena fell in step with the working men. "See you soon—Doctor Drew." Selena touched her lips, now burning from that lovely kiss. It was chaste, however, beneath that sweet kiss, Selena sensed unleashed passion. It was hard to tell whether it was hers, his, or both. She pulled the scarf over the bottom half of her face and trudged toward Victoria Street, quickly enveloped by a group of gas workers. As they peeled off toward a pub on Great St. Anne's Lane, she glanced behind her to see if the doctor was following her.

He wasn't. Exhaling in relief, she ducked into another alley heading toward Westminster Abbey. The bells of the Great Clock of Westminster, which some Londoners now called Big Ben, chimed *Westminster Quarters*, then three single strikes. It was three o'clock. What little Drew revealed—yes, she referred to him by his first name, and why not since they had kissed each other—had her concerned. Her husband, in name only for quite some time, was dying. Alone. A stab of guilt slid in under her ribs. And Celia was in London? How? What about *her* ill husband? Those two salient items were enough reason for Selena to follow up on her promise to contact Drew.

The strange emotions tearing through her were confounding, indeed. She thought of the kisses they'd shared. Perhaps her heart wasn't as dead as she'd thought. Her growing feelings for the doctor caused her to suffer a sliver of guilt regarding Barnsdale. But Selena had other concerns, like what to do next. Her time was growing short; she understood she had to return to Chapel Street soon. But she had more to do, like wrapping up her plans for the few families she assisted. She couldn't allow Sharpe to hamper her goal. The rookery boss's determination to find her was an annoyance to her, nothing more.

Nor could she let her attraction for Drew Hornsby get in her way.

DREW STOOD AGAINST the wall, allowing the workers to pass. He briefly considered following Selena, but she was soon swallowed up in a sea of peaked caps. She'd asked him to trust her. But did he? Not fully; he did not know her at all. Yet, he had kissed her. It was unwise not only because it had revealed his attraction to her but also because she was married and coming out of a possibly abusive relationship. Who knows what damage had been done to her? Yet, he hadn't been able to help himself, revealing his complete lack of experience as far as women were concerned.

Once the alley emptied, Drew headed toward Annie's room. There, he found the children sitting at the table, eating the meal Selena had brought. Annie had a plate on her lap.

"Have some, Doctor. 'Tis good food," Annie offered.

"Thank you, Annie, but I've eaten. It's all for you." Drew laid his hand against Annie's forehead. "Warm, but not horribly so. I want to take your temperature. I have a gadget here called a thermometer." Drew opened his bag and showed Annie the six-inch-long item. "I stick this under your tongue, and you cannot eat or speak for nearly five minutes. It takes your body temperature and tells me how bad your fever is." He shook it briefly until the temperature needle rested at 98.6 Fahrenheit.

"Cor, blimey. What will they think of next? Go on, then, Doctor." Annie opened her mouth, and Drew slipped it under her tongue.

"You can close your mouth and breathe normally." Drew pulled his pocket watch from his vest pocket and noted the time. "Will you seek out Teddy Chisholm, then, Jimmy?"

"Aye, Doctor. I'll go tomorrow morning. I have to drop some of the mending Mum finished at the tailor's. She was feeling much better this morning," Jimmy replied.

"That's good to hear. And you and your sisters are well?"

"I feel good," Sally replied. She pointed at the younger girl. "But Jane says her throat is sore."

"Is that true, Jane?" The girl, no more than six or seven, nodded. "I will check you next. Meanwhile, eat up. Hearty food keeps you strong."

He took the thermometer from Annie's mouth. "99.9, Annie. As I suspected. A slight fever. We want to keep that fever manageable." He laid a packet of powder into Annie's hand. "Add about 20 grains to tea and take every four hours. It's willow bark. It will keep your fever down and ease any aches and pains."

"Oh, aye. I have those."

Drew examined Jane first by listening to her chest, then by taking her temperature and looking down her throat. He patted the sweet girl on the head. "Finish your meal, Jane. Then get under the covers on the other bed like a good girl."

Drew leaned in and whispered in Annie's ear, "I believe Jane is developing bronchitis. It is nothing you did or did not do. It happens when people share a room or a house, and it can hardly be avoided. Do not blame yourself. Her fever is about the same as yours, and her throat is slightly inflamed. Has she been coughing?"

Annie looked worriedly toward her youngest daughter. "No. Not yet. Oh, my dear girl."

"It could be a slight chill or cold, as they call it now. Do not worry." Drew turned and reached into his bag, then handed his card to Jimmy. "Lad, if your mother or sister worsens, come and fetch me. I'm less than three miles away. I'll leave another packet of willow bark powder. Twenty grains for your mother, ten for your sister. Every four hours. If Jane starts to cough, apply mustard plasters to her as well. I'll return the day after tomorrow. Again, come fetch me if they worsen. If I'm not home, my housekeeper, Mrs. Evans, will tell you where I am. Can you handle this, as well as working in the morning?"

"Aye, Doctor. Finnian's isn't far, just the next street over. I'll wait to attend school in the afternoons until Mum and Jane are better."

Drew patted the boy's shoulder. "Buy food from Teddy's kitchen and bring it to your family—stews and the like. Teddy may even give you leftovers for a cheap price. Keep them warm and fed, and keep this place and yourselves clean and tidy. It makes a world of difference when battling a sickness, whether serious or not. Do not drink water from the public tap unless you boil it first. Feel their foreheads. If it's burning hot to the touch, come and fetch me. Keep the door locked."

Jimmy smiled up at Drew. "Aye, Doctor. I'll take care of them, don't worry."

Drew packed his medical bag, waved to the Critch family, and entered the hall. Shouting above stairs reached his hearing, then, a noise that sounded like a physical fight, with two men yelling epithets. It was a blasted shame that a good family had to endure such spartan and filthy lodgings. All he could hope for was that the bronchitis would not turn serious. He had witnessed entire families wiped out by such lung-borne illnesses. Walking along the street to hail a cab, he decided to visit Liam and Celia. He had to tell Celia that he had found Selena.

Perhaps Celia could offer him insight on how to approach the wayward and alluring duchess.

CHAPTER SEVEN

S INCE IT WAS Monday, it was not all that busy at the Crowing Cock. Drew arrived in the East End at about four in the afternoon so that the luncheon rush would be over. Most of the customers remaining were enjoying afternoon tea, with three-tiered trays filled with sandwiches, scones, and other delicacies. Drew inhaled. The cooking smells in Liam and Celia's place were always enticing. They must have served beefsteak and onions earlier because the mouth-watering scent lingered in the air.

Enya, the head waitress, smiled as she approached him. "Good afternoon, Doctor. Here to see Liam and Celia?"

Drew removed his derby hat. "Yes, if they are available."

"Come through the rear, Doctor." The staff knew he and Liam were half brothers, as they had recently publicly acknowledged it. Enya showed him into the kitchen.

Liam turned from the stove and gave Drew an exaggerated bow. "Why, Sir Drew. How kind you are to bless us with your presence."

Enya chuckled as she returned to the restaurant floor.

Drew blushed at the attention but was glad to see Liam joking. When they had first met a few months ago, Liam had been far too serious and brooding, to boot. Drew was also often referred to as far too solemn—it must run in the family.

Celia threw her arms around Drew's neck, stood on tiptoes, and kissed him affectionately on the cheek. "Never mind him. We are extremely proud. You deserve it."

"Thank you. It was wholly unexpected. The title has more to do with my ties to the Hornsbys than anything."

"That's not quite true. I'm sure your work at the free clinics factored into the decision. It said so in the paper." Liam winked teasingly. "Morrigan? Please take over the stoves. Fiona? Bring tea and sandwiches to the staff dining room and take over Celia's station, if you please," Liam ordered.

"Aye, Liam," Fiona answered, quickly gathering a teapot and mugs on a tray. Fiona was Liam's manager, and Morrigan, the former waitress, was training to work in the kitchen. Liam's staff was loyal, and they thought of each other as family.

Drew laid his hat and doctor's bag on the dining room sideboard, removed his black wool coat, and hung it on the hook by the door.

Once seated, Fiona entered and laid the large tray on the table. "I've got to return to my station. Orders are piling up. Congratulations, *Sir* Drew." Fiona gave a little curtsy, and Liam and Celia laughed.

"Just call me Drew, Fiona. And tell the rest of the staff to do the same."

Fiona waved as she disappeared into the kitchen. Celia poured the tea, and platters of sandwiches and biscuits were passed around. Drew was starving.

"What news? You must have some," Liam said as he added milk to his tea.

Drew told them about being placed on retainer to care for the Duke of Barnsdale and his diagnosis.

"So, he *is* going to die?" Celia asked softly. "Your initial diagnosis was correct when you saw him last month."

"Yes, he will die. Sooner rather than later. There is nothing to be done."

"I wish Selena would reach out to me. I can't help but worry about her safety." Celia sighed, her concern for Selena palpable.

"Well. That is the main reason I came by today. I found her."

Celia dropped her spoon, which landed on the china plate with a clink. "Holy crow! Where? How?"

Drew told them everything he knew, including her general location, how she was referred to as the Golden Angel, her charity work, and her disguises.

Liam whistled. "Devil's Acre? Sharpe's stomping grounds? Is the woman mad? Do you think the duchess will get in contact with you as she promised?"

Drew bit into his cheese and onion sandwich, chewed, and swallowed. "What do you think, Celia? You know her better than anyone."

Celia sighed plaintively. "It has been nearly fifteen years since I've seen her, except for your aunt's tea party and the next day at Corrine's. Corrine and I were shocked at her aloofness. She was never like that in school." Celia smiled slightly. "Selena could be mischievous, not in playing cruel tricks, but sneaking into the school's larder late at night to bring us treats. We were diligent to ensure no one found any biscuit or cake crumbs in our bed. Selena was a year older than us and taller. She protected us from the older girls. Selena was tough but had a heart of gold. So, I am not surprised to hear she is doing charity work." Celia took a sip of tea. "Do you think she will she get in touch as she promised?

"I believe so, but it will be on her schedule."

Selena was thirty-one years old. He would have guessed younger. "That is what I am fearful about, that she will not reach out to me until it is too late. Tell me more about her," Drew asked, genuinely curious.

"Selena's grandfather is Viscount Weybridge—"

"Good God! Sorry to interrupt, but I noticed Viscount and Viscountess Weybridge at a recent social event. They were with Viscountess Chesley. I heard afterward that they were asking questions about Barnsdale's illness and the duchess's disappearance."

Celia shook her head. "How typical of the upper crust. While I adore Selena, her parents and grandparents are snobs of the first order and rather loathsome, to be truthful." Celia placed two sandwich wedges on her plate. "They're not a close family. She rarely saw her grandparents because Selena's father and his parents were estranged. I believe the viscount frowned on his son's choice of bride."

"I cannot believe those toffs gossiping, and about their grand-daughter, no less," Liam interjected.

"It is the way of things in society," Celia replied. "Selena's father is the second son and has no chance of becoming the heir as his older brother has three sons. Selena has an older sister, but I've never met her. Katherine, or as her parents called her, Kitty. Selena sometimes called her Kit. Kit defied her parents, eloped with a man they deemed beneath her, and moved to New York. Selena tried writing her, but Kit never answered her letters or any of the parents' letters either, after an initial one or two. That inflamed Selena's parents more."

"In what way?" Drew asked.

"Selena's parents dreamed of their beautiful daughters each marrying a duke. They never let up. It became worse when Kit departed, for they focused all that unwanted attention on Selena. She loathed coming home during school breaks because they constantly invited the few eligible dukes they knew over for tea. When she was seventeen, her parents settled on Barnsdale. What did they care that he was twenty-five years older? This happens often within the upper classes. Unfortunately, it was my fate, as well." Celia frowned, no doubt recalling how her aunt and uncle had pushed her into a marriage with a much older earl. "Selena was adamant she would not marry Barnsdale, but when it comes down to it, young women have no options." Liam took Celia's hand and squeezed it affectionately.

"Nonetheless," Celia continued, "Selena came to tea at Corrine's the day after your aunt's tea party. As I said, she was not the schoolgirl we remembered. She did not want to be touched. Corrine asked her if Barnsdale had hit her..." Celia's eyebrows furrowed as if deep in thought, then shook her head. Changing the subject, she added with a smile, "We talked about what we'd called ourselves in school—the Bluebells. We chose that name for our mutual eye color and because bluebells symbolize humility, constancy, and everlasting love. It's what we wished our futures would be." Celia's smile disappeared. "Selena bitterly stated that none of it came true for her. Corrine had mentioned that her arranged marriage wasn't what she'd hoped for and that she had found another man—Mitchell, we now know—attractive. She asked us what she should do."

"Did you or the duchess give advice?" Drew asked.

"Selena spoke first and most forcefully on the subject, suggesting a solicitor. She said, 'Save yourself before you become a hollowed-out husk devoid of emotion. Like me.' It hurts my heart to repeat it. We asked her about Barnsdale again. Selena said she hated him because he was cold, harsh, and controlling. She started doing charity work last autumn with the nurses of St. Thomas's Hospital in the early evenings to escape him. 'I cannot bear to face him,' was her exact quote. Selena stated she had an appointment with a solicitor in two weeks. I suggested Corrine take a lover. It wasn't a cheeky recommendation. I was in deadly earnest. But Selena's response…"

"What was it?" Drew asked, his voice barely above a whisper, his interest piqued.

"Selena said, 'After what I have endured with Barnsdale, I want no other man to lay a hand on me ever again.' I should not be repeating such a private conversation. I feel terrible for doing it. But, does it give you any insight into her current actions?" Celia asked.

It did. And yet, Selena had kissed him. "As a physician with university training, I have a certain knowledge of psychological issues, especially concerning trauma and stress, as I've observed plenty at the free clinics. Mental health is fast becoming a serious area of study, as it should be. I will offer my opinion, but I am not sure it holds merit."

"Please do offer it," Celia urged.

"Perhaps this is a separation of sorts in the duchess's mind. She had to escape Barnsdale's presence regardless of his health. That charity work with the nurses must have assisted her in healing some of whatever Barnsdale damaged, because the duchess is doing it in earnest now. Although, why Devil's Acre? It could be a random pick, as it's near the Barnsdale residence. Still, why travel to the East End when there is poverty and helplessness right under the nose of Westminster proper? The bigger issue now is that the duchess has stirred Lucian Sharpe's wrath. He's ordered his gormless gang to search the streets for her."

"To what end?" Liam exclaimed.

"I asked Teddy Chisholm that very question. He believes the angel is interfering with Sharpe's opium trade and thieving schemes, which means a drop in his income."

"Oh, no! Selena *is* in danger!" Celia's hands flew to her cheeks, her eyes wide with concern.

"I am tending patients there, and I'll watch out for her." Drew looked at his hands. "There are times when I regret not stopping by the Barnsdale residence after that initial meeting last April. However, I firmly believe doctors should not insert themselves into patients' private lives or pass moral judgments. Many doctors act with too much authority and intrusiveness, usually without the patient's consent. Thankfully, newer physicians like myself were taught differently. The duchess bade me not to return or inquire further. Even still, I slipped her my card, a breach of my own code."

"You did all you could," Celia said softly. "It must be difficult to deal with all the misery and grief you're exposed to."

"Very often. I try to remain detached, maybe more than I should, but it's not always possible. I'm cutting back on my workload. I have decided to take most of the summer off. I plan to return to Kent to stay with family and perhaps spend time at one of our cottages. Thanks to my family, I'm fortunate enough to be able to afford the luxury of a self-imposed rest."

"You deserve it," Liam replied. "No one ever thanks you for

working yourself into the ground. Celia and I also plan to step away from our punishing schedule, at least for a little while."

"Very wise. Now, as for the duchess, perhaps I should not have released her in that alley, but I wanted to gain her trust. I did not want to try to restrain her or act the bully, for she's had enough of that."

"You did right," Liam observed. "Speaking of bullies, have you had a good look at Sharpe? Remind you of anyone? Damon Cranston, the new Duke of Chellenham? Mitchell? *You?*"

Drew was aghast. "You're not suggesting he's a duke's bastard like us? This city has a population of close to six million, maybe more. What are the odds we'd come across him? Besides that, isn't Sharpe too old?"

Liam shrugged. "Sharpe told me once his mother was a young under-house parlor maid in a fancy house, but was turned out onto the streets when she claimed she'd become pregnant by the master's son and heir—a boy of barely sixteen. She said the youth never knew about the pregnancy as the parents covered it up."

"This is incredible. I can scarcely credit it," Drew murmured.

"And you speak of odds? I sat down one night and did the math," Liam said solemnly. "If the dead duke procreated with abandon from age fifteen until he died, we could be talking of hundreds of descendants. Perhaps a thousand—or more. I'm sure there are plenty more offspring he knew nothing about. Who knows? Maybe I'm seeing Edward Cranston's filthy fingerprints on every person I see with golden hair, blue eyes, and better looks than most. Regardless of his street upbringing and life, you can't deny that description fits Sharpe."

"The fates would not be that cruel, would they?" Celia cried.

"Yes," Drew replied. "The fates can be that cruel—and cruelty certainly describes the late Duke of Chellenham. The late duke's selfish eugenics leanings and his scheme to profit from it caused chaos...but also brought us all together. As far as Sharpe, I suggest we keep that information to ourselves for now. In the meantime, I will do all I can to find the duchess again. I wanted to tell you in case she contacts you."

"I will let you know if I hear from her," Celia stated. "And I will write to Corrine right away. I hesitated because she and Mitchell were still on their honeymoon, but I cannot delay any longer. Too much has happened. We could use Mitchell's police detective skills right now."

Drew could not argue with the logic of that statement. Corrine and Mitchell were due to return to London in two weeks anyway. As to Selena, what he had discovered made her all the more fascinating. It also filled him with sorrow. His heart ached to know that she described herself as a hollowed-out husk, devoid of emotion. But one thing he knew now for sure—Selena *was* in danger.

And Drew was determined to protect her.

LUCIAN SHARPE HAD no illusions about his character or lack thereof. His ex-housemaid of a mother had given birth to him in some squalid room, then immediately turned to gin for solace, effectively ignoring Lucian. He was born in Devil's Acre and had witnessed many changes since the 60s—the slow-moving clearances, the multiple outbreaks of cholera and typhus, and the multitude of rats, fleas, criminals, and prostitutes. What a place to call home.

Still, home it was, and it was also his kingdom. But Lucian possessed the intelligence to realize the area was near its end. He had recently received written notice that the tenements would be razed on Great St. Anne's Lane starting in April. All the housing on Perkin's Rents would also be torn down by the autumn. They would continue westward until they reached Duck Lane in the spring of 1900, where it would be renamed St. Matthew Street. He had one year remaining as the king of this dank rookery he called home. Because he owned property throughout the area, the London County Council had offered him money for his piles of rotting boards and crumbling bricks. It wasn't much, but more than he had expected. Lucian was in no position to refuse, thanks to the Housing of the Working Classes Act in '85, which gave the LCC the power to compel the sale of properties.

But where should he go? This question had plagued him for years. At thirty-eight years of age (or however old he was, he had no clue), did he really want to start over, fighting other criminals and thieves for ever-shrinking parcels of territory?

Bloody hell, no.

Secretly, Lucian had had enough of this life. He stood, heading toward the corner of his dark room above Finnian's Chop House, and lit the small gas cooker to heat water for his tea. He had rooms like this all over Devil's Acre, for he had never stayed in one place for long. He had started making plans seven years ago by hiding away every cent he made until he opened an account under an assumed name at the London and Westminster Bank last year. The account held a healthy balance. He also had another business—and a different persona, should he need them. It depended on the circumstances. But in any case, Lucian knew he would need more than one option for his new life.

Through the years, he had conducted business with dodgy aristocrats, like the Earl of Darrington, where he had also received many valuable tips for stocks and investments, which increased his wealth even more. But even these originally cash-strapped peers, Darrington included, were getting out of the game. The earl had recently told Lucian he was scaling back on his smuggling ventures because of family problems. Which meant Lucian's income would take another hit.

Yes, it was time to cash in his chips and move on. But where?

While he didn't give a toss about what happened to the men who followed him, it was only fitting that he looked after his newfound son, Teddy. Lucian already had a few ideas. The fact that the lad had turned a profit at the chop house in less than two weeks showed that he could invest in the boy's future by buying him a restaurant similar to what Liam Hallahan ran. Lucian never said so aloud, but he had been impressed by Hallahan's scheme to turn a rundown pub and brothel into a popular working- and middle-class eating establishment. Why not do the same? Lucian already had his eyes on a few locations. But beyond securing Teddy's future, Lucian didn't care about anyone in Devil's Acre. Let the place be demolished—it was nothing but a muddy marshland.

Meanwhile, he had other ends to tie off before escaping, including finding the Golden Angel. Usually, he wouldn't care if some altruist flitted about the streets giving bread to the poor. But this woman was hurting his bottom line. He'd lost three good cutpurses due to this woman's interference. The loss of income was a problem enough, but he'd be damned if he let some angel of mercy get the better of him. His underlings would lose all respect for him and no longer fear him. Lucian needed to wrench every last penny out of this place before disappearing for good. Besides, it kept his inept gang of thieves busy looking for her. What he would do when he located her was another story.

Despite of his notorious reputation, Lucian had never committed or ordered murder. He had learned early on that while you could participate in nearly every crime and vice known to man, committing or participating in the murder of another human being was a line, once crossed, you could never return from.

First off, if caught, you were hanged. If the police didn't scoop you up, the stigma and whiff of murder followed you everywhere. While it caused fear among criminal peers, that sort of filth was not easily scraped off, whether you changed your name or not. His soul was dark enough without adding killing to his sins.

Lucian poured hot water over the tea leaves in the strainer. There were many options for the angel once she was located. He could sell her to a rival gang…though that was low, even for him.

He could demand that she pay a penalty. Or maybe he would release her with a warning. Lucian snorted. What happened to her depended on his mood whenever she was caught. What mattered in the end was shoring up his future, not some fool lady giving bags of pennies to the dregs of society.

But first, he had to get his house in order. Lucian had recently decided to raise the rents in all of his buildings, as well as the prices at the chop house. It would only amount to a few pence, but they would add up swiftly enough. He would demand a higher quota from the pickpockets and thieves, which meant there could not be any interference from outside influences. His future was at stake, and he was not about to let anything or anyone jeopardize it.

The Golden Angel had to be found and dealt with, as soon as possible.

One way or another.

CHAPTER EIGHT

SELENA FELT WORSE that morning than she had the day before. Despite following Penny's advice to stay indoors, her condition had not improved. The onset of increased body aches and sneezing confirmed her worst fear—she was falling sick.

What to do? Try to hide it from Penny? That was not likely, as her maid was attuned to every change in Selena's appearance, mood, and overall well-being. Usually, she was grateful for it, but today, it would make it difficult to do the things that needed to be done.

Shivering, she turned over and pulled the quilt up to her neck. Her sister, Katherine, entered her thoughts again. How was she doing? Was she happy, at least? For the longest time, Selena had resented her for abandoning her to their parents' machinations. Yet she'd also admired Katherine for having the courage to follow her heart, although it was clear across the ocean. The gossip regarding that scandalous elopement among the elites was fierce, and her viscount grandfather had blamed his son for allowing such scrutiny on the family, which had widened the chasm between her grandparents and parents.

Unfortunately, it had also made her parents rabid about pairing her with a duke, regardless of her feelings. Oh, she'd fought back. There had been many fierce verbal rows over the years. Her parents, driven by their ambitions, relentlessly pursued a high-status match for her. Finally, when she had turned twenty-two, her parents gave her an ultimatum: Marry Barnsdale or be kicked to the cobbles and disowned. Selena was so weary of it all and disgusted by her parents' selfish behavior that marrying Barnsdale had seemed the only escape. Why Barnsdale waited all those years—well, she was a trophy for him to obtain. He had told her so, and more than once. Did peerage males still place bets at their exclusive clubs over trivial items such as who would marry a particular young lady? Selena would not be surprised.

Once married, Selena soon learned that being kicked to the cobbles would have been a preferred fate. But that was a statement from someone who had never experienced genuine hardship. Her volunteer experiences with the St. Thomas's Hospital nurses showed her the suffering beyond her sheltered life. Nothing could have prepared her for the blunt reality of Devil's Acre, and her first day traveling about the few streets remaining in the slum had certainly opened her eyes. The abject misery she had observed, from the malnourished children to the desperate mothers, caused her to cry herself to sleep when she was alone in bed that night. The stench of poverty and despair clung to her, starkly contrasting with the heavily perfumed air of upper-class homes. So much for thinking she'd prefer to be kicked to the cobbles instead of marrying Barnsdale. No, life on the street was far worse.

When she fled Barnsdale, Selena decided to make a differ-ence—for herself, and for others. She needed to give her life some meaning. And helping others seemed the most worthwhile way to do it.

Too many people needed assistance, and not all would accept it. So Selena located a few willing to take charity and get references from those who knew of others in dire need, and those who would keep their mouths shut. It became clear by the third day, when she heard of the criminal who had a tight grip on Devil's Acre, that she would have to wear disguises. Did the whiff of peril add to the exhilaration she received from helping others?

It certainly made her feel alive for the first time in years. But nothing had cleared those cobwebs from her soul like assisting those who gladly accepted the help. Selena understood she could not do this for much longer, especially after hearing from Drew that her husband was, indeed—dying. Even though she had Penny checking the newspapers for the duke's death announcement, she'd never fully believed he was *that* ill. And Celia was in London? What was going on there?

Selena fully intended to contact Drew, and it would be soon. She wanted to hear more of the current news.

But it's not the only reason.

She had kissed him on the cheek. *How shocking.* The doctor was beyond handsome, but it was more than that. It was the caring way he had treated her when he'd called at her house last year, and offered to help her. Selena was still moved and grateful.

Nothing showed the deterioration of her mental state at that time so much as the way she'd treated him. When she'd discovered his aristocratic ties, she'd immediately pushed him into the enemy column. She regretted that. The kiss she gave him on the cheek was a thank you in one way and an apology in another…but there was more to it. She was attracted to him.

There. Selena admitted it.

However, she would tuck away that admission for now, as Selena had too much else to contend with. The weightiness of her responsibilities and the uncertainty of her future all seemed to press down on her, threatening to overwhelm her.

A fierce sneeze caught her off guard, and she reached for the cotton handkerchief on the bedside table. Then, a coughing fit wracked her body. Her lips turned downward in disgust as she glanced the phlegm on the handkerchief—greenish yellow. *That* could not be good. Suddenly, Selena heard footsteps heading for her door. Penny had the ears of a great horned owl.

The bedroom door flew open. "You *are* sick! I thought as much." Penny marched to her bedside and felt Selena's forehead. "Warm, not hot. You stay under the covers, and I'll bring you a full breakfast."

"I don't think I can manage—"

"Nonsense. Feed a fever, my mum always said. Here, sit up." Penny fluffed the two pillows behind her.

"I thought the saying was feed a cold, starve a fever?" Selena sniffled.

"Well, I believe my mum, as she was never wrong about such things. I'll get another blanket as you must stay warm, Mrs. B." Penny stopped and stared at Selena. "Wherever did you get the name of 'Mrs. Beecham, widow of a sea captain'? Was it from the book you told me about?"

"Yes. *The Buccaneer and the Lady.*" It was a rousing adventure romance, with the young, widowed Mrs. Beecham finding love again with a handsome pirate with a heart of gold and long golden hair to match. Did the attractive Doctor Hornsby remind her of the fictional pirate? Perhaps—at least in her dreams.

"Well, you won't be running about those horrid streets for many days to come; I'll hazard to guess," Penny declared, her hands on her hips.

"But people depend on me. Children. Entire families. Maybe you can—"

Penny held up her hand. "No, Mrs. B., I will *not* deliver baskets for you. As much as I feel sorry for the unfortunate people, I'll not risk my life—and neither will you. You're worn down to a nub. I can hear how stuffed up you are. You need hearty food, warmth, and rest."

"Penny, I could not rise from this bed if I tried." And that was an accurate declaration. Everything ached, from the hair on her head to the tips of her toes. Oh no, she hadn't caught bronchitis from Annie Critch, had she? Selena recalled Annie's wheezing and ragged breathing. She inhaled and exhaled. No discernible rattle as yet, but it would come. Of that, she had no doubt. In a rush to heal what ailed her inside, she'd neglected to look after herself. Keeping a punishing schedule and not dressing to reflect the inclement weather had caught up to her. Frustrated, Selena wiped her nose. Acting impulsively had brought her to this sorry state, that and her implacable stubbornness.

Several moments later, Penny entered the room holding a tray. "Sit up further. That's it." Penny laid the tray on her lap. What Selena could smell of the food made her stomach churn. "There's a fried egg, just as you like, with bacon, toast, and a chunk of Lancashire cheese. It took some doing to find that type of cheese, but I did over in a shop near Westminster Abbey because I know how you like it."

"I appreciate everything you do for me, truly. But I am unsure how much of this I can eat," Selena stated wearily.

"You must try. At least some of the egg and cheese. Sip some tea." Penny exited the room and returned carrying a wooden chair from the table. She placed it by Selena's bedside and sat upon it.

"You're going to watch me eat?" Selena asked incredulously.

"I am, Mrs. B., for I know this much. You'll only grow sicker and weaker if you refuse food. I will speak plainly: Your charity mission must end, sooner rather than later. You've done as much as you can. Now, you must place all your energy into getting well. Besides, that money you took from the duke's safe must be running out."

Selena bristled with defiance. "There is still some money left. I will decide when this 'charity mission,' as you call it, is at an end. Not *you*."

Penny folded her arms. "Yes, *Your Grace*."

Selena sighed. "I'm sorry I sounded imperious. I hate being sick. And there is still much for me to do." She picked up her fork and knife and cut the egg into small pieces. Spearing a portion, she placed it in her mouth and chewed. "There. I'm eating some of the egg, and thank you for cooking the yolk hard. Barnsdale's cook would never do it, so I had to switch to scrambled." Selena sipped her tea, then broke off a piece of cheese. "Imagine, I could not even get my eggs cooked as I wished in that house. Barnsdale ruled everything, including me."

"I understand," Penny replied with genuine empathy. "You

were under his thumb. I've something important to say: You said Doctor Hornsby told you the duke is dying. You should be there when he takes his last breath. If you wish to further your charity work after he passes, you can do so. Widows have more power than a married woman." Penny exhaled. "And before he breathes his last, you should empty the safe before the lawyers get their hands on it. You may need that money. Who knows what the duke will leave you in his will?"

Selena halted the fork before her lips. Could he leave her nothing? It was possible. She must shore up her future. She reflected on Penny's statements as she ate the fried egg. Do more charity work after Barnsdale passed? Yes, she could do that.

"I can't believe I just suggested further thievery," Penny murmured, shaking her head. "But then, we've already done it, haven't we? In for a penny, in for a pound—literally. I never asked, did your father pay the duke a dowry?"

"No, not that I'm aware. Instead, my greedy father managed to finagle a payment out of Barnsdale. I am not sure how much, I never asked. A few hundred pounds? I never saw a penny piece." Selena sighed as she popped more of the egg in her mouth and chewed. "Still, what you suggest has merit. I cannot depend on Barnsdale leaving me a stipend. We must look to the future." It was a stark realization, but the time had come to do just that. She had put it off long enough.

"It wouldn't hurt to grab a few more items to sell while we're at it," Penny murmured.

"Penny!" Selena was taken aback. "You're suggesting I rummage through Barnsdale's possessions while he's on his deathbed?"

"It sounds heartless to my own ears, I'll grant. But I've read in the papers how widows are often left with next to nothing, even in the peerage. Don't let that be you. It will mean returning to your parents, who will no doubt nag you to remarry the first unmarried male aristocrat who strolls by."

"I just turned thirty-one. They can hardly force me to do

anything." The thought of returning to her parents caused a shiver to coil down her spine. Throughout the entirety of her marriage, she had only seen her parents twice. As far as Selena was concerned, they were out of her life.

Penny curled her lips. "They forced you at age twenty-two, and if you come back to them without a farthing, they will force you again. You felt you had no choice the first time, either."

Selena bit into the creamy cheese. "I wanted to get away from them more than anything."

"And you would likely agree to a second marriage to get away from them again," Penny said decisively.

Yes, history could repeat itself, which was sad to say. Women had no power, not without money to live on. Her friend laid out the options, and deep down, Selena knew it was entirely likely that her parents would use her again to further their own causes. There was no use putting off the decision any longer. She reached for the handkerchief and blew her nose. "Very well. We will return to Chapel Street as soon as I recover from this chill." She pushed the tray away. "I cannot eat any more of this. I'll cast up my accounts if I do."

"Finish the egg, at least," Penny coaxed.

Selena sighed, then stuffed what was left of the fried egg into her mouth. She could hardly taste it. After Penny took the tray and left the room, she started coughing. Then she heard it, a faint wheeze on each exhale.

Oh, blast it.

Four days later…

DREW SAT IN his study, trying to work out his schedule for the coming week, but his mind drifted toward Selena Seaton Woodhouse. It had been five days since she'd promised to contact him. How much longer was she going to wait? Unless the runaway duchess had no intention of reaching out. No, he had the distinct impression she spoke the truth, not so much to see him but to discover more about Barnsdale and Celia. Drew dipped his pen into the ink bottle and wrote in "Bethnal Green Clinic" under Tuesday and Wednesday, and "Liam's clinic" under Thursday.

Perhaps using Celia as dangling bait had been underhanded, but Selena had acted interested enough that Drew was positive she'd send word. But here it was Saturday, and nothing. He had already seen Barnsdale this morning, but should also stop by tomorrow. So far, the morphine shots were keeping the edge off the pain, but for how long?

Under Sunday, he wrote, "Devil's Acre" and "Barnsdale." He must see Annie Critch and her daughter, Jane, first. Annie had slightly improved, but the child's fever hovered around 100°F for two days. Drew had managed to locate samples of the new aspirin powder that was not yet available to the public. He would use it for Annie and Jane when he saw them the next day.

The bell sounded, and Drew could hear the grumblings of his housekeeper, Mrs. Evans, as she headed for the door. He continued writing in his calendar until Mrs. Evans announced, "A Miss Holdsworth to see you, Sir Drew. Says it's urgent."

Drew's head shot up as he locked gazes with the worried, middle-aged woman standing next to Mrs. Evans. "Penny Holdsworth?"

"The very same, Sir Drew," the woman replied. "I've come concerning a lady with whom we are both acquainted."

"That will be all, Mrs. Evans."

His housekeeper's eyes narrowed, giving Miss Holdsworth dubious looks. "You'd be wanting tea, I suppose."

"I can't stay very long," Miss Holdsworth replied.

"No tea, Mrs. Evans. And please close the door behind you."

Drew rose from his chair and followed behind Mrs. Evans, effectively closing the door on her heels. His housekeeper sniffed and muttered, "Well!" but continued down the hall.

"Please take a seat, Miss Holdsworth." She sat before his desk, so Drew sat opposite. "Tell me the problem."

"I found your card some months ago among the duchess's belongings. I never let on that I knew where it was, but I had to come. Especially when she told me about running into you while delivering food. The duchess has been ill this past week and she's growing weaker by the day. I tried yesterday to call in a local doctor or send someone for an ambulance wagon, but she insisted I do no such thing. This morning, she was hot to the touch, as if flames were burning inside her." Penny rubbed her gloved hands together in worry. "You must come, Sir Drew. Please!"

"Call me doctor, Miss Holdsworth. Did you come by hansom cab?"

The maid nodded. "I shouldn't have left her."

"Where is the duchess staying?"

"We're renting a couple of rooms on Victoria Street."

"Do not admonish yourself for leaving her. We are only a few miles away." Drew stood, hurried to the side table, and opened his cabinets, gathering the necessary items. "The duchess is coughing?" he asked as he placed items in his case.

"Yes. And wheezing something terrible. I'm worried."

"Then let us depart immediately." Drew hurried toward the door, opened it, and entered the hall. "Mrs. Evans!" he yelled.

His housekeeper emerged from his bedroom, dusting rag in hand. "Aye, Sir Drew?"

Since he had been made a baronet, his housekeeper had insisted on calling him that, even though he kept gently reminding her not to. "I am off to see a patient."

"And where will you be if anyone comes asking?" Mrs. Evans inquired.

"I cannot say. Tell anyone I will return in several hours, and before you leave, Mrs. Evans, please have a pot of your delicious beef marrow broth ready. I will pick it up when I return."

Drew did not wait for a reply. He slipped into his coat,

grabbed a hat, scarf, and gloves, checked if Miss Holdsworth followed, then stepped into the snow-covered walkway and waved towards the approaching hansom cab.

Selena sick? Drew's heart banged furiously against his ribcage in worry.

CHAPTER NINE

T HEY ARRIVED AT the six-story brick building less than seven minutes later. Drew followed Miss Holdsworth to the third floor. The structure was no more than forty years old and kept in reasonable tidiness and repair, starkly contrasting with where Annie Critch and her children lived. This was a place for the increasing number of laborers and middle-class people who comprised an ever-growing section of London's population.

Miss Holdsworth fished the key from her cloak pocket and unlocked the door. Drew was hit with a blast of cold air as soon as they entered.

"My mum always said to sweat out a fever, but it didn't seem to work. So I opened the windows, what few we have. I hoped the cool air would bring down her temperature."

Drew followed the duchess's maid to the back bedroom. "You were correct, Miss Holdsworth."

"Please, call me Penny." She stood aside so Drew could examine Selena. "Mrs. B has been tired and sniffling for more than a week. She's been doing too much. I told her more than once."

"Mrs. B.?"

"She did not want me calling her 'Your Grace,' in case someone might overhear, so she came up with a name: Mrs. Beecham, widow. I've called her that for over two months. It's become a habit now."

The duchess writhed on the bed, covered in sweat, mumbling

something Drew could not make out. He immediately located the thermometer in his medical bag, shook it, and stuck it under Selena's tongue.

"Drew?" she rasped.

"Yes, Selena. Please do not talk; stay still so I can take your temperature." He tore off his overcoat and outerwear and handed it to the maid, then grabbed the chain on his watch to pull it from his waistcoat pocket and snapped it open. Drew could feel the heat radiating from her, and it sent a swift stab to his heart to see her in such distress.

"First names, already," Penny murmured. "That was quick doing."

Drew ignored the succinct observation. "Penny, is there a tub in this flat?"

"Yes, Doctor. I have to fill it. We live in a part of the building that doesn't have a tub hooked up to pipes. That costs more. But we have pipes hooked up to the sink in the kitchen and a water closet between the kitchen and parlor area."

Selena moaned, and with his free hand, Drew gently pushed away the matted golden-red hair from her forehead, then laid his hand against it. As Penny said, it was as if flames danced under her skin. "Is there any place nearby that delivers bags of ice?"

"Yes, I think so. Not far from here."

"I will need several bags to fill the bottom of the tub. I will only immerse her for a few minutes to jolt her body temperature, as I believe it's not a good idea to leave someone on ice long-term." Drew had learned in university that plunging in ice cooled the body temporarily but often triggered a rewarming effect, which could cause the body's temperature to climb higher than it had been originally. That was something he wished to avoid. Besides, he had aspirin powder, which was far more effective than ice baths or sweating out the fever before a roaring fire.

Selena moaned again, and Drew caressed her forehead. "There, there... Be calm. I am here to help." Selena sighed and stilled. Drew checked the thermometer. "103.5°F. We must bring this temperature down immediately. Set up the tub in the kitchen, then have someone deliver the ice. Do you need any money?"

"No, Doctor. I have enough. I'll go right this minute." Penny's voice caught. "I should have come to you sooner, but she insisted she wasn't sick. The duchess can be stubborn. She hid her handkerchiefs, if you can imagine. I found them this morning, filled with yellow-green phlegm. I knew then she was more ill than she admitted."

"It could be bronchitis. One family she delivers food to has it. The ice, Penny."

"At once, Doctor."

Penny disappeared into the parlor, and a few moments later, Drew heard the door slam.

Selena's head lolled about on the pillow, her skin flushed. "Everything…aches."

"I know," he soothed as he removed his coat and rolled up his shirt sleeves. "Why did you hide that you're sick?"

"I did not want to burden—" A violent coughing attack interrupted her reply.

Drew reached into his bag and laid a cotton handkerchief next to her mouth. He gently wiped it when he was done. "Your mucus suggests bronchitis, and we certainly do not want it to become more serious in nature, like pneumonia. Do you have a headache?"

Selena nodded. Her breathing was ragged, and she wheezed with each exhale, which had Drew concerned. It could already be pneumonia, as she seemed far sicker than Annie and her daughter. "Have you vomited?"

Selena groaned and shook her head. "I'm hot one minute, c-c-cold the next."

"That is undoubtedly a symptom of a high fever. We must bring your fever down before we can treat your chest congestion. Penny has gone for ice. It will mean a quick dip in an icy bath to shock the fever. After that, it will be tepid baths. I brought aspirin powder, which will assist in lowering the fever."

"Aspirin?"

"It's new, so new that only a select few doctors have access to it. It will be released to the public this spring and dispersed through apothecaries. I hear they are developing a tablet form, but that is a way off... I am boring you." Drew kept talking to keep her mind focused. Selena was restless. Her eyes darted about the room, her limbs slack but moving enough to show her agitation—another common symptom of high fever.

"Boring? Never," she rasped. "And you have the rare powder. Well done, you. You're like a pirate, capturing and hoarding your treasure." She giggled wheezily. "Captain Hornsby." Selena dragged out the last syllable of his name for several seconds. "Such a busy bee. Buzz, buzz, buzz."

Drew's eyebrows shot skyward. Had delirium set in? It could occur with a high fever.

The giggling ceased. "I'm afraid. Hold me."

Without hesitation, Drew sat on the edge of the bed and gathered her into his arms. She was so hot, he felt the burning heat of the fever through his clothes. "I'll get you through this, Selena. I promise."

"Aye, Aye, Captain," she murmured. "So tired."

"Sleep, Selena. Take a rest."

THE SLOOP-OF-WAR SHIP creaked as it rolled and pitched in the rough sea. The gathering dark clouds showed a storm brewing over the horizon, just as Captain Hornsby predicted. Selena watched as he stood on deck, legs spread to keep a steady stance, his long golden hair blowing in the strengthening wind. He wore tight black trousers, leaving nothing to the imagination, high boots, and was shirtless except for a vest, showing his muscular torso and arms to advantage. The captain looked every inch the late 18th-century pirate he was, or privateer, as he kept correcting her.

"Heave to, you scurvy rats!" the captain yelled. "Mr. Baines, batten

down the hatches. There's a black squall coming."

The barrel-chested, bald first mate nodded. "Aye, Aye, Captain. All hands on deck!" he shouted louder than the captain. Selena stood aside as the rest of the crew scrambled from below.

"Bosun, look lively!" Captain Hornsby ordered. "Compass reading."

"Northwest by north, sir!" Baines replied.

"Get to stations! Slack away the mizzen and main sheets. Staysails aft to keep her head in the wind."

"You heard the captain!" Mr. Baines ordered.

The shoeless sailors climbed the rigging ropes so fast that Selena could not believe her eyes.

"Rig and man the pumps, Mr. Baines. Bring the yards about sharp."

Mr. Baines repeated the orders, and the remaining crew went about their duties.

"Miss Seaton!" Captain Hornsby thundered as he strode toward her. "This is not the time to be on deck. Get below!"

Selena was set to argue, for the gathering storm did not appear serious. But with one glance into Captain Hornsby's clear blue eyes, she knew the weather was about to turn. She'd started as a captive, taken from her uncle some weeks ago in Port Royal. As soon as the captain discovered she was the granddaughter of a viscount, she became more of a passenger who just happened to be worthy of ransom. He gave up his cabin to her, treated her with respect, and saw to her comfort. Underneath the outer pirate persona lay an honorable gentleman. Wasn't that what Selena had always longed for? Decent, noble, and whatever other synonyms fit. And, of course, tall and handsome. Captain Hornsby encapsulated all that and more.

They were heading toward Liverpool to meet her grandfather. He'd agreed to the price, whatever it was.

He took her arm. "You're not safe up here. Go to the cabin and stay put." It started to rain, not heavily, but enough to convince her the captain spoke the truth.

Good heavens, but he was attractive. Standing close like this had her heart doing backflips. She stood on the tips of her toes and kissed his cheek. "Good luck and stay safe."

When she turned to head below, he grabbed her and brought her *against him. The captain slipped his arm around her waist. She could feel the solidness of him—and that hard part of him that caused her to moan slightly.*

"You call that a kiss?" He captured her lips and kissed her so deeply and furiously that she thought she would swoon. His tongue tangled with hers, their passion matching the swirling storm fermenting around them.

Selena ran her fingers through his long, golden hair, returning the kiss as she ground against him. No doubt the crew watched them, but she didn't care. The captain trailed hot, urgent kisses along her neck. "We don't say good luck, but fair winds and following seas."

"Good to know," she moaned as his hand trailed over her hip.

The ship rolled violently to the port side, enough to break them apart. Selena lost her footing and tripped over a coiled rope, and when the sloop rolled in the opposite direction, she went over the side. Her fall seemed to happen in slow motion. She could see the captain leaning over the side, his arm outstretched, saying her name, but she could not be sure as the wind carried the words toward the increasingly rainy horizon. A clap of thunder sounded from above.

When Selena hit the water, it was so cold that it took her breath away.

SELENA AWOKE, DISORIENTED. She was drowning in an icy sea. Her arms flailed, desperate to reach the captain's outstretched arm. Everything was dark and cold, as if death surrounded her, pulling her into its icy grip. It looked like she was about to die, just when things had turned interesting between her and the handsome pirate captain. Weeks she'd waited, wanting him to kiss her, hold her in his arms. And now *this*. She struggled to regulate her breathing as the frozen water seeped into her bones. "Help! Help me, Captain!"

Was she dreaming? Enacting a scene from the buccaneer book she was reading? Or was this real? Warm arms gathered her close and elevated her to safety. Selena knew that from now on, being held in this man's embrace would mean that all was right with the world. Nothing or no one would ever harm her again.

CHAPTER TEN

DREW LIFTED A disoriented Selena from the icy bath. He had only left her there for a few minutes, but her fevered response showed that she was in distress. Her arms slipped around his neck, and she held tight, shivering in his arms.

"Are the towels in her room?" Drew asked the maid.

"Yes, Doctor."

After Penny returned and before the ice arrived, Drew had traveled to his residence and collected the bone broth, extra blankets, towels, other relevant items, and a medium-sized basin.

Selena's eyes remained closed as her teeth chattered. He laid her on the towels on the bed, then covered Selena with more.

"Help me, Captain?" Drew questioned as Penny assisted him.

"Oh, that. It must be the book she's been reading. Remember I told you that the duchess called herself Mrs. Beecham, the widow of a sea captain? It's from one of her favorite books—a romantic adventure. She read quite a bit to escape her life with Barnsdale."

And she'd called him a pirate captain not long ago… "Dry her off, then cover her with the blankets. I will retake her temperature."

Penny tsked. "The poor dear. Look at the goosebumps on her skin. She's shivering something awful. And she's only wearing a thin chemise. How improper."

"You can change her into her nightgown after I take her

temperature. Is the broth heating on the stove?"

"Yes, Doctor," Penny replied.

As Drew shook the thermometer, Selena murmured, "Fair winds and following seas."

That must be quite the dream she was having. Drew slipped the thermometer under her tongue and marked the time with his pocket watch.

"Is she all right? Her eyes are closed," Penny asked worriedly.

"I assume the duchess is in that fevered state similar to twilight sleep." He pulled the thermometer from her mouth and studied it. "102.2°F. Better, for now. You can change her, and I will add some aspirin powder to the bone broth. I brought an invalid cup to use." Penny gave him a questioning look. "It's a partially covered teacup with a spout, much like a teapot. It's less likely to spill."

"I've never seen one. Luckily, I've never been that sick. Neither has the duchess until now. Will she get better, Doctor?"

"I will do all that I can, Penny. I'm going to fetch the broth." Drew departed and headed to the kitchen area. He glanced around the small flat. Not very fitting for a duchess with its combination parlor and kitchen, but it had a fireplace and a water closet. He stirred the broth, poured some into the invalid cup, and added some aspirin powder, mixing it until it dissolved.

Penny had Selena dressed in a fresh nightgown when he returned to the room. "Let's have her sit up partway. Are there any more pillows?"

"No. We only have one each."

"Then we'll use some of the extra blankets I brought. Give me a hand." Drew placed the invalid cup on the table, and together, they made Selena comfortable.

Penny gathered the damp towels in the dimly lit room. "I'll place these by the fire to dry. Then I'll make tea." She hurried from the room, the sound of her footsteps echoing in the quiet flat.

Drew sat on the edge of the bed and then shook Selena gently. Her eyes opened slightly. "You have to drink this, Selena. It has the aspirin powder in it." He placed the spout against her lips. "Sip it slowly." He laid his free hand against her forehead. Still hot.

"I can't," she rasped.

"You *must*. It will assist in bringing the fever down."

Selena opened her mouth slightly, and Drew tipped the cup so some of the broth pooled on her tongue.

"Now swallow. Good. We will take a moment and do it again. You are very brave."

A tear trickled from the corner of her right eye. "No, I'm not."

"You are. Never doubt it. I'll stay here through the worst of your illness, I promise. I will see you well," Drew reassured her. He meant it and would stay by her side no matter how long it took.

Selena nodded. "Thank you."

Drew sat patiently for twenty minutes, assisting her with the broth. Then he stood and covered her with another blanket. "Try to sleep." Selena closed her eyes and drifted off immediately.

Drew closed the door partway.

"Come sit at the table, Doctor," Penny instructed. "I've made a pot of tea and some sandwiches. I hope you like shrimp. It's all I had, as it's the duchess's favorite."

"Thank you. And I do like shrimp." Drew looked around for his suit coat as he removed it before placing Selena in the ice bath.

"Don't worry about your coat. I hung it up. You don't need it. It's unbearably hot in here anyway," Penny said.

True enough. Drew sat as Penny poured the tea.

"I've finally convinced the duchess to return home. I've tried for weeks. But when you told her the duke is definitely dying... He *is* dying, yes?" Penny questioned.

"Yes. The duke has a month, maybe less. The cancer is far advanced, and there are other complications. It's hard to gauge the timeline on these matters as everyone reacts differently."

Penny tsked. "That man coughed violently for well over a year. The duchess had suggested he seek medical care more than once, but he was determined not to go—such a wretched, obstinate man. I'm sure you witnessed that last year when you came on the medical call. I never liked him. A terrible thing to say about one's employer, although he did hire me as a lady's maid for the duchess."

"I'm glad you have been with her, especially the last couple of months," Drew replied, reaching for a sandwich wedge.

"I like that you haven't asked why she left. In my few experiences with doctors, they poked their nose in. You're not like that. Anyway, the duchess explained her reasons to me. I only worry about what the solicitors and society say about her absence. I told her she should ask a doctor for a note explaining she needed a long rest." Penny stared at him over the brim of her teacup, unblinking.

"Ah. And you wish me to provide said note."

"I know it's asking a lot," Penny replied. "And truly, the duchess does need a rest. It's not a lie, Doctor."

"I do not think it wise that the attending physician to the duke—and particularly one being paid by the duke—sign a doctor's letter concerning the duchess's absence, especially when I told servants and the nurse, I had no idea where she was. There would be too many questions. The duchess does not need that kind of scrutiny."

"Oh," Penny replied, disappointed.

"However, my family is involved with a wellness clinic in Hertfordshire, the Bevan Sanitorium. Family members and friends working there could provide such a note at my request."

Penny's eyebrows raised. "It's not an asylum, is it?"

"Not at all. It's a serene place of rest where some go when overwhelmed by life's complications. It's placed in an idyllic country setting, where people of all societal stations retreat to get their bearings. The duchess can tell anyone who asks probing questions that she was recommended there by one of her friends, which brings me to another topic. The duchess recently reunited with her school chums."

Penny nodded as she sipped her tea. "Yes, the duchess told me about them. Countess Winterwood and Baroness Addington."

Drew smiled slightly as he placed two sandwich wedges on his plate. "Quite a bit has occurred since the ladies met for tea in November." Without going into too much detail, Drew told the maid of Corrine and Celia becoming widows and their new marriages to his friends. Drew decided not to mention the men's blood ties as the duke's bastards. "Celia lives in the East End and is very worried about her friend. When I tell her about the duchess being ill, she will drop everything and come to the duchess's side because that is Celia—generous, cheerful, and kind. She would gladly say she recommended Bevan Sanitorium."

Penny nodded. "I'm pleased to hear the duchess's friends found happiness."

"You have tended and cared for the duchess all these years, Penny. Why not accept assistance? Lady Corrine will return to London from her honeymoon in two weeks or less. The duchess needs their support. Along with yours, she can face what lies ahead."

Penny wiped a tear from her cheek. "Yes. Tell Lady Celia to come if she wishes. I welcome it, and so will the duchess." Her voice trembled with what sounded like a mix of relief and apprehension.

"Good. After we finish eating, I would like you to take the basin, fill it with water from the tub, sit by the duchess's bedside, and use the cloth to sponge cool water on her face and chest gently. I will go and fetch Celia. It's early evening, and the restaurant is closed for the day. When I return, I will make up mustard plasters to loosen the congestion in her chest. She will need more baths. The ice should be melted by then."

"Between me and Lady Celia, we can handle things."

"I am staying through the night."

Penny raised an eyebrow. "You care for her. I sense the attraction between you. It's not wise, Doctor. She's a married woman and a duchess. I mean no disrespect."

Drew could become angry over the implication that he was beneath Selena, but he understood the maid meant no harm. "I'm here in a medical capacity. You came to *me*, and I intend to see it through. At least until the fever breaks."

"Yes. Of course, Doctor. Forgive my loose tongue. It can be unruly at times. I know it's not proper for a lady's maid to be so forward, but I adore the duchess. I consider her a dear friend."

"I will wager that the duchess feels the same for you," Drew murmured.

"I want there to be no tittle-tattle over you or the duchess, that's all. You're a good man, Doctor. I sensed that from the start. I'll wager the duchess sensed the same thing, the first moment she met you." Penny stood. "I'll fill the basin. You finish your tea."

As he completed his meal, Selena's well-being consumed Drew's thoughts. He was determined to keep his feelings in check for her sake, as the last thing he wanted was to bring any unwanted scrutiny. The future was uncertain, but his focus remained clear—getting Selena well was his top priority.

SELENA GROANED AND opened her eyes. Everything was blurry, so she could not see much. The first thing that hit her was the rolling body aches, which made every muscle and tendon throb horribly. Someone was sitting in a chair beside the bed. "Celia?" she croaked.

"Yes, it's me, Selena. We've all been so worried about you. Corrine sent a telegram. She and Mitchell will be leaving for London the day after tomorrow—or whenever they can arrange travel, depending on the weather. They're in Pevensey Bay, in

Sussex. Detective Sergeant Mitchell Simpson of the Metropolitan Police is her new husband. Quite the story there—and I have quite a tale to tell, but when you've recovered." Celia squeezed her hand affectionately. "I'm rambling. We will see you well." Her words were filled with love and reassurance, comforting Selena in her weakened state.

Oh, how she had missed her friends. "I'm so glad you're here." Selena glanced at the window. "How much time has passed?"

"It's thirty minutes past noon the next day. I have taken the day off from the restaurant and will stay with you. You still have a fever, but it is less serious than last night."

Restaurant? Whatever did she mean? Selena recalled people coming and going from her room at various times. Still, the one she remembered most had the gentlest touch as he wiped her fevered brow and fed her bone broth, whispering words of encouragement in his deep, empathetic voice. "Doctor Hornsby?"

"He stayed with you all night and hardly left your bedside. He departed a couple of hours ago to attend to other patients, and then he will get a few hours of sleep before he returns here later in the afternoon."

Drew stayed all night? Everything swelled up and burst forth in a surge of emotion. Selena did something she had not done for many years—she cried. The sobs ended in great gulps of air. Then she started coughing. Penny rushed into the room.

"There, Selena. Calm yourself," Celia urged as she held her hand tighter. "You're not alone. Not any longer. You have people who care for you, and we will see you through this illness and what lies ahead." Celia released her hand and snatched a handkerchief from the table, then leaned in to dab the tears from Selena's cheeks. "Take a deep breath and exhale. Good. I have brought plenty of food from the restaurant. My husband, Liam, is an excellent chef. There is chicken soup, rolls, scones, seafood chowder with plenty of shrimp, and some cold ham and cheese."

"It's a wonderful feast," Penny added. "Perhaps we can give

you chicken soup and a roll later. But first, I have bone broth with aspirin powder. The doctor said I should serve you some as soon as you woke. I'll go get it." Penny hurried from the room.

"Penny must have been a comfort to you these past years," Celia said gently. "She is very devoted to you."

Selena sniffled and nodded.

"After the broth, you must sleep. Drew says it assists with the healing. He also instructed me to place a fresh mustard plaster on your chest. I'll go and get it." Celia patted her arm. "All will be well, dearest. Wait and see."

After her friend left the room, Selena choked back another sob. For the first time since her marriage, she did *not* feel alone. Yes, she'd had Penny during those years, but now she had her friends, including Drew. Her dreams were full of him in whatever incarnation, either the dashing pirate captain or the compassionate, passionate doctor. To be attracted to a man at this juncture of her life was not wise. Yes, Drew had taken over her dreams, fever or not.

Before Selena could explore that attraction—and she *knew* it was mutual—she had to return to her role as the Duchess of Barnsdale. And that might be the most challenging thing of all.

CHAPTER ELEVEN

REW ARRIVED AT the Victoria Street flat at four that afternoon. He had not eaten much the past twenty-four hours and had had even less sleep, although he managed to nap after seeing other patients this morning. The enticing scents of chicken soup and fresh bread were welcoming.

After Penny took his hat, coat, and medical bag, he pointed toward the bedroom.

"Selena is sleeping," Celia replied. "Come, have something to eat."

They sat at the small table while Penny served chicken soup with rolls and cold ham. Once she poured the tea, Penny joined them.

"I sent a telegram to Ryan Wollstonecraft at the Bevan Sanitorium," Drew announced as he buttered his scone.

"Wollstonecraft? Like the author of Frankenstein, Mary Wollstonecraft Shelley?" Celia asked.

"The very same, although distantly related. Ryan's uncle is the Earl of Carnstone. The Wollstonecrafts of Kent are family friends and have teamed up with the Hornsbys over the decades in many endeavors, such as the free medical clinics where I often work. Ryan works as a physician at the sanatorium in Hertford-shire. I sent a telegram requesting a letter regarding the Duchess of Barnsdale and the dates in question. I told him I would explain later. Thankfully, he replied immediately and said the letter would be sent by train. It should be in London by tomorrow night. He will ensure that the story of her staying there will stand if anyone investigates."

"Oh, what a relief!" Penny exclaimed. "I was that worried."

"So, Selena is returning to the Barnsdale residence... But why, exactly?" Celia asked. "I am not being sarcastic. I truly wish to know."

"To sit at the dying duke's bedside, showing support—" Penny began.

"I did that," Celia replied, frowning. "Sorry to interrupt, but I sat at my husband's bedside for years, and how did he repay me? He left me out of the will, and I had no dowry to live on, and there were no dower rights I could claim. I was left with nothing."

"I'm sorry to hear that, my lady!" Penny gasped. "What if Barnsdale does the same?"

"Please, call me Celia. Only through the generosity of my husband's distant cousin and heir was I given a stipend, but until then? I was thrown into the streets." She paused, thinking. "Is there an heir?" Celia asked.

Penny sipped her tea. "I've never heard talk of one. I don't think so. It's only males in the family, traced back to the previous dukes, correct?"

Celia sighed. "Yes. There must be a direct link to any previous dukes."

Penny shrugged as she took a spoonful of soup. "There's been no mention of distant cousins or great uncles, but who's to know?"

"The solicitor will have to search the extended family tree, which may take some time. If there is no heir, everything entailed will be turned over to the crown," Celia sighed. "You're right. Selena should return and stand her ground, or the duke's solicitor will claim desertion, and society will turn against her. When the duke dies, all eyes will turn on her. She does not need the added stress. It's best that her absence be explained."

"My thoughts exactly," Drew replied.

A moan sounded from the bedroom, and Drew jumped to his feet. "I will attend to her."

When he entered, his heart squeezed in empathy for Selena, who thrashed about in her sleep. Nightmares, no doubt. After locating the basin, Drew filled it with cool water and returned to the bedroom, closing the door partway. He sat on the chair, dipped the cloth in the water, and gently dabbed her forehead. In the past four years in his duties as a physician, he had seen patients as ill as this recover swiftly, and others continue to spiral downward to the point of no return. He prayed Selena was in the former. Losing a patient was upsetting enough, but to lose Selena? It would devastate him.

Selena's eyes fluttered, then she sighed. "Drew."

"Yes. I'm here."

"Annie and her daughter?" she rasped.

"On the mend. Jane's temperature hovers near normal. They will have to stay in bed for a few more days. And so will you."

"The families I deliver food to—" Selena coughed.

"Try not to talk too much. Your health is my priority. Do you understand you cannot assist everyone?" Selena nodded. "For I will tell you, it's a bitter pill to swallow. I realized that soon after becoming a physician. I help who I can when I can, but I also know I have to look after my own physical and mental health. It would be best if you did the same," Drew whispered compassionately.

"But they need help. Annie and her children..." Selena said. "And there are others..."

"I understand. And you can help them...once you've recovered. I'll ask my father about the current status of Devil's Acre. He's quite knowledgeable on these critical matters. Then you can plan from there." He continued to trail the cool cloth across her forehead, temple, and cheeks as he spoke.

"And Barnsdale?" Selena whispered.

"The morphine shots are keeping the pain controlled, but

barely and not for long. I will have to start using a more potent mixture of opiates soon, which means he will be unconscious more than conscious. He is nearing the end."

Selena sighed. "I'm returning there when I recover."

"Penny told me. I believe it's wise. I have undertaken something on your behalf." Drew informed her of the letter coming from the Bevan Sanitorium.

Selena grasped his hand. Her skin was cold, and she shivered. "Thank you so much. Will you hold me? Please?"

"Of course." Drew set the basin and cloth aside, then sat on the bed beside her, pulling her into his arms. Selena laid her head against his chest as he pulled the quilt to her chin. "Better?"

"Yes. You're so warm. I feel—safe." The tips of her fingers stroked his chest, causing his heart to stutter. Then she ran her hand along his arm. "I cannot stop touching you."

"Then, don't." Drew did the same, caressing her cheek, running his thumb along her lower lip. He gently kissed her forehead. "Relax."

Selena gazed up at him, and the air around them crackled with desire. He wanted to kiss her deeply, run his hands over her curves. She must have felt his arousal as she was all but pulled into his lap. But this was not the time and place to explore such yearnings.

"Sleep, sweetheart," he murmured huskily.

Drew held her closer. Selena felt so right in his arms. Of all the women in London, a married duchess had touched his heart. But it was more than her delicate beauty. Her vulnerability stood out, alongside her stalwart bravery, and Drew found that mixture potent. It released emotions he had never experienced for a woman—desire, admiration, and a fierce need to protect her. All this was beyond his instincts as a physician and as a man. The compassion he felt toward most patients was heightened with her.

Drew would do anything to keep her safe.

Slowly, he, too, drifted off to sleep.

HE WAS SHAKEN awake by Celia.

"Sorry," she whispered. "Two hours have passed. Penny says it's time for more broth and medicine."

"Yes, of course." He gently laid Selena against the pillows and blankets. She never stirred. "We should allow her to sleep another hour."

Drew followed Celia into the parlor, closing the bedroom door behind him.

"You should head home and get a proper sleep," Celia urged kindly. "You look exhausted."

Drew rubbed his eyes. "I am, rather. I will go home and set my alarm clock. The bell is loud enough to wake me. I should return here by eleven, then I will escort you home. Thank you, Celia, for assisting. You have been a big support."

"Selena is recovering, then?"

"Yes, she is. I believe by early next week, she will be over the worst of it."

Drew could see Celia had more to say or ask, but she refrained, and Drew appreciated it. He and Selena cuddled together—in bed? A professional in the medical field would never do that. He should have called Celia or Penny in the room to comfort her.

But Drew could not refuse Selena anything.

Six days later...

SELENA SAT UP in bed, eating a delicious meal prepared by Celia's husband. He had delivered it when Celia visited, and good heavens, but he was handsome with his dark hair, fair skin, and clear blue eyes. The love and respect Liam and Celia shared were evident, and although she was happy for her dear friend, it caused a brief spasm of longing.

Could it be just a few months ago that Selena had declared

her heart dead and that she did not want to be touched? It seemed so long ago. Gains had been made, however. Still, she was worried. Would returning to Chapel Street somehow undo all she had accomplished concerning her intellectual and mental well-being? Selena could not allow it. If she could gather the daring to continue with her charity work even though the rookery boss wanted her gone from the area, surely she could stand her ground with her dying husband.

A knock sounded at the door, and Selena could hear muffled voices. Penny opened the bedroom door. "Lady Corrine Simpson."

A rush of emotion tore through Selena, and she held out her hand. "Corrine!"

Her friend rushed to her side, took her hand, and squeezed it. "My dear Selena."

"May I take your cloak, Lady Corrine?" Penny asked. "And would you like a cup of tea?"

"Yes, to both, Penny, thank you." Corrine handed Penny her burgundy wool cape, sat beside Selena, and retook her hand. Penny departed, closing the door partway. "Mitchell and I arrived in London last night. I went immediately to Celia to catch up on the news. Are you feeling better?"

"Yes, with regard to my bronchitis and my melancholy mood as well. I'm afraid I was not in a good place when I visited with you and Celia last November. I apologize for revealing so much and saying things I did not mean. I've already apologized to Celia."

Corrine patted her hand. "If we cannot confide in our friends, who can we share our secrets with? Real friends say they are sorry. So I will do the same. I want to apologize for not writing all those years ago. You sent a few letters, and Celia sent even more, but I ignored them because I was ashamed."

"Of what?" Selena whispered.

"My father lost everything. And since my brother was too young to take the reins, I became responsible for earning a living.

I trained to become a nurse." Penny entered the room, took Celia's tray, then brought another with a teapot, mugs, and a plate of biscuits. Then she closed the door behind her. Corrine explained how she worked as a nurse in an army hospital, workhouse infirmary, and clinics to keep the wolf from the door, but her arrogant father kept spending money, increasing their debt.

"By the time Travis Addington came to me with his marriage proposal and offered to clear my father's arrears and pay a stipend toward the viscountcy, I was so weary that I agreed. My brother will be the viscount one day. He can handle that end now and in the future. There's more, of course. I will tell you how Mitchell came into my life the next time we meet. I want Celia to hear it, as well. And we definitely want to hear about Celia's adventure. Have you met her husband?"

Celia nodded and smiled. "Very handsome."

"And he cooks! What more can a woman want?"

Selena laughed, and then she stopped. "That is the first time I have laughed in ages. Thank you for that."

"We will laugh more in the future, I promise. I'm so pleased we have renewed our friendship. The Bluebells are together again."

"Yes, we are. I'm pleased, too." Selena sobered. "I read of the baron's murder in the paper. I should have reached out. I *am* sorry. But I had just left Barnsdale and decided I must remain focused on myself. That sounds utterly selfish now that I say that aloud. Forgive me."

Corrine tilted her head, giving Selena a wistful look. "All three of us were in a melancholy state, Selena, in untenable situations and unhappy marriages. It's time for us to move on. You still have Barnsdale to deal with. It will not be easy to return and play the role of the supporting wife. You are very courageous in doing so."

"It is tempting to stay right here in this flat and wait for him to die. He does not deserve any comfort from me." Selena poured the tea, added the milk, and passed Corrine the cup. "But I must face my past if I am to move into the future. I have no idea where I stand with regard to the dukedom. I believe the solicitor is searching the family tree for an heir, but why haven't they done it before? Who knows? The dukedom goes back a few centuries. I should be there to ensure my rights—if I have any." She smiled. "Now, enough about me. Tell me a little about your detective sergeant. You can save the good parts, like how you met, when we are with Celia. But what is he like? And are you happy?"

Corrine blushed, then smiled. "I thank Providence he came into my life. I love him so much. He was a support and a protector, comforted me when I needed it, and spoke the truth when I needed to hear it. He and Liam Hallahan are half brothers to Drew Hornsby."

Selena nearly spat her tea across her bed linens. "What?"

"It's no longer a secret. All three men are the illegitimate sons of the late Duke of Chellenham. That horrid man left progeny in all corners of England, I'll be bound. They only recently discovered they share a bloodline. They have become friends and act more like brothers with each passing week. Wait until you meet Mitchell. His resemblance to Drew is quite noticeable, Liam, too, if you look close enough."

"Unbelievable," Selena whispered. What a revelation. It appeared there were more than a few layers to the good doctor.

"When are you returning to Chapel Street?" Corrine asked, pulling Selena from her thoughts.

"The day after tomorrow, if I receive medical clearance."

"Celia and I will be offering our support. You are not alone in this, Selena," Corrine reassured her.

Selena smiled. "I welcome it, and I am comforted by your support. It means the world."

"And Drew will offer support as well?" Corrine interjected with an eyebrow raised.

"Doctor Hornsby has been a friend and a good doctor."

"Nothing more?"

"No," Selena answered a little too swiftly. "I am still married." Selena exhaled shakily, her inner turmoil evident in her trembling breath. Her true feelings, a tumultuous mix of guilt and desire, were more than mere words could express.

Corrine took her hand. "Believe me, I know how you feel. I was still married to Addington when I first met Mitchell—the conflicting feelings of culpability and yearning were overwhelming. I will say no more about it. When you are ready to discuss it, know Celia and I are here for you."

Conflicting feelings described how she felt perfectly. But it all had to be set aside. Whether Selena was strong enough to do it remained to be seen.

Chapter Twelve

D REW ARRIVED AT the Victoria Street flat just before noon to examine Selena and give her the all clear to return to the Barnsdale residence. Thankfully, her wheezing cough had lessened, and she had regained most of her strength. They hadn't had much opportunity to speak this past week because of her illness and all the comings and goings. Drew was pleased that everyone had rallied around Selena, giving her hearty meals and keeping her company.

He knocked on the door, and Corrine answered. "Oh, Drew. How lovely to see you! Come in." She stood aside to let him pass. "I am about to depart. Penny has gone to the shops to buy a few necessities. How are you?"

"A little tired, but well enough. How are you settling in?" The new Baron Addington had gifted Corrine with her late husband's residence.

"The baron's staff managed a miracle in our absence. All of Mitchell's furniture is in place. I need to attend to a few details, and everything will be settled by the end of next week. Thank you again for lending us the cottage in Pevensey Bay. It was perfect, at least up until the snowstorm." Corrine took his arm and pulled him toward the kitchen area. "At Liam's request, Mitchell is contacting his fellow officers to gather information about Sharpe regarding his criminal doings and background," Corrine murmured.

"Good. I have also contacted my father, Viscount Hawkestone. He's returning to our country home next week. Before he departs, he is collecting data about Devil's Acre and its future, if it has one," Drew whispered.

"Brilliant. I will inform Mitchell. I must dash."

Drew followed Corrine into the parlor, where she picked her wool cloak from the hook by the door. He set his bag aside and assisted her.

"Penny should return shortly," Corrine said as she slipped on her gloves. "I've already said my goodbyes to Selena. I think she is looking much better. But you are more equipped to make that observation." Corrine kissed his cheek. "Talk to you soon."

After closing the door behind Corrine, Drew grabbed his medical bag and headed toward Selena's bedroom. He found her sitting upright, wearing a dressing gown. Her lovely hair was styled in an upward sweep, with a few curling tendrils framing her face.

He must have been staring, for she said, "I have had a bath and my hair washed. I look and feel halfway human today, and I hope presentable." Selena gave him a brief, teasing smile, which enhanced her natural beauty.

"Yes," Drew murmured. "Extremely presentable." His heart raced at the sight of her, but he quickly composed himself. It was best that he slipped into physician mode instead of letting his feelings show. "Still coughing?"

"A little. It gets better each day."

Drew pulled his stethoscope from his bag. "Undo the button on your dressing gown, if you please." He sounded officious to his own ears. Once he had the equipment in place, he breathed on the chest piece and placed it against her skin. "Breathe in. Hold it, now exhale. Again."

"There is still a slight wheeze, isn't there?" Selena asked worriedly.

Drew placed the stethoscope into his bag. "Yes, but there is a great improvement. You've had bronchitis for close to two weeks. The worst is over. The congestion has loosened, and you certainly have more energy. However, the cough can linger for up to six weeks."

"I am relieved to hear that," Selena said as she rebuttoned the dressing gown. "About the worst of it being over, not the coughing."

"You may return to Chapel Street the day after tomorrow, but continue to rest for at least another ten days." Drew pulled an envelope from his bag and laid it on the bedside table. "Here is the letter from the Bevan Sanitorium, if anyone asks."

"I cannot thank you enough for all you have done," Selena said, her voice quivering with emotion. Her gratitude was profound, and it touched him. "Can you stay until Penny returns? I have an idea to share with you."

By rights, Drew should leave. Being here with Selena was not a good idea, and he wondered if Corrine had departed earlier than needed to leave them alone.

"Of course." He sat on the chair by her bed. "What is it?"

"This flat. The rent is paid until the end of February, and I have enough money for three more months beyond that. I wish for Annie Critch and her three children to stay here until I can find her something else. Do you think it is a good idea?"

"Your intentions are compassionate, and I admire and respect that. But I must be blunt. Annie and her children do not pass as middle-class or even the laboring class. They are dressed in rags. Their present living situation is not ideal. Even though they now have soap, keeping the place clean and sanitary is next to impossible. Fleas, rats, mice, and other vermin permeate the building. The landlord of this set of flats would take one look at them and turn them away. It's not fair, but that is how it is."

A furrow knotted between her brows. "No, it's *not* fair. But we can buy them appropriate clothes, and you can ensure they do not carry unwanted visitors like fleas. Jimmy can still work at the pub—has he started employment there?"

Drew pushed his glasses up his nose with the tip of his index finger. "Yes, he has. And doing well, by all accounts. Teddy gives him leftover food to take home, so the family eats better."

"Well, there! He will only be a little farther away from going to work. And better food means improved health. Annie can continue with her mending for the tailor shop. The girls can go to school. The furniture in this flat comes with the place, and I can leave the blankets, pillows, dishes, and other kitchen items for them to keep. Although some of the blankets and other items are yours." Selena exhaled. "There is only one bedroom, but it's large. We can arrange small beds for the girls, and Jimmy can sleep on the sofa."

"Who is the landlord?"

"I am not certain. The manager of the building lives on the top floor. Mr. Colin Caywood. He collects the rent and takes care of any issues. I can tell him my cousin and her children need a place to stay."

Drew folded his arms. "I believe we should both meet with the landlord. I can throw my aristocratic ties around, being the son of a viscount and nephew to a duke. I was just made a baronet. That title has some sway, as well."

"I never got a chance to congratulate you. Penny read the news in the paper. Then I became ill. You deserve to be made a baronet. You are a wonderful, caring doctor."

"Thank you."

"Drew?"

"Hmm?"

"I like you—very much," she whispered.

His heart sped up at the words and the tender way she conveyed them. "I like you, too. Very. Much."

Selena sighed forlornly. "It is all we dare say right now, isn't it?"

Emotion surged through him, and the urge to say, *I absolutely adore you. You have enchanted me. Body and soul,* danced on the tip of his tongue. But he willed the words away. "Yes. It's all we dare," he replied gravely.

"How old are you? I meant to ask it earlier."

"I am twenty-five. I turn twenty-six at the end of March."

Selena's eyes widened. "Oh, my word. I turned thirty-one last month. I am a little over five years older." Selena looked distressed.

"Is that an impediment to friendship? Or something more—hypothetically speaking."

"Well, yes," Selena murmured. "A woman involved with a younger man—hypothetically speaking—would be frowned upon by Society, and so would the union. If one existed."

"But a man twenty years older, or in the case of Celia, thirty-five years older, can take a much younger wife, and no one turns a hair. Personally, I do not care what society thinks of my choices concerning my life, including my choice of a partner."

Selena nodded. "I know you're right. Even though I outwardly declare I don't care what people say, I occasionally worry too much about what others think. It's a habit hard to break. I will endeavor to change that."

Drew took her hand, and she laced her fingers through his. "And what do you think of a younger man as a lover?"

Their gazes locked. The air crackled with electricity as their mutual attraction took on its own life force. He acted boldly saying that, but it slipped out before he could stop it. How many times had he dreamed of such? Selena in his arms—and his bed.

"I suppose," Selena replied breathlessly, "it would depend on the man."

Good God. Blood rushed to his shaft, and every nerve ending sizzled. Drew had to stop this right here. Reluctantly, he tore his gaze from her, and it landed on the book on the bed. He sat upright and grimaced at the tightness of his trousers. Thankfully, he still wore his long coat. Drew released her hand. "What are you reading?"

"*That* is a definite change in subject. *Our Mutual Friend*, by Charles Dickens. Celia brought it to me. It is one of her husband's favorite books."

"Allow me to head upstairs and see Mr. Caywood. Hopefully, I can arrange for the landlord to see us tomorrow. If you like, I can read to you when I return. I have no further appointments this afternoon."

Her face lit up, and the dazzling smile nearly blinded him. She was so beautiful, as much inside than out, maybe more so. "I would like that. Please stay for supper. Celia brought a large pot of seafood chowder."

"I will stay." Without thinking, he kissed her hand, then swiftly released it.

"I will come with you." Selena swung her legs around the edge of the bed. "I should be up, anyway. It will take me a moment to change."

"It's unnecessary," Drew said, then rubbed his bearded chin. "But perhaps you should be there since you're the occupant. Have you met with Caywood before?"

"When we first arrived." She opened the drawer of the small dresser. "There it is. I wear this large shawl over my head to hide my hair. I came to Devil's Acre a few times before renting this flat. I soon learned that my shade of hair attracted attention. I've been covering it up ever since."

"Very wise. Although, I think Sharpe and his minions are aware because they know you as the Golden Angel."

"Exactly why I hide it. I'll join you in the parlor."

Drew stepped outside to allow Selena to change clothes. He glanced around the flat. It was spacious and more comfortable than where Annie and her children stayed. Why couldn't they live here? Perhaps he should involve Liam and Celia's charity initiative. And why not? He sat on the board.

Selena opened her bedroom door. She wore a modest gray wool gown with a scarf wrapped around her head. She lifted the oversized shawl to cover the scarf. "I am ready," she said. "It's best you do most of the talking, Sir Drew."

Drew chuckled as they climbed the stairs to the top floor, and Selena directed him to the correct flat. He knocked. The door flew open, and an older man of medium height and graying hair looked Drew up and down. "What is it? Looking for a place, are you?"

"No. I am with Mrs. Beecham, who rents number 314. We wish to speak with you regarding renting that flat and to make an appointment with the landlord. We have a proposal."

"And who are you?" Mr. Caywood snapped.

"Sir Drew Hornsby."

"Allow them to come in, Caywood," a deep voice boomed from inside the flat.

"It so happens the landlord is here today." Caywood opened the door wider and stepped aside. "Mr. Luke Caspian. Through here, please."

Drew and Selena followed Mr. Caywood into the parlor. A tall man stood at the window with his hands clasped behind his back. Warning bells sounded in Drew's head. The man had golden hair.

No. It can't be.

The man turned around. The landlord was smartly dressed in a dark-gray afternoon suit any wealthy businessman would wear. Drew clutched Selena's arm as if to warn her not to react.

The man standing before them was none other than Lucian Sharpe.

CHAPTER THIRTEEN

S ELENA GASPED BUT quickly covered it by coughing into her handkerchief. Luckily, Drew gave her a few seconds' warning by applying pressure to her arm. She kept her head down, not only to show deference but also to avoid his attention.

"Caywood, offer our guests a seat," Sharpe ordered.

The manager led them to the sofa and then stood aside.

"And how may I assist, Sir Drew?" Sharpe asked as he sat opposite in a leather wing chair. The corner of his mouth twitched slightly. Selena couldn't tell whether it was annoyance, amusement, or a mixture of both.

"I am a physician and Mrs. Beecham is my patient. She has been unwell for the past two weeks and wishes to return to her family to recover fully."

Selena coughed, allowing the men to hear the palpable wheezing rattle in her chest.

"Mrs. Beecham's rent is paid until the end of the month, and she requests that an acquaintance, a distant cousin and a worthy woman, and her three children be allowed to move into the flat. Mrs. Beecham is willing to pay upfront for a further six months."

Six? She barely had enough money for three months' rent.

"Indeed?" Sharpe's gaze slid to her, and Selena gave him a wan smile. The way he studied her made her entirely uncomfortable. She sniffled, wiped her nose, and looked away, keeping the handkerchief close to her face to hopefully obscure her features.

"Mrs. Beecham is paying for three of those months, and I'm arranging payment for the other three, through the Hallahan Initiative, a charity I'm affiliated with."

"Hallahan. I see. And what happens when the charity runs out in six months? How is this family to live?" Sharpe asked pointedly. "I don't fancy tossing a woman and her three children to the cobbles. But I will do it for nonpayment of rent."

Selena did not doubt it for a minute.

"Well, the lad Jimmy is working at Finnian's Chop House under the manager, Teddy Chisholm," Drew said. "He earns a shilling a week while training, which will soon rise to three and six weekly. Mrs. Critch mends for a tailor shop and earns a few shillings a month; the initiative will find other work for her."

Sharpe crossed his legs. "That will not be enough to cover the weekly rent, let alone for a month. I'm here today to discuss rental increases with Mr. Caywood. Instead of a weekly rent of three shillings for that particular unit, I am raising it to three and eight, starting next month."

Selena silently fumed. What a miserable man Sharpe was.

"We can cover that. I can assure you that the family is re-spectable and clean. Surely, you can offer a slight discount because we are paying upfront. Mr. *Caspian.*"

Sharpe's mouth quirked. He got the message. *Allow the family to stay and for a discount, or your real name might be revealed.* Selena felt Mr. Caywood had no idea of the landlord's criminal alter ego.

"We can come to an agreement. When are you leaving, Mrs. Beecham?" Sharpe asked, sliding his intense gaze to her again.

Selena wiped her nose. "The day after tomorrow, Mr. Caspi-an. The Critches will move in the same day."

"Caywood, work out the rent for six months—March until the end of August. Give a four percent discount."

"Right away, Mr. Caspian." The manager disappeared into another room.

"Mrs. Beecham, there is no need for you to stay," Sharpe purred in a honey-smooth voice. "I can conclude the negotiations with Sir Drew. I wish to stipulate this, however. This building will not become a dumping ground for charity inclinations and projects, regardless of who is behind them."

Selena fought her annoyance, trying to keep her face neutral. Sharpe was loathsome despite his handsome countenance, faux veneer of respectability, and upper-class accent. His eyes were not what she would call dead, but they were undoubtedly frosty.

"Your message regarding the charity has been received, Mr. Caspian. However, I will wait here until the deal is finalized," Selena replied firmly.

"Suit yourself. Are you paying cash, Sir Drew?"

Drew reached into his coat's side pocket and pulled out a roll of notes. Selena's eyes widened at the thickness of the roll, but soon schooled her features. Had Drew borrowed money from his father?

"Yes, I will pay in notes, Mr. Caspian," Drew answered indifferently. "I will require a receipt."

Mr. Caywood entered the room and handed Sharpe a paper with the amount for total rent due, for him to inspect. "Very good. Hand this to Sir Drew."

Drew looked it over. "That is satisfactory."

Sharpe stood. "I will write the receipt myself." He departed as Drew peeled off numerous notes and placed them on the table before him.

Mr. Caywood swiftly gathered them up. "Do you require change, Sir Drew?"

"Keep it as a commission on the deal. And your word that you will not harass the Critch family in any way." Drew handed Mr. Caywood his card. "If you have any problems, contact me."

"You have my word, Sir Drew."

Sharpe reentered and handed Drew a folded note. "That concludes our business. For today, at least. Mr. Caywood will visit Mrs. Critch to go over the tenancy rules. Give the keys to the new occupants when you depart. Good afternoon, Sir Drew. Mrs. Beecham."

A firm dismissal if Selena ever heard one. Candidly, she wanted to leave this man's presence. He made her uneasy for reasons beyond his blatant, barely hidden criminality. Still, she could not pinpoint exactly what caused such thoughts.

Drew took her arm as they headed downstairs. Once outside her door, Drew unfolded the note. "He wants to see me tomorrow afternoon at his office in Finnian's Chop House."

"Heavens, what for?"

"To warn me, no doubt. To keep quiet about his secret identity. This paints a curious side to Sharpe. He is more intelligent and shrewder than I initially believed."

"Why an alter ego?" Selena whispered as she unlocked the door.

"To have a legitimate side of his business. To escape into another life when the time comes." They entered the parlor. "Enough about Sharpe for now. This building's rents are more expensive than I thought."

Selena removed her shawl and scarf and laid them across the back of the sofa. "And I am in one of the cheaper units. Perhaps this is too middle-class for the Critches, and I feel terrible for saying it. I want them to feel comfortable and safe, if only for six months. And seeing Sharpe owns these flats, the sooner we make other arrangements, the better."

"Why the Critch family out of all the families you assisted?" Drew asked.

"I sensed an innate goodness in them. In better circumstances, Annie could have worked in a dress shop. She is very talented with a needle. Jimmy is a good lad, eager to help his family. The girls are sweet. Annie says her husband abandoned them several months ago. She heard he went to Liverpool to get a job on one of the steamships. She soon realized he would not send them money or ever return." Selena joined Drew on the sofa. "I know there are many families in this predicament. I want to do something for at least one family, more than a loaf of bread and a sack of pennies. I want to give them a fresh start. There are one or two others I want to check in on when I'm fully recovered."

Drew laced his fingers through hers. "Then we shall do all we can to assist."

"The Hallahan Initiative is real, then?"

"Yes, indeed. Liam and I, as well as Celia, are just getting it off the ground. We plan to have many aristocratic patrons, so we can certainly afford to assist Annie Critch and her children. We will find them a satisfactory situation before the six months are up."

"You mentioned moving to them, when you last visited?"

Drew nodded. "They were most anxious to find someplace else, and I'm sure they will enjoy living here. They are very grateful for the opportunity and eager for a better life. Isn't that what we all want at the end of the day?"

They still held hands when Penny came through the door, carrying two baskets. She stared at them, raising her eyebrows.

Drew immediately stood. "Allow me to help you with those."

"Doctor Hornsby is staying for supper, Penny," Selena said.

"Oh, is he, now?"

Selena gave Penny a warning look.

"And he is more than welcome," she added brightly, handing Drew a basket.

"The Critches will take possession when we leave, the day after next. It is all arranged. They will be staying here for at least six months," Selena said.

"That's good to know. I bought the food staples you requested to get them started. Flour, tea, sugar, butter, vegetables, a packet of digestive biscuits, bacon, eggs, and some cheese." Penny pulled a small paper bag from her basket. "And some lemon drops for the children."

"How thoughtful. The next step is clothing," Selena stated.

"Celia has boxes of clean, used garments," Drew suggested. "I will pick them up tomorrow and take them to Annie."

Selena clapped her hands together. "I am so pleased this is coming together. Let us get supper ready."

AFTER A DELICIOUS meal of Liam's seafood chowder, Selena sat upright in bed, listening to Drew read to her from *Our Mutual Friend*. His voice was deep and melodic, and he gave emotion to every passage. The unlikely love story between Eugene and Lizzie struck a chord. They came from such different backgrounds and social situations, yet Lizzie's nursing of Eugene from a near-fatal attack drew them closer, enough that they could admit their feelings and be married. Lizzie's love and devotion brought Eugene from the brink of death.

Although Selena was not fatally ill, she felt as if Drew's tender care and consideration had brought her back to life, and in more ways than one. Her heart beat with decided purpose, allowing emotions she thought gone forever to reemerge.

DREW CLOSED THE book as Selena dashed a tear from her cheek. "How romantic. Celia's right. This book is entertaining and dramatic. There are so many varied characters from all walks of life. Have you read it before?"

"Yes. I quite enjoyed it. The book is a stinging rebuke of society's so-called respectability and monetary and class values. It also shines a light on dishonesty and complacency."

"I find Eugene and Lizzie's love story particularly touching, seeing that they were from different classes. If Eugene hadn't been attacked, would they have found their way to each other? Knowing society as I do, I suspect not. Would there not be too wide a chasm?"

"If two people are in love, I believe there should be no impediment to their hearts joining as one," Drew murmured. "None at all."

That emotional statement made Selena's heart speed up. "You truly believe that?"

"Yes. I only have to look at our friends to see the proof. A detective and a baroness? A chef and a countess?"

"A doctor and a duchess?" Selena added softly.

Drew closed his eyes. He was about to say something, probably to dismiss any possible connection because of her married state. And he would not be wrong. *However…*

"Corrine told me that you, her husband, and Celia's husband recently discovered you are half brothers. How did that come about? I know you are adopted."

Drew's eyes snapped open. "I am a bastard. One of the duke's bastards. The late Duke of Chellenham's, to be exact."

Selena nodded. "Corrine told me. Not all the details, but the general facts. And it does not matter to me. Perhaps you will tell me all the particulars sometime in the future, as I want to know you better."

"Selena—"

"I know. Let me say this. I am married. Unhappily, but married. My husband is dying and will pass soon. It's a stark fact, but there it is. Until then, we will act as polite strangers when you come to tend to the duke. We will not exchange longing looks or touch each other in any way. You will act every inch the professional you are, and I will act as the cold duchess everyone expects to see."

"I *am* genuinely sorry I said that," Drew murmured. "It's not true. Not in the least."

"It was said long ago, or so it seems. Much has happened since then."

"Yes. Much."

Selena took his hand. "But when the duke *is* gone, I will toss aside that life gladly. I do not care about proper mourning any more than Celia or Corrine did. My happiness is more important. I want you to court me. I want us to know each other better. I want—you."

"God, Selena," Drew moaned.

"Kiss me," she whispered. "As if it might be the last time."

"But it won't be," he replied huskily.

"No. It will not be. I promise that if nothing else."

Drew sat on the edge of the bed, cupped her cheeks, and took complete possession. The kiss was, in turn, sweet but ferocious, tender but passionate. It took her breath away. It was everything she had dreamed of and more. His tongue swept through her mouth in a commanding way and she eagerly returned it. There was so much longing and desire in that one kiss that Selena did not want it to end. He only ceased kissing her when they heard Penny's footfalls heading in their direction.

Drew stood. "Goodnight, Your Grace."

Selena touched her lips, her eyes filling with tears. "Goodnight, Doctor Hornsby."

He exited the room, and when she heard the outer door close, she allowed the tears to flow. Selena did not sob uncontrollably. She wept because she was falling in love, and while that filled her with joy, it also terrified her.

Penny sat in the chair and patted her hand. "It will be all right, Your Grace. You'll see. All will work out fine, just as you wish it to."

Pray, let it be so.

CHAPTER FOURTEEN

Drew entered Finnian's Chop House at one o'clock sharp the next day. Jimmy Critch was standing in the corner, clearing tables. The lad waved when he saw Drew, so he headed in that direction.

"Hello, Jimmy. How are you doing?"

"Good afternoon, Doctor Hornsby." Jimmy winked. "Teddy said to say that when customers come in."

"Well met. How are you fitting in?"

Jimmy nodded. "All's well, Doctor. I start school next week in the afternoons. It's closer to where we're moving to on Victoria Street." Jimmy looked around, then said in a lower voice. "I cannot thank you enough, and the Angel and whoever else. We're only there for six months, but I promise we'll be the best tenants."

"Think of it as a place of rest, so your family can regroup and plan for your future. No more worrying over the rent, buying food, or staying warm, at least for the time being. Everything will be provided in the short term. Your sisters will go to school, too. Now, I'm here to see the owner."

"Sharpe? He's upstairs. I'll show you the way. He said you'd be coming."

As they headed toward the rear of the pub, Drew said, "I dropped off boxes of clothes to your mother. You're ready to move tomorrow?"

"We can't wait to get out of there. We'll toss the old clothes and leave behind other bits and bobs that aren't worth bringing. Teddy gave me the afternoon off, so we can finish getting ready. Teddy's been good to me and sends leftovers home with me nearly every night, and for nothing!"

They climbed the narrow stairs and entered a darkened hallway. It had all the makings of a Dickens's villain's lair in Drew's mind. Dank, cobwebs everywhere, and candles lit in wall sconces cast eerie shadows to dance on the walls.

Jimmy knocked. "Mr. Sharpe. Doctor Hornsby to see you."

"Come in." Jimmy opened the door and then stepped aside. "Thank you, Jimmy. Take a seat, Doctor Hornsby."

Drew sat before the small desk, waiting until Jimmy closed the door before he spoke. "To whom am I speaking to today, Sharpe or Caspian?"

"Does it matter?" Sharpe replied laconically.

"Enough so I can gauge the level of threats to expect."

"Tsk, Sir Drew. I assumed better of you. I did not call you here to threaten you, but merely to ask if you would keep my other life private. As a favor. And in return, I will allow your charity family to squat in one of my middle-class apartments."

"They are hardly squatters, but I won't argue the point. I assume you have other buildings, perhaps some in Devil's Acre?"

"Not for long. This entire area will be gone in less than eighteen months. I have been planning my exit for some time. Caspian is only one of the few names I use. So, will you keep my secret?"

Drew stared at Sharpe closely. By God, he looked so like Damon Cranston, the new Duke of Chellenham. Liam was right. The resemblance was uncanny. The jaw had sharper edges, his eyes were a little larger, but everything else was a near match. "The Duke of Chellenham."

Sharpe started, his eyebrows shooting skyward. "What the bloody hell?"

"The name is familiar, correct?"

"What is this?" Sharpe growled.

Then it is true. "I've heard a little of your background. Your mother was a parlor maid in a wealthy man's home—"

"My late mother was a gin whore who lied to get whatever she wanted. If you think I believed her drunken ramblings, you're not as smart as I thought," Sharpe barked.

"I found it hard to accept, as did Liam. We only recently discovered it."

"Hallahan—and you? What is your game here?"

Drew shrugged. "No game. I just wanted to let you know there are quite a few of us—the duke's bastards. The late duke left offspring all over England. It was all part of his twisted eugenics plan. If you want to know more, Liam and I can provide information."

Sharpe pounded the table, clearly agitated. His detached reserve had disappeared. "Never mention this again. Not to me or anyone. If you repeat this lie or tell anyone of my legitimate business name, I will hunt you down and rip out your tongue. You wanted a threat? You got it."

"Fair enough. I'll keep quiet about all of it for one other request. Leave the Golden Angel be. If this slum is going to be gone in eighteen months, what do you care if someone gives food and pennies to those in need?"

"The bitch is interfering with my business," Sharpe grumbled. Then his eyes narrowed. "You know who it is."

"No, my patients have told me about her, though they say she hasn't been around much lately. Maybe she heard of your threats and that your men are searching for her. Regardless, let it go. You have my word. I will say nothing about our dealings or conversations."

"Agreed. Then we have nothing else to say. Don't come here again."

Drew stood. "Goodbye, Sharpe."

He turned and departed, waving to Teddy on his way out. Drew did the math in his head. The previous duke had been fifty-seven when he died. Sharpe claimed to be either thirty-eight or nine. That would have made the duke about sixteen when Sharpe was conceived. It all fit. Drew could only hope that Sharpe kept his word about the angel. Selena was returning to her role as duchess for the next while, so she'd be out of Sharpe's clutches. But on the outside chance that Sharpe learned who the angel was, Selena would be protected, thanks to his pact with Lucian.

But at that thought, a warning bell clanged in his mind. He didn't wholly trust Sharpe. So he'd just have to make sure Selena stayed out of Devil's Acre.

LUCIAN SAT IN his chair for a long time, Hornsby's shocking declaration still reverberating in his head, causing a dull throb behind his eyes. He was immediately transported back when his mother had taken him to Clarendon Place in a fancy neighborhood. Lucian had been nine. It was a few months before his mother had died. They had hidden for hours in a green area on the street, and he remembered being cold and hungry, but that was all he recalled of his miserable childhood anyway.

Finally, a fancy carriage pulled up in front of a white town house with black wrought iron balconies. His mother grabbed Lucian's frayed collar and stepped onto the walkway opposite. "There he is," she spat. "That's your father. Miserable sod."

Lucian watched a tall man with golden hair climb out of the carriage. The clouds parted, and the sun caught him in a shimmering light. The man was beautiful, like a painting of an angel Lucian had seen in a tattered book once.

"You look like him and all, no mistake," his mother murmured. "The Marquess of Brookton, heir to the Duke of Chellenham. Aye, that's him. Take a good gander, lad."

The marquess held out his hand and assisted a woman out of the carriage—and then another. They giggled as they each sidled up to him. One stroked his chest while the other ran her hand down his upper thigh. They weren't fancy ladies from a ballroom. Instead, they looked like the ones living on Lucian's street.

"He's got a taste for it now," his mother muttered. "Women from the lower classes are vulnerable and flattered by his attention. They're easy prey." His mother stepped forward, then stopped, as if she contemplated confronting him but thought better of it. "I never should've brought you here. Forget you ever saw the evil man." His mother grabbed his hand and pulled him away. He turned, watching the man slip his arms around the two women as he led them to the front door. So that was his father.

Lucian had hardly listened to anything his mother said during his brief time with her. Why bother when she was drunk more often than most? But he had taken her warning to heart. He locked away this incident as he had many aspects of his early life and never sought out his father, even when he became a duke. He had read Chellenham's obituary and tossed the newspaper aside, feeling nothing.

Hornsby and Hallahan, possible half brothers?

It didn't seem likely—or did it? And there were more besides?

That fit with his mother's declaration. Just how many by-blows were there? There must be hundreds if Lucian tripped over them everywhere he turned. Was that why he and Hallahan could speak with such ease? Because they shared a bloodline? Lucian did not go out of his way to make friends, but he always thought he and Hallahan had made some sort of…connection, if he were to put a name to it. But Hallahan banned Lucian from returning when he took over the pub and brothel and started renovations. The rejection stung and solidified his initial belief that keeping people at a distance was a better way to live.

A knock sounded at the door, pulling him away from his troubled thoughts.

"It's Madden."

Lucian was not close to any of his men and trusted them even less, but Madden had proved loyal these last few years. "Come in."

"A woman to see you, lookin' for a room."

"Why bother me about it? Take care of it," Lucian thundered.

Madden closed the door. "You'll want to see this one. I know you like a pretty face. This woman is beyond that. You've got to see her to believe it."

"Fine. Send her in."

Madden opened the door and waved to someone. A woman crossed the threshold wearing a threadbare and faded black wool dress. She wore a shawl over her head, so it wasn't easy to see her face. Madden departed and closed the door. As soon as he did, the woman lifted the shawl from her head and rested it on her shoulders. She looked up, and Lucian inhaled sharply.

Stunning. There was no other word to describe her. With dark auburn hair and a figure that would make any man weep, her face was beyond perfection. Shockingly, his heart stumbled at the sight of her, a feeling he had never experienced before. Lucian quickly arranged his features to show his usual indifference.

"You want to rent a room?"

"Yes, for me and my son. He's fourteen."

Fourteen? How old *was* she? Her accent was strange, almost nonexistent compared to everyone else in England, but it was there, nonetheless.

"Where are you from?"

"I was born here but have lived in America for nearly fifteen years. I'm a widow. Can you rent me a room or not? I have money, though not a lot."

"Your names?"

"Kit Greenwood. My son's name is Duncan. I need a room to get my bearings and decide what to do next. I was told you're the man to see."

Lucian watched her closely. He couldn't tear his eyes from her glorious face. She spoke firmly and didn't act afraid of him. "I am. Do you need a job as well?"

The woman nodded.

"Ever work in a pub?"

"Yes."

As long as Lucian owned Finnian's, he'd never employed women because he did not want the bother that came when men had had too much to drink and wanted to grab at the barmaids. But he might make an exception here. Her presence could definitely boost sales.

"My son manages this place; I own it. I might be able to get you a few shifts. Regarding a room, I have one available next street over. Four pence a week." He had gone soft. Usually, he charged sixpence. "It's only one room, and there are no cooking facilities. Madden will escort you. Madden!"

The door opened. "Aye, guv?"

"Take Mrs. Greenwood and her son to the Critch room and tell her the tenant rules. The Critches should be moved out by now. And Mrs. Greenwood? Be here at ten in the morning in four days to discuss employment with my son. Do you follow?"

"Yes. Thank you." She lifted the shawl over her head and departed.

Lucian exhaled. He seemed like every other fool, turned by a pleasing face and figure. Only once had he lost his head over a woman, as much as he allowed himself to lose it. It had been one of the prostitutes at the Crowing Cock, back when it operated as a brothel and pub. He had asked the woman to move in with him. Thankfully, she'd said no. He wouldn't allow himself to succumb to such weakness ever again. Nor would he allow anyone to claim family ties, however dubious.

Lucian was a lone wolf and determined to remain that way.

Woe betide anyone who crossed him or interfered in his life.

CHAPTER FIFTEEN

"Your Grace, it is good to see you," Yarrow exclaimed as he stepped aside to let Selena in.

"And you, Yarrow. Penny relayed my instructions, I trust?" Selena removed her gloves and passed them and her cloak to the footman.

"Yes, Your Grace. I have placed your belongings in the gold guestroom. The nurse will stay in the adjoining room, as you instructed."

Selena picked that particular oversized guestroom for the separate sitting room and its location at the end of the hall, far away from Barnsdale. "And Penny is in the room across mine? I am not fully recovered from my illness and need her nearby."

"All is in order, Your Grace. Penny is upstairs unpacking your belongings. Would you care for tea?"

"Yes. Please bring it to my room, along with a cup for Penny. And the duke?"

"He is sleeping, Your Grace. But Nurse Gretchen can update you on His Grace's condition."

Once on the stairs landing, Selena paused and inhaled, holding her breath for a moment before exhaling slowly. With her shoulders back, she determinedly strode toward Barnsdale's room. The nurse stood when she entered the room.

She curtsied. "Your Grace."

"Nurse Gretchen. I'm pleased to meet you." Selena's gaze slid over to Barnsdale's bed, and his gaunt and ghostly appearance nearly caused her to gasp aloud. The man looked terrible, far worse than when she'd last seen him over two months ago. His eyes were closed. "How is the duke doing?"

Barnsdale's eyes snapped open. "Nurse," he rasped. "Leave us."

Selena's first instinct was to grab the nurse's arm to keep her in the room, but Selena steeled her spine. She turned to the nurse. "I will speak to you later. Thank you."

The nurse nodded and closed the door behind her.

"So, the bitch returneth," Barnsdale snarled, his words dripping with venom and resentment.

"Yes. Still a miserable bastard, I see. Even in dying, you remain true to yourself."

His milky gaze slid to her. "Grown a backbone, I see. Where were you, not that I care?"

Selena pulled the chair over to the bed and sat on it. They might as well get all this into the open while he could still carry on a conversation. "I needed to get away from you before I broke into pieces. A friend recommended a place of rest in Hertfordshire. I have been there for the past two months. I feel much better and have come home to be the dutiful duchess everyone expects."

"And to ensure your societal status and see to it you are left money to live on, I've no doubt."

"Yes, that too," Selena replied bluntly, her words hinting defiance. "Although I care not what society thinks. Not anymore."

"There will be no money. I settled enough on you when we married."

Selena's eyebrows shot upward. "Settled? What *are* you talking about?"

"I paid your father a goodly sum, a price he said *you* named and insisted on. He put it into an account for *you*," Barnsdale snapped. He started coughing violently and shakily brought a handkerchief to his mouth.

Selena was utterly shocked. Money placed into an account? "I know nothing of such money," she said once he stopped coughing. "First off, my father threatened to turn me out if I did not marry you. Second, I knew you paid my father a small amount, but he never stated the value of the settlement, nor said it was mine. I am not aware of *any* account. Knowing my father, he placed the money in his keeping—for his use only."

Barnsdale's eyes narrowed as if gauging whether she spoke the truth.

"Why did you never mention it to me?" Selena demanded. "But then, when did we ever carry on a conversation of worth or any discussion at all? My father shrewdly calculated that you would never say a word; if you did, he would claim ignorance of the matter. How much was it?"

"Eighteen thousand pounds."

Selena's hand flew to her mouth. "My God! I swear to you, I knew nothing of this transaction. I assumed you bought me as one buys an expensive vase. I was a possession to you. Nothing more. So, I acted as a ceramic doll on display, showing no emotion. I gave you exactly what you paid for."

"And I assumed you were grasping and greedy since you demanded such an exorbitant amount. Regardless, you're whitewashing it, since I am lying here, dying. You never even tried to be a proper wife. All you showed me was your price tag," Barnsdale accused bitterly.

"That, as it turns out, was my father's price tag. And *you* never tried to be a proper husband," Selena shot back, her emotions churning. "Not ever. When our baby—"

Barnsdale clenched his fists and slammed them against the bedcovers. "Do not dare bring up that time!"

"I will! When I lost the baby at six months, I was devastated, drowning in grief. Not once did you offer sympathy or comfort to me. You blamed *me* for losing the baby."

"He was my son and heir. It *was* your fault!"

"How dare you?" Selena cried, all notion of keeping her emotions under wraps gone. "A woman has no control over such a happenstance. The doctor said it just occurs, often for no reason. Indeed, I know he told you that, because I was there when he did. The doctor also said he wasn't sure if I could have other children, but it was likely I could. He said I simply needed time to heal and to process my sorrow. And I did. I was devastated by the loss, mired in melancholy. Yet, you came to my bed—"

"And you promptly vomited all over the place!"

"I was sick, you daft man! I was in mourning!" Selena yelled. "Sick in body and soul. But you did not care. You never cared. You still. Do. Not. Care. It was all about your needs. Your son. Never a thought for me. Not once. I hated you for that. And when you no longer came to my bedchamber, I was relieved. I *rejoiced*." That barb was cruel and beneath her, but it was also true. "I should not have said that."

The room sizzled with tense emotion. Years of pent-up resentment—on both sides—were released. Their marriage had been an abject failure all around—a lack of communication, respect, and, most of all, a lack of love.

"You never liked my attentions," Barnsdale murmured accusingly. "Not from the very beginning."

They were going to go *there*. So be it. Well, she did broach the subject first. "I was a virgin. I knew nothing about intimate relations between a man and a woman. You were not gentle or understanding that first time or during the rest of your many visits. To you, it was rutting. There was no lovemaking involved. You held me in such contempt that you did your business, leaving me unsatisfied and resentful. We did not connect on any level, did we? We never confronted the problems. We only allowed the wound to fester. And oh, how quickly it decayed."

Pain radiated in Barnsdale's eyes, and Selena could not tell if it was from their heated discussion or his condition—or perhaps both.

"Do you wish me to fetch the nurse?" she asked gently.

"No. Not yet." He exhaled, his breath shaking. "We bungled this, no mistake."

"The marriage? Yes. There is fault on both sides, and there is no going back, I fear. Maybe we are selfish people, or just found ourselves in a terrible situation. But in the brief time you have left, let us deal with each other with civility. Or try to. Do not die with hate in your heart. What good will it do you now?" Selena paused. "I no longer hate you, Barnsdale."

Barnsdale turned his head away. "Leave me. Please. For now. And send for the nurse."

Selena stood. "Very well." *At least he said please.* She turned to depart, then stopped. "If only we'd tried. We could have been friends. We could have learned to trust and respect one another. We could have tried for another child. But all that possibility is gone. I am sorry for us both, but most of all, I am sorry for you."

"I don't want your pity," Barnsdale replied flatly.

"No, I suppose you do not. But I offer it, nonetheless. Good afternoon."

Selena exited the room and swiftly headed toward her old room. She knocked on the door, and the nurse let her in.

"I am sure you heard that entire exchange, as we were not exactly quiet. I ask that you not repeat it to anyone, especially the staff."

"I would never, Your Grace. As a nurse, I'm sworn to keep my counsel in all situations, medical and personal. You can count on me," the nurse replied.

"Thank you. May I call you Gretchen?" The nurse nodded. "Tell me of the duke's current condition."

"Doctor Hornsby was here this morning before you arrived, Your Grace. He said that starting tomorrow, we will increase the dose of morphine. That should take the edge off for a few days. It will not be long, I wager."

"Thank you for your kind care, discretion, and for being honest with me. I genuinely appreciate it. So Doctor Hornsby will be here tomorrow?"

"Yes, Your Grace. He usually comes late morning, for that is when the duke is the most lucid."

"I will meet with him then. The duke wishes you to attend to him. Thank you again, Gretchen." Selena departed.

Once in the gold guest room, she sighed shakily. She'd managed to get through the dialogue with her husband and she'd spoken the truth. Surprisingly, so had Barnsdale. As he said, they had bungled their lives together—and badly. They started their marriage under a cloud of resentment and wariness that only increased as the years ticked by. *A slow death.* Lack of communication had been the weapon of choice for the deed. Selena vowed that in her post-Barnsdale life, she would never hold anything back again, especially from someone she loved.

Penny came across the hall, carrying the tea tray. "I had the maid give it to me," she said as she placed it on the round table near the window. "Come and sit. That must have been difficult."

Selena exhaled as she sat. "Did you hear? I feel as if our shouting filled the house."

"No. I don't think the maid heard anything either, as she only delivered this a few moments ago." Penny poured the tea and passed the cup and saucer to her.

She offered Selena a sandwich, but she shook her head. "I could not eat right now. Perhaps in a few minutes. Would you mind terribly if I told you what was said?"

"You know you can tell me anything, Your Grace." Penny stood and closed the door. She grabbed a sandwich and bit into it. "I am all attention."

Selena gave an abbreviated version, leaving out the more personal aspects.

"Your father told Barnsdale you asked for eighteen thousand pounds, then never gave you any of it? I cannot believe the duke never mentioned the money," Penny said as she picked up her cup and sipped the tea.

"Barnsdale resented me from the time we exchanged our vows, thinking me covetous. I resented him for buying me as if I were a piece of merchandise, even though I did not know the price, and I resented that I had been pressured into the marriage. The poison spread, slowly turning into abhorrence on both sides. We were doomed from the start. We never talked, just inaudibly seethed. Stubborn and irrational, the pair of us. We never had a chance."

"You sound a little regretful," Penny said softly.

"Perhaps a little. I told him we could have been friends, but who knows? Perhaps not, as he is a thoroughly unpleasant man. It's all a moot point now. And as far as the money? Knowing my miserable father, it's all but spent. I do not know if it's worth pursuing." But maybe she should try, since Barnsdale had told her he wasn't leaving her anything. She kept that aspect from Penny. Why cause worry? Selena had to get through the next few weeks before stressing over what lay ahead.

Or thinking about where Drew Hornsby fit into that uncertain future.

MITCHELL WAS SHOWN in Drew's study by Mrs. Evans. Drew immediately stood and held out his hand. "It's good to see you. You look well." He pointed to the cane under Mitchell's arm. "You don't need it any longer?"

Mitchell took his hand. "Now and then. I can't walk long distances without it, but I'm doing better walking for short spurts, from the hansom cab to your study, for example."

"I am pleased. You will be able to return to work soon."

Mitchell sat on the sofa, and Drew sat in the leather wing chair opposite. A fire crackled in the hearth. "It depends on what my doctor says." Mitchell smiled, giving Drew a wink. Mitchell had stayed with Drew as he recovered during the late autumn. During that brief time, they became friends and more like brothers. They were also doctor and patient. "What I cannot believe is the transformation in Liam Hallahan. When I left on my honeymoon trip, he barely tolerated us. But earlier this week, he greeted my return with a handshake and a pat on the shoulder! It shocked me, but I welcomed it."

"Love can be transformative. Opening his heart to Celia opened it in other ways. Did you meet his young son?" Drew asked.

"Tommy? I did—a fine lad. As I said, I cannot believe all that has transpired since Corrine and I departed. Liam only recently discovered it?"

"Yes, some months before we appeared on the scene. Can I offer you a drink? Then, I will explain all that has occurred. A scotch, correct?"

"Yes, A scotch. It's bloody cold out. The wind cuts a person to the bone."

Drew poured them drinks, passed one to Mitchell, then started his narrative. He mentioned Lucian Sharpe in passing but did not say anything about Liam's theory of Sharpe's paternal blood link. Sitting here, looking at Mitchell with his blond, wavy hair and clear blue eyes, Drew realized the resemblance really could not be denied. And it went beyond hair and eye color (even though Liam had black hair). Their bone structure had subtle symmetrical features that clearly indicated a family resemblance. One would have to look closely, but it was there.

"Here's to Liam and Celia." Mitchell raised his glass. "May they be as happy as Corrine and I."

Drew raised his glass. "Hear, hear."

They took a sip. "Speaking of Lucian Sharpe, I have some preliminary information. I told Liam I would pass it on to you." Mitchell placed his drink on the table beside him, retrieved his notebook from his coat pocket, and flipped it open. "As far as I can tell, he was born in Devil's Acre to Ava Fahey on October 16, 1862. Sharpe will be thirty-seven this coming October. No father is listed, which is usually the case in these matters, as well we know."

Drew nodded, as no father had ever been named on his and Mitchell's records. But they knew of their father now. Sharpe's mother had an Irish name, which was the late duke's taste in young women. The more vulnerable, the better. "Sharpe told Liam he was thirty-nine."

"Unfortunately, many children raised in poverty have no idea of their birthdate. I never knew. The Simpsons picked a date for me."

That was undoubtedly true. "Why was his last name Sharpe on the registry? Don't illegitimate children usually take the mother's last name?"

"Sorry, I should have been clearer. Lucian Sharpe Fahey is the full name on the record. He must have dropped the Fahey part somewhere along the line. Get this: He hasn't been arrested for anything, not under Sharpe or Fahey. His record is spotless. I find that's the case in many of these rookery bosses. They have their henchmen do the dirty work so they can keep their hands clean. We only caught Danaher, the villain who shot me, because he came out from behind the curtain."

"What does Sharpe deal in?" Drew asked.

"Pickpockets, smuggling—and I know smuggling was more prominent decades ago, but it's still done for certain products—thieving and selling stolen goods along with selling certain low-quality opiates and gin. Gin is still the preferred drink among the lower classes because it's cheap. Sharpe stayed away from prostitution, and he's never been whispered about when it comes to murder. As far as the police are concerned, he's not a priority, as there are plenty of murderous ruffians to focus their attention on. It's probably why Sharpe has been able to operate for so long without incarceration."

"So, he's intelligent. Cautious." Drew already understood that much in his brief dealings with the man. The fact that Sharpe owned real estate and God knew what other investments proved that point. "My father has discovered some helpful information about Devil's Acre. Come this time next year, it will be no more.

The council will be changing the names of some of the streets. Notice has already gone out to the owners of those despicable shacks. They start demolition in the spring." At least Sharpe had told the truth about those details.

"Just like most of St. Giles and the Seven Dials area," Mitchell stated. "I was lucky I escaped the slum life when a good family took me in. You, too, eventually. However, I did my time as a young constable in the Old Nichol in the East End and other areas. I observed plenty, as I'm sure you have, at the free clinics and your life before the Hornsbys adopted you. Despite the newspapers sensationalizing slum life with sordid stories, plenty of good people try to survive in those untenable situations. Not everyone is a criminal or a prostitute who allows children to run feral through the alleys."

Drew nodded. "So many overly dramatic, repugnant stories have become entertainment. I have heard of slum tourists coming into the poorer neighborhoods to see for themselves if the stories they had read in papers or penny dreadfuls were true. We can thank Jack the Ripper for that aspect. Speaking of good people in unfortunate circumstances...." Drew went on to explain about the Critch family and Selena's part in the tale.

"Celia mentioned the charity work. Corrine and I wish to join the Hallahan Initiative. We may not be overtly wealthy, but Corrine still has contacts within the peerage." Mitchell tucked his notebook away and reached for his drink. "Do you think Sharpe is a danger to the duchess?"

"Perhaps not at this point. She has returned home and is beyond his reach...for now, at least."

"Acting as an angel of mercy in the Devil's Acre? A duchess? Celia and Corrine had nothing but glowing words for her. They said she was the leader of their group and she often looked out for them. I am blasted sorry to hear of the duchess's difficult marriage. Well, she'll be free from the duke soon enough."

Drew remained silent.

"You're not going to speak of her, are you?" Mitchell asked

softly.

"No," Drew replied. "I have tucked away my feelings regarding Selena for the time being. I believe it is the wise thing to do."

"Good luck with that. I'm not being glib. I was in a similar situation with Corrine. I understand the yearning, the holding back and protecting one's heart. Just know I'm here for you. Anytime you want to talk."

"Thank you. I genuinely appreciate it."

Being wise had not lessened his yearning. Drew desperately wished he felt free to discuss this situation with Mitchell, as his half brother had fallen in love with Corrine while she was married. He, better than anyone, would understand the guilt Drew felt about having deep feelings for a married woman, though he did his best to keep those intense emotions buried, fighting the ongoing impulse to pull her into his arms and kiss her soundly. Yes, they had kissed, but Drew wanted—more.

There was nothing else for it. Drew had to admit to himself that he'd fallen in love.

CHAPTER SIXTEEN

BEFORE DREW HEADED to the Barnsdale residence, he stopped in unannounced at Damon Cranston's Queen Anne's Gate home. Damon had told him to drop by without invitation, and there was no time like the present.

The butler opened the door to complete chaos. Children ran through the halls with gleeful abandon, with a laughing Damon hot on their heels. He stopped short when he spotted Drew.

"Sir Drew Hornsby to see you, Your Grace," the butler announced, ignoring the children gathering about him.

"Well met. Look, children, Uncle Drew has come for a visit. And he's now a baronet!"

Technically speaking, these four youngsters were his half-brothers and -sisters. This entire situation was complex. Damon had found these children at the late duke's foundling home. When Damon and his duchess, Althea, had discovered the blood ties, they'd adopted them, giving them the Cranston name if they wanted it. The youngest, Chloe, was five and called Damon "Papa" even though they were half siblings. So did six-year-old Jack. The older children called Damon by his name. This blood connection, this shared complicated heritage, bound them all together. There was no denying it. It certainly was not a twist that Drew had ever seen coming.

Chloe hugged Drew's leg, and he swiftly swept her up into his arms. She was a beauty with her golden ringlets. "Good morning, children."

Chloe hugged him. "Uncle!"

Drew was entirely charmed and embraced her in return.

"All right, that's enough," Damon ordered good-naturedly. "Go and finish your breakfast and report to the governess. And no running!"

Drew lowered Chloe to the floor, and the children waved as they headed toward the dining room. "I am sorry to show up unannounced."

"I told you that you didn't have to wait for an invitation. Come into my study. Have you had breakfast?" Damon called over his shoulder as he headed down the hall.

"Not much of one—"

"Kingsley! Bring tea, bacon, eggs, and toast to my study!"

"At once, Your Grace."

Once inside the room, they sat at a round oak table with two wing chairs. "I stopped by Hallahan's restaurant again, three days ago," Damon stated.

"Did you? For luncheon?"

"Yes, I had a business meeting with MacClery. Hallahan— Liam—came out to say hello." MacClery was the old duke's former butler and the man who now comanaged the Chellenhome Foundling Home. "We were both impressed with the food and vowed to return. Beefsteak, roasted potatoes, and other delightful fixings. Utterly delicious. You know, there are a scattered few of the progeny that have darker hair like Liam. It is rare, from what I've observed. The resemblance is there, nonetheless. Do the three of you still intend to approach any others?"

As Drew stared at Damon, he realized that his half brother's resemblance to Sharpe was uncanny. "With all that has happened the past two months, we haven't had a chance to discuss it. Truly? I am not sure. I'm here to ask a favor. It's confidential."

Damon crossed his legs. "Can you tell me the particulars?"

Could he? More importantly, should he? Damon was still

reeling from all the revelations after his father's death, let alone adjusting to married life and a ready-made family. "I am following a lead on a hunch, though I haven't informed Liam or Mitchell about it yet. It's probably nothing. But does the Chellenham dukedom keep records of staff through the years?"

Damon's smile disappeared. "Christ. You've found another one. And he or she is not on your list."

"It's Liam who first brought it to my attention. He chalked it up to seeing the duke's progeny everywhere. But it got me thinking."

Kingsley entered with a footman carrying a large tray. They efficiently set the table and laid platters full of food. Kingsley poured the tea.

"Thank you, Kingsley. Patrick. You may leave us. Do close the door."

The butler and footman bowed slightly, then quit the room.

The men served themselves. Famished, Drew did not hesitate to load his plate with scrambled eggs and slices of bacon.

"Liam brought it to your attention?" Damon asked as he sipped his tea.

"Yes. It concerns an acquaintance of mine and Liam's—a rookery boss in a notorious slum. He told Liam his mother worked in a wealthy home, and the son and heir got her pregnant. She was immediately turned onto the streets. This acquaintance's mother said the son and heir never knew of her condition, but who knows? The woman in question died when the rookery boss was nine."

"A rookery boss. That hunch is very vague. You must have been compelled to investigate for another reason," Damon said as he cut into his eggs.

"He has the stamp: golden hair, tall, blue eyes. His resemblance to *you* is quite startling. He looks more like you than the rest of us. The man will be thirty-seven in October. Mitchell found his birth registration for another reason, which I will explain later. I want to see if his mother's name is in the dukedom records."

"We certainly have records. We would need at least thirty-seven years ago. Kingsley!" Damon yelled.

The butler opened the door and stepped into the room. "Yes, Your Grace?"

"Bring the dukedom ledgers from 1860 to 1865."

"At once, Your Grace."

Once the butler departed, Damon said, "Can you reveal anymore?"

Drew cut into his eggs. "Not at this time. But I promise to disclose all when I am able."

"A criminal. Well, with my father's loathsome personality, it was bound to come out in someone. Perhaps the man's identity should remain a secret. Ah, here's Kingsley. Just place the books on my desk. Thank you, Kingsley." Damon stood and headed toward his desk as the butler bowed and departed. Drew came to sit before the desk.

"The name?"

"Ava Fahey."

Damon snorted. "An Irish name. Why am I not surprised?" he muttered as he flipped through the pages. Then he pushed a volume aside and opened another. "Here she is—hired on January 12, 1861, as an underhouse parlor maid. Ava Sharpe Fahey, age sixteen. The criminal's mother?"

"Yes," Drew replied solemnly.

"There is no next of kin listed." Damon flipped through the next volume and then stopped. "'Dismissed for thievery, June 2, 1862. No reference, no payment. Banned from the property.' When was this felonious boss born?"

"His name is Lucian Sharpe. He was born October 16, 1862."

Damon slammed the ledger shut. "The poor maid was obviously starting to show her expectant state, and when my grandfather discovered who the father was, they turned her onto the streets without a farthing. Typical."

Drew frowned. "The timeline seems to fit."

"My late father preferred seduction over force. He was sixteen at the time. I will wager coin this was not the first maid he dallied with, either." Damon exhaled. "Be thankful you never knew him. He was the worst of men. I've never met a more selfish, unprincipled cretin; he believed his physical perfection must be passed on, regardless of the cost, then sought to profit from his issue."

"I am definitely grateful. And now I understand why my mother moved us constantly, changing our name every few years. She was frightened the old duke would find us. I am glad he never did."

"Let's finish our repast, though I have lost my appetite."

So had Drew. Once they returned to the table, Drew said, "Your initial reaction is correct. I believe it wise to stay quiet about Sharpe for now."

"It gives one pause," Damon replied gravely. "Pursuing the identity of my—our—father's vast and varied offspring may not be prudent after all."

Drew was beginning to think the same.

SELENA HAD BREAKFAST in her room and then changed into a periwinkle-blue tea gown with puffed upper sleeves and pearl buttons. She had to admit she had missed wearing fashionable clothing for the past two months. The anticipation of seeing Drew had her heart pounding at a fast rate. She had to remain calm and detached and act like she barely remembered him, despite the swirl of emotions inside her.

As she entered the hallway, she heard the front door close downstairs. Had she missed Drew's visit already? She hurried toward Barnsdale's room.

"Good morning," Selena said brightly as she entered the room.

"Good morning, Your Grace," the nurse replied.

Selena's gaze slid to Barnsdale. He merely grunted in return. "Did I hear someone leaving?" she asked.

"Mr. Mecklenberg had a brief meeting with the duke," Gretchen replied as she smoothed the covers on the bed. "I must fetch fresh water and order some tea and chicken broth. I'll return shortly, Your Graces."

The solicitor. Once the nurse departed, Selena sat on the chair by the bed. "How are you this morning, or would you rather I not ask? And before you tell me that I do not care, so why bother to inquire, let me say this instead. If you would rather I *not* ask, tell me."

"Don't ask," Barnsdale barked. Then, he sighed. "Only because there is no point. I worsen with each passing day. It's not worth discussing."

"Fair enough. I will address any inquiries I have with the doctor. He *is* coming today?"

Barnsdale grunted in reply, then pointed to a piece of paper on the bedside table. "Take that."

"What is it?" Selena took the note from the table.

"The combination to my safe. Although, I'm sure you know it already, seeing a few hundred pounds was missing."

Selena remained silent.

"At least you don't deny it. I assume you needed the money for travel to Hertfordshire and other expenses. The contents of the safe will be yours. There are a few thousand pounds, some jewelry, and a few gilts."

"Gilts?"

"Government bonds. I've instructed Mecklenberg to place an addendum on the will. I won't leave you penniless. I also instructed him to visit your miserable father and discover what happened to the money." Barnsdale started coughing violently, and Selena grabbed a clean handkerchief and held it to his mouth. When he finished, she gently wiped around his lips. They had a slight blue tinge, which Selena knew from her time with the St.

Thomas's nurses meant insufficient oxygen in the blood. She set the cloth away, then, spying on a basin nearby, brought it to his bedside. She dipped a clean cloth in the cool water and slowly wiped his face.

"Is that too cold?"

Barnsdale closed his eyes. "No. It feels good."

"Thank you for the codicil. It will lessen my worry."

Barnsdale exhaled shakily. He opened his mouth as if to say something, but closed it again.

"Why didn't you seek medical attention when the coughing worsened?" Selena whispered.

"Hubris. I thought it was nothing and that I knew better than any physician. Listen. Mecklenburg thinks he's found an heir."

Selena froze, squeezing the cloth with her fist. "How can that be? Why did you not know about this before now?"

"It was three generations ago, or was it four? Some tawdry family scandal. A forgotten branch of the near-leafless tree. I want—I ask—you to look into this. You can use Doctor Hornsby as a witness. I need to know if this is legitimate; I need it double-checked. I'm asking a lot. It carries the weight of my family's history and future."

"You would trust me with this?"

Barnsdale did not reply. "I have no one else," he answered gravely. "And...I trust you." His words hung heavy in the air, revealing his vulnerability and need. It was surprising because Barnsdale had never shown any such susceptibility before. This was the first time they'd participated in a civil conversation. Because of that, she should remain gracious, but for him to say he trusted her at this juncture?

"Only because you need me to do this."

"Yes. I don't want—hate—between us. Not at the end."

Selena continued to blot the cool cloth gently against his forehead. She had spoken the truth when she'd told Barnsdale that she no longer hated him. But she still did not like or trust him. So why did a glimmer of compassion set alight inside of her, causing her to consider his deathbed request? By all accounts, she should refuse and curse him to a fiery hell if she were genuinely vindictive. It appeared her heart was not completely dead after all. Falling for Drew had obviously released emotions she had not felt for ages. This conflict within her was palpable, a true battle between her past and present. And an uncertain future.

"I will verify the information. Do you mind if I involve my friend's detective husband? He's on leave and doing private investigation work."

"Mitchell Simpson?"

"Yes. How do you know him?"

"I read the marriage announcement in the paper and recognized Addington's widow. You mentioned her once. Hire the man. I'll tell Mecklenberg to offer Simpson a stipend and that you will represent me in this matter."

Mentioned her once? It must have been when they first married. How surprising that Barnsdale would recall that insignificant detail. "Do you believe the information is faulty?" Selena asked.

"I don't know. I want the legitimacy of the claim checked. The dukedom should go on."

Though the man was dying, he had made her life miserable—even scheming to place her in an asylum—and that stark reminder should stay at the forefront of her mind. Barnsdale was not a friend. "I will do what I can."

The door opened.

"Doctor Hornsby has arrived, Your Graces," Nurse Gretchen announced.

"I will go and greet the doctor," she said as she stood.

"Thank you," Barnsdale whispered.

Selena found it hard to grasp that they had come to a truce—perhaps a shaky one, but an accord nonetheless.

Now, she had to act as if she hardly knew Drew. And hide the fact that she was falling in love with the doctor. Her feelings for Drew were not simple but a multifaceted mix of affection, attraction, guilt, and worry. However, as her future came into clearer focus, she knew the handsome doctor would be part of it. Of that, Selena had no doubt.

CHAPTER SEVENTEEN

REW STRODE ALONG the upstairs hall toward the duke's sick room. Selena emerged from behind the door and walked toward him. His breath caught in his throat. She looked stunning in the light-blue tea gown, with her golden-red hair carefully styled with a few wayward tendrils framing her beautiful face. He wanted to embrace her. He wanted to kiss her. Instead, glancing over his shoulder and seeing no one behind him, he held his gloveless hand to his side, the palm facing outward.

Touch me. Ease this ache of yearning.

Selena came nearer, and then she did the same, looking over her shoulder and holding out her hand. They passed by each other, their fingers trailing slowly across their open palms as the sparks danced between them. As the tips of their fingers touched, Drew closed his hand over hers and they turned to face each other, reveling in the momentary, heated connection. Slowly and reluctantly, he pulled his hand away, their fingers brushing across their palms in one last, desperate caress. The only one they dared to make.

"Good morning," Selena said, her words soft and shuddering. She took a deep breath and exhaled. In a steadier voice, she said, "I would like an update on my husband's condition."

Yes. Her husband. He must keep that forefront in his mind. Selena was married. A maid emerged from a nearby room carrying a bundle of linen. There was no opportunity for proper conversation or clandestine handholding.

"The news is grave, Your Grace. I have come with an adjusted dose of morphine for the duke. Then, I will use the Brompton Cocktail. It's a potent elixir of various opiates that are usually used toward the end of life."

"I thought he had two months or less?"

"It appears, Your Grace, the cancer is most aggressive, more than initially thought. At first examination, I believed it would take a few months. But the duke is weakening, barely keeping food down. His body is failing."

"I noticed his lips are light blue this morning."

Another maid passed them, carrying a basket of rags and cleaning materials. Drew waited until she passed and entered another room before replying.

"That means his heart is laboring, as I surmised from a recent examination," Drew murmured. "I believe his heart will give out before the cancer kills him."

"I see," Selena murmured. "Are you home early this evening?" Selena whispered urgently. "I won't stay long. We have things to discuss. Some of it pertains to the duke."

Drew nearly said no. Why tempt fate, for they had agreed to remain distant during the length of the duke's illness. As it was, they said they would not touch, and here they were, stoking the embers. "Bring Penny with you. Say you are attending to charity doings."

Selena gave him a puzzled look, then nodded. "That is a sensible suggestion. Come and see Barnsdale."

Selena led him to the room as the smell of carbolic soap and spray assaulted his senses. Drew firmly believed in bacteriology and germ theory and had instructed the nurse to keep the room as clean and sterile as possible. After laying his medical bag on the nearby table, he came to stand before Barnsdale. Selena remained by the door.

"Good morning, Your Grace. I will prepare your injection. On Friday, I will start the Brompton Cocktail I told you about."

"That bad, am I?" Barnsdale rasped.

"Yes, Your Grace. We are nearing the end sooner than I thought. Your organs are beginning the process of shutting down. Your heart, in particular, has me concerned." There was no mincing words. Drew believed in being honest with all his patients.

"My heart, eh?"

"Yes, Your Grace. We call it congestive cardiac failure. Already, there is fluid retention visible. If I may?" Drew pulled back the covers and pulled up the thin night rail. "Your legs are showing signs of edema, which is fluid trapped in the skin's tissue." The duke lifted his head slightly and looked where Drew had pointed. Drew then covered the duke.

"What's to be done?" Barnsdale rasped.

"I could try Southey's tubes inserted into the legs to allow some fluid drainage. It is not pleasant and will prove futile at this stage, as the fluid will build up again rather swiftly."

"That's it, then. I will die sooner than you thought. No draining. I should finalize my affairs, correct?"

"As soon as possible, Your Grace."

"Will you assist the duchess if I ask? It concerns a possible heir."

"I am at her service."

Barnsdale grimaced as Drew gave him the shot. Then, his eyes fluttered as exhaustion overtook him. The duke fell into a troubled sleep, his breathing labored. Waiting until the nurse returned, Drew escorted Selena into the hallway.

"He should sleep the rest of the afternoon," he murmured. "What time?"

"I'll be at your home at seven." Selena gave him a nod, then reentered the duke's room.

It would take all his inner strength not to reveal his growing feelings. But he had to try.

SELENA ARRIVED PROMPTLY at seven with Penny, and Drew showed them into the front foyer. His home looked like an upper-class town house with the requisite white-and-black marble floors and gilded wallpaper and trim.

"I inhabit the bottom two floors, and the third and fourth floors consist of two flats," Drew stated. "The smaller one has an entrance in the rear. The larger one has an entrance on the right side of the structure."

"You have tenants?" Selena asked.

"Not at the moment. I have been unable to find someone suitable."

Selena's mind raced with the possibilities. Dare she suggest it? "Would you mind if I had a look?"

Drew started. "May I ask why?"

"Once Barnsdale passes, I do not want to stay another night there. I do not care what society thinks. I only returned to ensure my future—no other reason. That may sound selfish, but I need to take care of myself. And Penny." She turned toward her lady's maid, who stood some distance away. "I never asked. Will you be staying with me? I often assume far more than is good for me. If not, I will understand completely. I will give you severance and a glowing reference. There is no worry on that score."

Penny stepped closer. "If it's all the same to you, Your Grace, I will stay in your employ. A widowed duchess needs a lady's maid. We've come this far together."

Selena laid her hand on Penny's arm and squeezed it affectionately. "Thank you. I appreciate it. May we see the flat, Drew? The larger one?"

"Of course. I'll fetch the keys. It is mostly furnished."

After Drew disappeared down the long hall, Penny raised her eyebrows.

"I meant what I said," Selena said under her breath. "I don't give a toss what anyone thinks about my living arrangements. Drew is a friend. And this is an ideal location."

"It's certainly a better address than Victoria Street. But can we afford it?" Penny replied.

Drew returned wearing his black wool coat, holding the keys in his gloved hand.

"I have news," Selena stated. "Barnsdale promised me the contents of the safe—money, jewels, and bonds. I will be hiring Corrine's husband, Mitchell Simpson, to look into certain matters, including ensuring the addendum or amendment to the will is in place. Barnsdale also asked me, with Drew's assistance, to verify the heir that has been found."

Penny gasped. "There's an heir? How?"

"A family scandal from three or four generations ago. I do not know the particulars as yet. I will see Mitchell and Corrine tomorrow. Are you available, Drew?"

"I am working at one of the free clinics until one o'clock, but I can meet you at the Simpson residence shortly afterward."

"Good. I will also need to hire a solicitor. I am wary of any deathbed promises," Selena stated. "I do not want to use the one I consulted when considering divorce."

"You should look after your rights," Drew replied. "I have a suggestion. It's regarding the Wollstonecraft family once again. Ronan Wollstonecraft just opened an office with two cousins, Rett and Bryan, who are working as clerks as they conclude their Certificate in Laws studies. I can give you their card before you depart."

"Brilliant. Let's have a look at the flat."

Drew led them outside along a small walkway that wrapped around the corner of the property. The entrance had been added on, probably with a foyer and stairs. "If you go through this door and up the stairs, you will arrive at the third level. Follow me." Drew turned a switch. "I had an electric light installed in this vestibule." Light flooded the area as they climbed the stairs. "There is another switch here to turn the lights off. The second key opens this door."

Drew stepped aside and allowed them to enter. Selena looked to her left. "And there?"

"A wall blocking off the stairs to the living area below. The modification is simple enough to reverse if I ever decide to turn this back into a single residence. Tearing down this wall opens up the stairwell. There is only gas lighting on this floor. A few servants' rooms are in the attic above but they haven't been utilized in years. I use them for storage. Later this spring, I hope to install telephones."

Penny and Selena followed him along the hallway. "There are two bedrooms, a study, a parlor, and a small kitchen with an adjoining dining area. There is a water closet and a bathing room."

Selena strolled into the parlor. The large room had a fireplace, a gold damask sofa, two matching wing chairs, and matching draperies.

"This and the study are the only rooms with fireplaces, but the other rooms have steam radiators."

"You have many modern improvements. And how much would you charge for this flat a month? If you were to rent it to anyone but me?"

Drew clasped his hands behind his back. "Fifteen pounds a month. But it's negotiable. I would say that to anyone."

"Would you take thirteen pounds a month?" Selena smiled.

Drew held out his hand. "I would. Shall we shake on the deal? It's a month-to-month lease. You will also have the use of my housekeeper, Mrs. Evans, a few days a week. You must pay for your firewood and coal. Electric and gas lighting included."

Selena slipped her hand in his. As always, she reacted to the warmth and strength of his touch. "Then it is a deal," she whispered. They stood for the longest time, their hands still joined, gazing at each other with a longing that tore Selena in two.

Penny cleared her throat, breaking the intense spell.

Drew released her hand and stepped back. "I have tea downstairs. Mrs. Evans prepared it before she left. Shall we go?"

Selena followed Drew downstairs, and he handed her the keys when he locked the outer door. "The place is yours," he murmured huskily, "for as long as you wish."

"Thank you." Selena closed her fist over the keys. All her belongings were still in storage from when the staff had packed her items from the adjoining bedroom. She would have them moved over here immediately.

Her new life was about to begin—now.

CHAPTER EIGHTEEN

B Y THE TIME they settled in the parlor, Drew's arousal had abated. All Selena had to do was touch him, the barest feather touch of their fingers, and he lost all control. He sipped the tea and frowned as it cooled far too much while they'd inspected the flat.

"I can make us a fresh pot of tea," Penny suggested. "Just direct me to the kitchen."

"That would be wonderful," Selena replied. "Thank you, Penny."

"Once in the hall, go to the rear, and there are stairs to your left that will take you to the kitchen below," Drew instructed. "The tea is clearly marked in a canister on the counter. I often make my own tea when Mrs. Evans is not here."

Penny lifted the tray and departed.

"How is your cough and breathing? It sounds much improved," Drew said.

"It is. It affects me more at night because I'm lying flat. But as you said it would, it's getting better. Listen, we are alone for a few moments," Selena said. "I have reached a tentative truce with Barnsdale. We had a frank conversation, the first one we ever had. He's asked me to supervise this investigation into the possible heir. I said I would be using Mitchell and you to assist."

"Yes, the duke mentioned he wants me to witness the doings. I said I would. How is it he never knew of an heir?"

Selena took a digestive biscuit from the plate and nibbled on it. "He said it was a scandal from generations ago, although he knew none of the details. I assume that branch was forgotten and ignored because there were enough direct-line heirs to choose from through the decades."

"Until there aren't."

"Yes. Barnsdale is the end of the road." Selena sighed. "I told him I no longer hate him. And I do not. I'm glad I returned and confronted him. It has lifted a ponderous weight from me. But not entirely. Will I ever feel like myself? I will never be the young woman who married him, but I want to feel some semblance of normalcy."

"In my medical studies, I learned from a forward-thinking professor that trauma causes injuries within that the eye cannot see. The wound is like a broken bone that mends but isn't quite the same. For example, a lingering pain when it rains reminds you of a physical injury. So, too, can certain situations remind you of the internal scars and tribulations you would rather forget. For the first ten years of my life, my mother and I lived in grinding poverty, constantly moving about because she was afraid my father would find us and take me away. My mum never told me that; I discovered that information later. When Mum lay dying, a vicar heard her plea and confession. He was Viscount Hawkestone, who later welcomed me into his family."

"Your father was a vicar?" Selena exclaimed.

"For two years. I will tell you about it someday. My father held that secret close, honoring my mother's wish that I not be informed until the death of my biological father. The Duke of Chellenham died this past autumn. When my father told me, I was stunned. Shocked. Resentful. But I resolved to push on with my life. Why hold grudges? My mother and Chellenham were dead. My father had kept his promise to a dying woman. I find that honorable. What I am trying to say is, that in here," Drew tapped his chest, "the injuries within will always remain, popping up occasionally when you least expect it."

"And do you have that internal scarring?" Selena asked, her voice laced with empathy.

"Yes. Sometimes I hold emotions deep within, which may outwardly cause me to seem or appear—"

"A little aloof?" Selena smiled.

"That is a diplomatic way to put it. For the longest time, I believed I did not deserve love. It was a strange reaction because I was given all the love a boy could wish for, first from my mother and then my adoptive parents, siblings, and extended family. As I grew older, I used that reserve to my advantage, especially when I became a physician." God above, he was laying his soul bare. "The scarring lessens with time. Yours will, as well. Talking about it is helpful. So is accepting friendship and love into your life."

Selena's eyes shimmered with tears. "As you have with the Hornsbys and your Chellenham half siblings?"

"Yes," Drew murmured. "I have a life rich with loving family members and friends, yet I've never been in a serious relationship before." He hesitated. "I've never been with a woman. At least, not in the most intimate sense." There. Yet another confession. It appeared he was laying his heart bare as well. It was not as if he'd never kissed another woman or touched her. He'd just never taken the final step—an actual joining.

Selena's eyes widened. "You certainly kiss as if you are very skilled."

Drew smiled. "Thank you. I've kissed a few ladies. The truth is, I have been too busy with medical studies and working at the clinics to go any further. I just attended a soiree with my father some weeks ago. That was the first time I've ventured into society in five years."

"And did you meet any eligible young ladies there?"

"None that appealed. You see, I spent much of the evening thinking of *you*. Since the moment we met last year, you've always been in my thoughts."

Selena blinked rapidly. "I have?"

Drew had come this far. "And you always will be."

Penny entered the room as Selena quickly dabbed the corner of her eyes, and the maid poured the tea.

"I brought some biscuits as well," Penny declared. "If you don't mind me asking, is this your home, Doctor? Do you own it? Or are you the manager?"

"It's mine," Drew replied as he sipped his tea. "My family gifted it to me when I turned twenty-one. It was a secondary residence in London that they no longer used. Since I would be practicing medicine here, I needed a place to reside. I decided to turn it into flats shortly after I graduated and came into my inheritance." Drew knew that speaking of money was bad form, but he wanted Selena to know he was not without resources. "If you wish, Penny, you can live in the small flat at the rear. It has one bedroom, a small kitchen, plumbing facilities, and a cozy parlor."

Penny stopped in mid-sip. "I-I never had my own place. How much for the rent?" Then she glanced at Selena. "I cannot consider it. The duchess employs me, and I should be nearby."

Selena touched Penny's arm. "You would be nearby to fulfill your duties but also have a space to call your own, not just a bedroom near me, but a place to make a cup of tea and sit in your parlor and do as you please. I think it is a capital idea. What is the rent, Drew?"

"How about fifteen pounds a month for both of them? You can decide between yourselves about the rent payment for the smaller flat."

Penny beamed. "Oh, my giddy aunt! And I feel giddy and all! Can we do it, Your Grace?"

Selena patted her maid's hand. "Of course. Drew, it appears you have rented both flats."

Drew was pleased. Once Barnsdale passed, Selena and her companion would have time to relax and refresh in their respective flats.

I want you to court me. I want us to know each other better. I want—you.

Selena's words from the other day echoed in his mind. There would not be a mourning period, so there was no impediment to their growing closer. But Drew would take this in increments, as Selena had been through so much already. The future looked bright, indeed. Full of possibilities.

As they parted by the front entrance, Drew dropped the smaller flat's keys into Selena's palm along with Wollstonecraft's card and then closed her fingers over them. He turned her hand over and kissed the top of her kidskin glove. "Until tomorrow."

He assisted her and Penny into the hansom cab and stood on the walkway, watching until the cab disappeared around the corner. He remained standing there until a gust of wintry wind nearly knocked him over. Drew did not feel the chill. Not at all. The warmth of love filled every part of him. He could finally admit it, as he stood standing in icy wind, as flurries tumbled gently from the sky.

Drew was deeply and irrevocably in love—for the first and last time in his life.

AFTER SELENA'S MORNING meeting with Mr. Ronan Wollstonecraft at his office, where she discussed her wishes and concerns regarding Barnsdale's legal promises and his impending death, she arrived at Corrine and Mitchell's home. Her friend gave her a tour of the spacious two-story town house. The residence was cozy and situated in an upper-middle-class neighborhood. Those snobs in society no doubt thought this was quite a comedown for a viscount's daughter and a baron's widow, but Selena had never seen Corrine so happy. She practically glowed.

Once they were settled into the parlor with the tea tray, Selena glanced at the mantel clock. It was five minutes past one. Drew was late.

"Something must have delayed him," Mitchell offered. "I

know Drew is punctual."

"How did you do it?" Selena asked softly, the words tumbling out of her. "How did you both resist the temptation of acting on your mutual attraction, though Corrine was married?" Selena blushed furiously. "I had no business asking that. Maybe you didn't resist. Oh, bother."

Corrine and Mitchell exchanged knowing glances.

"I'm not even sure what I'm feeling," Selena blurted out. "My emotions have been buried for so long, and I thought, well, dead. Yet, I told Drew I wanted to get to know him better and all that implies. Is it too soon? Should I retreat and get my bearings? How can I trust this rush of emotions? How does a person know they are in love?"

"My mother used to say if you have to ask that question, then you are not in love," Mitchell replied. Selena's heart sank. "But I don't think that's true. Everyone has doubts, especially when trauma is involved. You, Corrine, and Celia have suffered plenty. It's no wonder you're confused. It will all become clearer once Barnsdale dies." He paused. "Too blunt? Maybe. What do you owe him?"

Selena stared into her cup of tea. "I don't owe him anything. Not even my fidelity."

"As to your question, is it too soon?" Corrine interjected. "It's never too soon to embrace that rush, as you call it. Do not hold back. Life is too short."

"Yes, far too short. I only have to look at Barnsdale for that reality," Selena replied. "What has he got to show for his life but regrets? But I will make sure he faces death comfortably enough and see to his last request. But after he is buried, I do not want to give him a further thought. As each day goes by, I feel less guilty about that."

"Good," Corrine replied firmly. "What *is* Barnsdale's last wish?"

Selena gave them a quick synopsis about the possible heir and had just concluded when the bell rang. The maid entered the room. "Doctor Hornsby to see you."

Mitchell slowly stood, then carefully approached Drew, who removed his outerwear and handed it to the maid. Corrine had told her upstairs that Mitchell was using his cane less and less and how pleased she was with his progress.

Selena's gaze slid to Drew, and her heart skipped several beats. He had removed his glasses as they had melting snowflakes on the lenses. He was as handsome without the spectacles as he was with them. There was no doubt in her mind that she was entirely smitten with the good doctor. But in love? Yes, partway there, at least. She was holding back, just a little. Selena wanted to be sure of her feelings before acting on them.

Drew brought his case to the sofa and set it between them. "Good afternoon, Corrine. Selena. I am sorry I'm late. I decided to make a few stops on the way. I visited Mr. Mecklenberg's office, which I know was presumptuous of me, but I wanted to gather pertinent information about the heir in question." Drew opened his case, brought forth a ream of papers, and laid them on the sofa. Then he looked at Mitchell as he wiped the lenses of his spectacles with a cloth. "Did Selena fill you in?"

"Yes," Mitchell replied. "What did you find?"

"Mr. Kendall George Wood, age thirty-nine. He is married and has three sons and a daughter. He is the head schoolmaster, as of last year, at Harrow School," Drew replied as he slipped his glasses on.

"A prestigious position," Selena murmured. "Wood? Perhaps a shortened version of the family surname, Woodhouse?"

Drew gave her an admiring look, and she reveled in his approval. "Exactly. I posed the same question to the solicitor. He says it fits with the supposed banishment of a second son."

Corrine's eyes widened. "Oh, I do love a mystery!"

"Barnsdale's great-great-great-grandfather disowned his younger son circa 1749 and exiled him from the family," Drew continued. "The solicitor showed me the name in the family Bible with the line through it. James Nolan Woodhouse was the younger brother of Barnsdale's great-great-grandfather."

"There is no other male line except from the mid-1700s? How on earth can anyone investigate that?" Selena exclaimed.

"Luckily, James Woodhouse's marriage was recorded in the Bible before the name was struck through. There were plenty of female descendants through the years, though sometimes none at all from off-shooting branches of the Woodhouse tree. The only direct male line came through to the present-day Barnsdale. He was the only male child, just like his father before him. The duke has instructed Mecklenberg to have Mitchell and me locate the marriage certificates down through the line. And we must arrange a meeting with the headmaster, Kendall Wood."

"I concur," Mitchell replied. "He may have family papers and know a little history."

Corrine shook her head. "I cannot believe that after more than 150 years, only this man and Barnsdale remain?"

"Everyone else is dead. Mr. Wood's father died last year. His grandfather died ten years ago. Everyone else is gone, as far as Mecklenburg knows," Drew answered.

Mitchell stood. "Let's head to Harrow School immediately. We shouldn't be any more than an hour. Will you stay, Selena?"

She nodded.

A flurry of activity ensued, and after gathering coats, hats, and gloves, the men departed to hail a hansom cab.

Corrine poured more tea into their cups. "It's never dull, is it?"

Selena took her cup and sipped. "No." Then she sighed. "The only men in my life so far—my grandfather, father, and hus-band—are not honorable gentlemen. I never looked up to any of them. I assumed all men were like this. But they're not, are they?"

"No, my dear, they're not. But you have to search for one that is worthy. You could not look for a more honorable man to respect than Drew Hornsby," Corrine replied softly. "Or to love."

"He is five years younger. I keep saying I do not care what society thinks, but they gossip nonetheless."

Corrine smiled sardonically. "It can hardly be avoided. Ignore it. I was scarcely in society anyway, and Celia less so. You were probably exposed to it more than we were. That's why it keeps pushing into your thoughts."

Selena nodded. "Thankfully, it has not taken over all my views. I just agreed to move Penny and me into Drew's empty flats once Barnsdale passes."

"Good for you. You will be free from your past and able to come to know Drew better." She took Selena's hand. "I want to mention something. When you were sick with bronchitis, you mentioned you never got in touch when you read of Travis's murder. But you had. You sent your condolences in a card stating you were eager to renew our friendship, along with Celia. When I sent a reply, it was returned, saying you were traveling."

"That shows where my mind was when I ran away. I honestly forgot I replied to you. I am sorry." Selena shook her head. "I haven't been myself for several years."

"All I want is for you to find solace and peace, as Celia and I have, with an earnest man of honor. Drew is all that and more. He presents a contained air, which I suppose he must for his medical work. But I have the feeling inside that Drew is a man of great passion, waiting for the right woman to bring it forth. If the opportunity presents itself, discuss your feelings and doubts with him. If he loves you, he will understand."

"Thank you, Corrine. You are a dear friend."

Perhaps it was time to lay her cards on the table, emotionally speaking. Some uncertainty lingered, but Selena had lived in an emotional wasteland long enough. She only had to look to her friends to see how they'd shaken off the shackles of their previous miserable lives and embraced love.

When the time was right, Selena vowed to do the same.

CHAPTER NINETEEN

Drew and Mitchell were shown into the headmaster's office. Like all schools of this type, it consisted of a brick exterior, with dark wood paneling throughout the interior. Marble busts, portraits, and stained glass filled the halls. Students in black robes gave them quizzical looks as they were escorted through.

Mitchell stood by the long row of windows and glanced outside to the courtyard below. "Did you go to a school like this?"

"No. I went to Charterhouse," Drew answered, mentioning England's historic boarding school.

"Pardon me, Sir Drew," Mitchell teased. Then he sobered. "Good on you for getting a first-class education. It must have been difficult."

"I did not go from the streets right into school. I had a tutor for eighteen months, as well as my ex-governess mother making sure I learned my lessons. But when I did attend, it *was* quite an adjustment. Eventually, I felt comfortable enough to rub elbows with the elites, to a point. I wasn't born into it and was sometimes made to remember that. But I got through it relatively un-scathed."

The door flew open, and a harried man in flowing black robes, with numerous books under his arm, strode into the room. "Please sit, gentlemen," he said firmly as if speaking to unruly pupils. He placed the books on a nearby table and laid his academic cap beside them. Then Kendall Wood took his seat behind his ornate desk. He was tall and slender, with brown hair and a thin mustache. Was there a resemblance to Barnsdale? It wasn't easy to ascertain. "I have fifteen minutes to spare. I am told you are with the police. Does this have to do with a student here?"

Mitchell sat next to Drew, facing the headmaster. "I am Detective Sergeant Mitchell Simpson with the Metropolitan Police, and this is Doctor Drew Hornsby, Baronet." Drew smiled inwardly at Mitchell's introduction, making it plain they were professional men and should be treated as such. "You will need to give us more than fifteen minutes."

"Sergeant. Sir Drew. Why are you here?"

Mitchell glanced at Drew and said, "It has nothing to do with a student. The Duke of Barnsdale has tasked us to investigate his family tree…which brings us to you."

Wood sat back in his chair, looking puzzled. "I do not see how. I am not related to a duke."

"We have evidence to the contrary, Mr. Wood," Drew replied. "The duke is dying and has no heir. It is the common practice to have an heir apparent and, if possible, an heir presumptive in place—if they exist. The duke had neither. But in order to find another heir, it means that it is necessary to locate one directly related to a previous duke. Has anyone in your family mentioned the possibility?"

Wood blinked several times. "You're telling me I am the heir to a dukedom? It is not possible. I don't want it. No, indeed. I categorically refuse it." The visible tension in his shoulders and the furrow in his brows showed he was unnerved by the information.

Drew felt sympathy for the man. The news was shocking, indeed. But this was not the reaction Drew expected from Mr. Wood. "You could refuse. The title becomes dormant until you die, and then everything passes to the crown, but as long as you live, you will be the title holder and responsible for the upkeep. It is the law. You would have to hire someone as an overseer and still sign papers related to dukedom. For all that, you might as well become the duke and take advantage of the title, money, property, and prestige. Think of your family. Your three sons. They will be heirs. Would you deny them such a bright future?"

Those words hit home as a shuddering breath escaped Mr. Wood. "Tell me how this is possible."

Between Mitchell and Drew, they explained the bloodline through the previous dukes and what information they'd found.

Wood rose from his chair and opened his door. "Grant, cancel my appointments for the rest of the afternoon. Reschedule what you can," he said gravely to his assistant. He shut the door and returned to the desk, flopping into his chair. "I cannot take this in. Why didn't my father or grandfather tell me? This makes no sense. My great-great-grandfather's name was crossed out in the family Bible?"

"But not obliterated. The former duke wanted to show his disdain but not cut that bloodline entirely from the family in case a situation such as this might occur in succeeding generations," Drew replied.

"Maybe your father and grandfather had no idea they were related to a duke," Mitchell interjected. "After all, your great-great-grandfather changed his name from Woodhouse to Wood. Who knows what caused this rift? But if you are in line for the dukedom, we need to confirm it. Do you have any family papers that might help us corroborate what we suspect?"

"Oh, I have them. Everything you might need. Marriage, birth, death certificates. It was implied through the generations that these papers should be kept safe and protected. And yes, the documents go back to the mid-1700s, but no earlier. Now I know why. My God. I don't know what to do." Wood's agitation was apparent as he wrung his hands incessantly.

"Do you have a residence here on the grounds?" Drew asked.

"Yes, Harrow provides one for the headmaster."

"The family tree showed many female descendants through

your line. Are any living?" Mitchell asked. "They may know something of the ancestral scandal that caused the family rift."

That was smart—question other adjacent members of the family, Drew thought. But then, Mitchell *was* a detective.

"Yes," Wood replied. "My great-aunt Helen lives with us. Come, we will go immediately." Wood tore off his robes, hung them on the hook, and slipped into his overcoat. "A dukedom," he murmured worriedly. "I have no clue how to go about it."

"You hire a staff, a competent one," Drew suggested. "And a steward to manage the dukedom. But first, we must verify."

Wood froze, his hand gripping the door handle. "I do not want this. Not at all. But in the end, I have no choice, do I?"

"Talk it over with your family. As I said, you *can* refuse. You will still be legally referred to as a duke, but you do not have to call yourself one. You can deny the entailments and inheritance. Ultimately, it comes down to the obligation of family and title, as well as the future of your immediate family, and generations to come. It will not be an easy choice," Drew said solemnly.

"When is life ever easy?" Wood responded sardonically.

How true.

⟫⟫⟫⟪⟪⟪

SELENA AND CORRINE drank two pots of tea, waiting for the men to return. Three hours had passed, and Selena was becoming worried. Corrine had rung for the maid and asked for a third pot with sandwiches since it was teatime. While they were alone, Selena heard all the details from Corrine about her and Celia's adventures, meeting Mitchell and Liam, and falling in love.

"I will float away if I drink anymore," Selena smiled.

"I imagine Mitchell and Drew will return—" The sound of men coming through the front entrance and hallway halted the rest of Corrine's sentence. Once the tea and sandwiches were served and the men had come into the room and taken seats,

Mitchell and Drew told them everything they had discovered.

"Mr. Wood *is* the heir?" Selena exclaimed.

"It appears so. He's speaking to his wife and sons at the moment," Mitchell replied. "He doesn't want it, but as Drew explained to him, refusing would mean denying his sons a future. If they wish it."

"Will he stay on as headmaster?" Corrine asked.

"I can't see that happening," Drew replied gravely. "If he were a knight or baronet, perhaps he could continue. But a duke? It is a powerful position and a high rank within the peerage. Serving in the House of Lords would leave him no time to be headmaster."

"And what of the scandal?" Selena questioned.

"His great-aunt had heard whisperings through the years about an unforgivable scandal, but no one knows what happened. It had to be something severe enough for the duke to cut his second son from the family. I guess we will never know," Drew added.

"We stopped by Mr. Mecklenberg's office to bring him up to date. He will take it from here. Easiest thirty pounds I ever made," Mitchell stated. "Maybe I should stay a private investigator; it could prove lucrative."

"My love, you have ambitions," Corrine interjected. "And they will only be realized with the Metropolitan Police."

"See how well she knows me?" Mitchell beamed. "After such a brief acquaintance and whirlwind marriage." He reached for her hand, and she took it. "My soulmate. My very heart."

Corrine blushed prettily. "You're embarrassing Drew and Selena."

Selena was not the least bit embarrassed. Instead, she was touched that they felt comfortable enough to express their feelings in front of her and Drew. After an animated conversation and finishing the platter of sandwiches, Selena stood. "I must return to Chapel Street. Barnsdale should be told of the developments."

Drew stood as well. "I will come with you as I am due for a medical visit with the duke."

With goodbyes said and coats and hats firmly in place, Drew assisted Selena into the hansom cab. Luckily, it was completely enclosed to protect them from the weather and offer a modicum of privacy.

"I am not looking forward to the conversation," Selena murmured as the carriage moved along the cobbled streets.

"Would you like me to stay when you tell him about the heir?"

"Yes, since you spoke to Mr. Wood, I believe it best. I am not sure I can handle this."

"You can handle anything," Drew replied firmly.

"Can you handle me?" Selena asked softly. "Everything I bring to the table, good and bad?"

"Yes. I can and I will."

"Because you are a physician and mend broken things? Nurture and stitch up all the wounds, no matter how deep? Why?"

"Because I am in love with you."

Drew said it so matter-of-factly, with such resolute belief that Selena was stunned. Had she misheard him?

"I did not mean to tell you that in such a casual way," Drew said soberly. "I wanted to wait until you were free to consider it. I expect no reply. I want you to know that I believe in you, admire your courage and honesty, and only feel alive when you are near. Like now."

Selena's heart swelled with emotion. "Thank you for believing in me and for loving me. No one has ever said those words to me before. Can you imagine? I come from a very emotionally restrained family. We did not speak of such feelings."

"Not even with your sister?"

"How did you know about her?"

"Celia told me. She said she ran away, causing a scandal, and that you have had no contact with her."

Selena sighed. "Yes, not in more than fifteen years. It is as if

Kit has fallen off the ends of the earth. She wrote once when she arrived in New York, but not since. I wrote to the address she gave, but there's been no reply."

"What was the scandal, if you do not mind me asking?"

Selena smiled at the memories flooding her mind. "The worst, as far as my parents and grandparents were concerned. Kit ran off with the footman. She was barely eighteen. Kit said in her letter that she married James Greenwood once they got off the ship. But then, who knows if they actually married? There is no proof. But it worked for her. It was her way of thwarting my parents' plan to marry her off to an aged duke. And I believe she was in love. Perhaps I should have done the same, but Kit snatched the only handsome footman my family employed."

Drew chuckled lightly, and Selena joined him.

Then, she frowned. "As for *my* marriage, well, it started out on a foundation of mistrust and resentment and went downhill from there. We hardly spoke and when we did, it was certainly not of our emotions. While I welcome such forthright discussion and hope we continue in that vein, I will hold my reply for a time."

"I understand," Drew murmured.

"You're perfect, aren't you?" Selena smiled affectionately. "I had an inkling that might be the case, the moment we met."

"No. Far from it. I have faults, some small, some larger. Sometimes I don't listen, like when I slipped you my card last year during the examination. You told me not to get involved, but I gave you the card nonetheless. I broke my own rules, and I am sorry."

"If you only knew how important that card was. It gave me the strength to finally leave Barnsdale. It gave me hope, reminding me that I could call on you if I were in dire straits. I kept it close, using it in the same way a ship's anchor offers security in stormy seas."

"Is that why you called me Captain Hornsby?" Drew's sensuous lips curved into a teasing grin.

And how she wanted to kiss him right at that very moment. Her cheeks brightened with embarrassment. "I called you that when I was sick? How mortifying."

"Tell me about it, please."

"It's from one of my romantic fantasy stories. You were a captain on a pirate ship, and I was your captive guest. You gave up your cabin for me, and even though you treated me well, you had an aura of danger about you, with the long hair, one earring, and bare chest except for a vest. Standing on the deck with the wind whipping about your masculine, muscular frame, you were so very commanding. A storm was brewing, and you shouted orders. Then, you kissed me. But the ship rocked violently, and I fell overboard into the icy sea."

Drew smiled. "That must have been when I briefly plunged into the ice bath." He paused, his expression turning reflective. "I must be a rather dull fellow in your eyes that you felt you had to make me a pirate in your dreams. Nevertheless, I am flattered."

"Dull? Heavens, no. Not to me. You are a breath of fresh air after the treatment I've received from the men in my life. Your steadfastness, sense of duty, honesty, and honor appeal to me more than some brooding rogue with a dark past. Those types of men are fine for some ladies, but not for me. It's a definite plus that you are quite gorgeous. And the way you kiss and look at me with such longing... It turns me to jelly inside." She paused. So much for waiting to voice her emotions. She might as well plunge onward.

"I want to say so much more. I admire the work you do for those less fortunate, the free clinics, and the fact that you go to Celia and Liam's once a week to administer medical care to those living in terrible situations. I love that you drop everything to assist people you've just met and accept them unreservedly as friends and family. I love—you. I—"

Before she could speak another word, Drew placed his hand on the back of her head and pulled her in for a devastating kiss that caused her breath to cease. He expertly caressed every inch of her mouth, and Selena's tongue wrapped around his in return. As she'd said, the man could kiss. They continued for several moments until they noticed the cab had come to a stop.

The driver banged on the roof, a not-so-subtle hint for them to disembark. Drew broke the kiss, then ran the pad of his thumb across her lower lip. She loved it when he did that.

"In we go," he murmured. Drew reached for the folding doors, and Selena took his arm.

"I want us to hold nothing back from now on," she murmured. "We will always speak our minds, no secrets, no simmering resentments, all the cards on the table. I cannot endure another lonely and empty relationship like the one I am about to leave. Even if Barnsdale were not dying, I would be seeking a divorce. I know what I want."

"Good. I know what I want as well. I have for some time. I pledge to be an open book to you. In private, I will hold nothing back. Not ever. No secrets, no antipathy. You have my word." Drew smiled. "Speaking of holding nothing back, I haven't had a chance to tell you how my meeting with Sharpe went."

"With everything going on, I completely forgot. What did he say? Did he threaten you?"

"Not really. To sum it up, as long as I keep his legitimate doings to myself, he will leave the Golden Angel alone."

Selena exhaled. "What a relief."

"I quoted Thoreau to our friends, but it also applies to us."

"What quote?"

"Well, it goes like this. 'There is no remedy for love but to love more.' I will love you more than you ever thought possible." He swung open the folding doors and stepped onto the walkway. Then, he held out his hand.

Selena took it. *Yes, love more.* It was exactly what she needed to hear.

CHAPTER TWENTY

AFTER REMOVING THEIR coats, Drew followed Selena up the stairs to the duke's bedroom. Nurse Gretchen stood as they entered the room, laying her needlepoint aside. Drew's gaze slid to the duke. Barnsdale slept fitfully, his breathing labored. Drew pointed to the connecting room, and the ladies followed him.

"How is he?" Drew asked the nurse in a low voice.

"The duke's breathing worsens by the hour. He couldn't even manage to take broth today," Gretchen replied, her voice filled with worry.

"I will start with the Brompton Cocktail today. Nurse, could you bring the ingredients into this room and lay them out? I'll mix it shortly. It's in the box I brought yesterday."

"Right away, Doctor."

They headed into Barnsdale's room, and he and Selena stood by his bed. The nurse gathered the equipment and the box and hurried into the other room.

"Barnsdale," Selena shouted, stirring the duke awake. "We have news."

The two of them explained the situation, including Drew's meeting with Mr. Wood at Harrow School.

"Will he accept it?" Barnsdale asked.

"I believe he will. He has a wife, three sons, and a daughter, and will want them to benefit from the dukedom," Drew replied. "It will be quite an adjustment for him, going from being a headmaster to a duke."

"He has three sons?" Barnsdale gasped. He closed his eyes. "Oh, thank God."

"Would you like for me to send for Mr. Mecklenberg?" Selena asked.

"Yes. I need to know if it's finalized. Everything pertaining to my will."

"Do you want to meet Mr. Wood, Your Grace?" Drew questioned.

Barnsdale shook his head. "No. Not like this. Helpless and dying. I need to know the man's final answer right away. There's. Not. Much. Time." Barnsdale gasped for air.

No, there was not much time left at all, Drew thought grimly. After he mixed the drug cocktail and gave the duke the injection, he joined Selena in the sitting room.

"The tea tray just arrived. Please stay if you are not needed elsewhere. I've sent the footman to fetch Mr. Mecklenberg. Barnsdale?"

"He fell asleep. Giving him the cocktail means he will be asleep more than he's awake going forward. Considering the pain he is in, that is a blessing."

Selena poured his tea and passed him the cup and saucer. "I wished a lot of things to befell Barnsdale through the years, but not this, not to die in agony."

Drew was about to reply when the butler came into the room. "The Honorable Mr. Samuel Seaton to see you, Your Grace."

Drew gave her a questioning look.

"My father. I have not seen or spoken to him for close to five years. Show—"

A portly, older man of medium height burst into the room. "How dare you send an army of solicitors to my home?" he boomed. "Where is Barnsdale? I demand to see him!"

Selena sighed. "Thank you, Yarrow. I will take it from here."

Yarrow quit the room, closing the door behind him.

Her father pointed at Drew. "Who is this, another pettifogger? I cannot abide disreputable solicitors!"

"Sit, and I will answer your questions. And keep your voice down, Father. Barnsdale is extremely ill. This is Doctor Hornsby, baronet. Doctor, my father, Samuel Seaton. Sir Drew is not just a physician but a friend and confidant," Selena explained calmly.

Already, Drew did not like this man. He hadn't seen his daughter in five years, and yet he berated her and showed a complete lack of respect. Drew gave a brief nod of acknowledgment—it was more than the man deserved. To hell with parlor manners.

Seaton sat in the wing chair opposite Drew and Selena. "Ill? How ill?"

"He is dying. Cancer of the lungs," Selena replied tonelessly. "Why are you here?"

Seaton waved his pudgy hand dismissively toward Drew. "I will not discuss family business in front of the hired help, baronet or not."

"You will, or I will have Yarrow show you out," Selena replied determinedly. "You come here after all this time to make demands? After the way you left things?"

Seaton snorted. "I don't know what you are on about."

"You came here after I lost the baby and blamed me for it!" Selena cried. "It was bad enough that Barnsdale blamed me, but my own father?"

Baby? Drew's heart squeezed in empathy.

"You had one duty: to provide an heir. You could not even do that," her father accused. "You shamed your mother and me."

"Shame?" Selena cried incredulously. "I had a miscarriage. It happens all the time, and it was not my fault. How dare you fault me on this?"

"Even your disgraced sister managed to have a child, and who knows how many others. But not you."

"Kit had a baby? When?" Selena asked softly.

"We received a letter a year after she left. It was a boy. They named it Duncan."

"You never told me of this letter," Selena accused.

"It was addressed to *me*. Besides, your mother and I didn't want you to get any silly notions of running off as your sister had. We haven't heard from her since. Who knows if she and the boy survived?"

"I can't believe you didn't inform me," Selena murmured. "How utterly cruel. But that has been your behavior toward me my entire life. Say your piece, then leave. I want nothing further to do with you."

Selena's father sputtered. "That Mecklenberg the J—"

"Stop right there. Do not say one word against him. I will not tolerate any bigoted language. This is my home. Keep your foul opinions to yourself. I heard enough of them growing up."

Seaton snarled but nodded. "He accused me of theft and threatened me with court action!"

"You told Barnsdale I asked for eighteen thousand pounds when I did no such thing."

Seaton's gaze slid to Drew. "Again, I will not discuss this before a stranger. Who is this man to you?"

"I am her friend," Drew replied sternly. "You had best speak to your daughter respectfully, or I will throw you out myself." By God, he was tempted to do it. Right this minute. What a miserable excuse of a man.

Seaton's bushy eyebrows shot skyward. "Friend? That is rich."

Drew moved forward as if to stand, but Selena touched his arm briefly to halt him.

"The money, Father? Where is it? Why did you not tell me about it?"

"I thought Barnsdale would have told you. Indeed, he must have at some point. I kept it in a separate account. But you never came to claim it."

"And again, I say *you* never informed *me* of its existence. Where is the money?"

Seaton squirmed in his seat. "It was my responsibility as steward of the money to see its continued growth. I invested some of it, and took a fee for my efforts."

Drew did not like the sound of this.

Yarrow knocked and entered. "Mr. Mecklenberg is here, Your Grace."

All the blood drained from Seaton's face.

"Good. Show him in. We will settle this here and now, Father. You can tell the solicitor your tale."

Mr. Mecklenberg sat in the wing chair beside Seaton and laid his valise at his feet.

"Yarrow, bring a fresh pot of tea and more cups."

Yarrow bowed. "Right away, Your Grace."

After the butler departed, Selena pointed to Seaton. "My father was about to explain what happened to the money he was supposed to have set aside for me. How is it you never followed up on the status of the marital settlement, Mr. Mecklenberg?" Selena asked pointedly.

"As to that, Your Grace, I can claim ignorance of the entire transaction, as I only became the duke's solicitor eight years past. I only learned of it two weeks ago when His Grace informed me of it. There is no contact or written agreement among the duke's papers. Unless your father has a copy."

Seaton shook his head. "I signed nothing. It was a transaction between two gentlemen. I asked the duke for an amount I thought fair. I took a fee of two thousand pounds off the top and put the rest into an account. After a few years, I decided to grow the amount and make some investments. I figured I could make a little money on the side with each return on the investments, as I was doing all the work! At first, some of the investments paid handsome dividends. But, then—well—"

"How much is left in the account, Mr. Seaton?" Mr. Mecklenberg asked coldly.

"A little under six thousand pounds," he murmured.

Selena inhaled sharply. "Oh, Father. How could you?"

"How was I to know some of those railway schemes wouldn't pan out? I wasn't the only one who lost money. Then, the house needed a new roof, and other assorted expenses cropped up. I had every intention of replacing the money, but everything I had invested showed a loss. They added up. It is not my fault the economy turned sluggish eight years ago."

Mr. Mecklenberg reached for his valise and removed a sheath of papers. "The duke has instructed me to recover all monies possible. He has made a written and official statement claiming he gave you eighteen thousand pounds before his marriage to your daughter."

"You have no other proof that the duke gave me the money. I could claim the money is mine, and you have no way to gainsay it," Seaton replied stubbornly.

"That is true," Mecklenberg replied. "But I will bring about a court case that will tie you up in litigation and court costs for years. A signed and legal declaration from a duke of the realm will carry a good deal of weight. You will lose everything; I will see to it, no matter how long it takes."

Seaton's complexion turned even paler, if that were possible. His voice trembled as he asked, "What do you want me to do?"

The solicitor pushed papers across the table between them. "Sign this agreement. It will transfer the remaining money to a trust that my office will administer. In exchange, the dukedom will not bring charges against you."

At that moment, Yarrow entered the room with a footman who carried a tray.

"How am I to live?" Seaton whispered. "I have no income."

"I hear you were a solicitor yourself some years back," Mecklenberg stated. "I would suggest you hit the law books and reacquaint yourself with the rule of law. You know I will win if I take you to court. This deal is more than fair, even though I advised the duke against being so magnanimous. I wanted to take your house and possessions as recompense."

"I will sign," Seaton said, his voice shaky.

"Yarrow, please fetch pen and ink for my father," Selena asked.

In a flurry of activity, the old tea tray was removed, and the new one was placed on the large table. Then, a pen and ink set was brought in, and Seaton signed the papers. Mecklenberg swiftly gathered them up and put them in his leather case.

"Yarrow, escort my father from the premises," Selena said flatly.

Father and daughter did not exchange a look or a word. Mr. Seaton stood, shoulders slumped, and followed the butler through the door. Yarrow closed the door behind him.

"Would you like a cup of tea, Mr. Mecklenberg?"

"I have time for a quick one, Your Grace, thank you. What I did not tell your father is that I already acquired a freeze on the account from a judge acquaintance of mine. If he goes to the bank directly from here and attempts to withdraw money, it will not be allowed."

Selena poured the solicitor a cup of tea and passed it to him. "Very shrewd."

The solicitor sipped his tea. "Good and hot. I also wish to tell you, Your Grace, that your solicitor, Mr. Wollstonecraft, was at my office this morning. I gave him the appropriate papers concerning the section of the will pertaining to you. I told him I would inform you of the final will since I was coming to seek the duke's signature this afternoon. I also have news concerning the heir."

"Can you tell me?" Selena asked.

"Of course, Your Grace. After much deliberation with his family, Mr. Wood has decided to accept being the heir apparent. He has agreed to keep me on as the principal solicitor for the dukedom."

Selena clapped her hands together. "I am pleased to hear that. Barnsdale will be relieved to hear the dukedom will continue."

"He will, Your Grace. I hope you will not think this too forward of me, but I informed Mr. Wood of your predicament regarding the marriage settlement. He wishes to give you two thousand pounds when you become the dowager duchess, then a monthly stipend of eighty pounds a month until you remarry—if you ever do so. I am also to find you appropriate accommodations when the time comes."

"As to that, I already have a place rented. I plan to move into a flat at Gloucester Square as soon as the duke passes. So Mr. Wood can take immediate possession here, if he wishes. You can consult with Mr. Wollstonecraft about any arrangements. Please thank Mr. Wood for me. His gesture is generous and appreciated."

Mr. Mecklenberg took another gulp of tea. "I will inform him, Your Grace. Now, I must get these papers signed."

Drew stood. "I will take you. I should check on my patient before I leave. Your Grace, I will come to see you before I leave."

Drew led the way, and when they stepped into the room, Drew was surprised to see the duke awake and taking broth from the nurse. "Mr. Mecklenberg is here, Your Grace. There are papers to sign. And he has news."

The solicitor stepped forward. "Mr. Wood has agreed to become the next Duke of Barnsdale, Your Grace. The dukedom is safe."

Barnsdale's eyes fluttered shut in a moment of relief. "Thank God," he murmured.

Drew bowed, quit the room, swiftly descended the stairs, and returned to Selena. She was sipping her tea when he entered. He sat next to her. "Barnsdale was awake and greatly relieved to hear Wood agreed to be the next duke."

"I am glad."

Drew took her hand, offering a comforting touch. "I'm sorry you lost your child. How far along were you?"

"Six months," she whispered sadly. "The baby was a boy. The doctor said it was possible that I could have more children, but he wasn't sure. You should know that now. It could factor into our future. I was going to tell you about it eventually. It still is painful to talk about."

"I imagine so. I do not see how this factors into our future. I will love you and want you regardless of whether we have children or not. I am sorry your husband and father blamed you. As a physician, I can say unequivocally that a woman has no say over such an event. Often, there is just something wrong with the pregnancy or development of the fetus, and it is nature's way of terminating the pregnancy. It is nothing you did, believe me. Were there any complications? Such as abnormal bleeding?"

Selena shook her head. "No. Not at all."

"Then I do not think you need to worry. When the time comes, you can be examined by a doctor. I know of one who specializes in women's health."

Selena took his hand and squeezed it. "Thank you for your compassion. If only—if only—"

"Barnsdale or your father had been as understanding? I'm ashamed of my fellow men for acting so cruelly at such a vulnerable time. There is no excuse. I'm also sorry about your father's behavior and not telling you about your sister. I could tell you were upset."

"God knows where Kit is. I hope she and her family are safe somewhere."

Drew kissed her hand, then released it. "I should go. I'll return tomorrow. Rest, and know that some of your burdens have been resolved."

"Yes, I will certainly sleep better tonight. Goodnight, my dearest."

Drew stood, closed his eyes briefly, and let the endearment wash over him. Then he met her intense gaze as he gathered his coat and doctor's bag. "My heart."

He strode into the front hallway, and Yarrow assisted him into his coat and handed him his hat and gloves. Drew didn't feel the cold when he stepped outside into the blowing snow.

If everything fell into place, perhaps he and Selena could find lasting happiness. And that thought warmed him most of all.

CHAPTER TWENTY-ONE

A S FOUR DAYS swiftly passed, Selena found herself in a whirlwind of preparations for the next chapter of her life. Sorting through her possessions, she set aside items for donation, a process that stirred a mix of emotions within her. It was a peculiar juxtaposition—the clerks from Mecklenberg's office conducting an inventory room by room, while Barnsdale lay upstairs, his life slipping away…and Selena conducting an inventory of her own.

With permission, she gathered the quilt her late maternal grandmother had given her as a wedding present and other gifts she wanted, like a decanter set, a mantel clock, and a painting she liked of a serene country setting. She also had to oversee Penny's possessions, which were set aside and not included in the dukedom inventory. Earlier in the day, two footmen delivered two of her many trunks to her flat at Drew's.

Also, with this physical inventory and organization came a certain cataloging of her emotions. Particularly her feelings toward Barnsdale. She did not like him—she had never liked him. He was a man devoid of warmth and generosity of spirit. He possessed a cruel streak and a spitefulness that, over the years, reminded her of Dickens's Ebenezer Scrooge. Selena doubted even visits from three ghosts would make Barnsdale change his ways. The proof was clear: He was dying more or less alone, with no friends or family to mourn him.

Despite the tentative accord she had reached with her husband and the pity she felt for his wasted, barren life, Selena was resolute. She would not mourn his passing, nor feel any guilt over it. Her feelings for Drew Hornsby were right and just. Her marriage with Barnsdale had ended long ago, the final nail in the coffin being the blame he'd put on her over the loss of their child. Despite her own mistakes, Selena was self-aware enough to know where the errors lay, and she was determined not to repeat them.

A furious pounding at her bedroom door jarred her awake. Then the door opened, and someone stepped inside.

"Your Grace?"

It was Penny. Her maid turned the knob on the wall sconce and muted gaslight filled the room, causing her to blink.

"What is it, Penny?"

"Nurse Gretchen says the end is near. She has sent for Doctor Hornsby."

Two days ago, Drew stated it would probably happen late at night. "What time is it?"

"Half past three."

Selena stood, grabbed her dressing gown, and slipped it on, tying it around her waist.

"Do you want me to come with you?" Penny offered.

Selena patted her maid's arm affectionately. "Thank you for offering, but no. Pack up the remainder of our possessions, including the bedding that belongs to us. Be ready to depart as soon as we are able."

Selena headed down the hall. By rights, she could stay in her room and wait until Barnsdale passed. But that wasn't in Selena's nature. Regardless of their shared horrid past, she would not let the duke die alone. She entered the dim room, and Barnsdale's rasping breathing filled her hearing. The man was struggling for every breath. The nurse stood by his side, glancing at Selena as she approached. Gretchen shook her head. So, this would be the duke's end.

His gaze darted about, his eyes glassy. "Selena," he croaked.

He hadn't called her by her first name since the first few months of their marriage. "I-I-I'm s-s—" Barnsdale bit his lip so hard that a dot of blood appeared. Even with his last breaths, he could not bring himself to apologize. Well, he was true to his character, if nothing else.

"Let go, Lombard," she urged gently. This was the first time she had ever used his given name—a tragic statement on their life together. "Let go and find the peace you never found on this earth. Go, now. There will be no more pain."

A single tear escaped his left eye as his body shook from coughing. Then, with one last shuddering exhale, he lay still. The nurse stepped forward and laid two fingers on the right side of his neck.

"He's gone," she said solemnly, the weight of the words hanging heavily in the air, marking the end of a tumultuous chapter in her life.

The first rush of emotion that covered Selena was a profound sense of relief. Relief that Barnsdale was finally free from his pain and that she was free from him. The desire to leave this house immediately was overwhelming, but she knew that the rituals had to be observed.

Selena turned to find Yarrow, the long-serving butler, standing in the doorway, wearing his dressing gown. The man showed no emotion, but butlers rarely did. "Yarrow, please fetch Mr. Mecklenberg and have him contact the undertaker as agreed upon."

"At once, Your Grace."

Selena faced the nurse. "Gretchen, I cannot thank you enough for your dedicated care and compassion. You are indeed an angel of mercy. You made his last days as tolerable and comfortable as you could. I am confident he appreciated it."

Gretchen smiled slightly. "The duke was not an easy man. A few times, I was tempted to quit because of his temper. But I could see the emptiness of his life, no doubt of his own making, and I decided to stay and ease him into passing. In fact, Doctor

Hornsby asked me to stay and gave me those exact reasons. We take an oath to care for our patients regardless of their disagreeable nature. If the doctor could do it, then so could I."

Selena nodded, not sure of what else to say. It was an accurate depiction of Barnsdale. Disagreeable to the very end. At least, the duke had generously left her something in the will and instructed his solicitor to recover what money he could from her father. She supposed it was Barnsdale's way of making amends, even if he could not say the words aloud.

Drew entered the room, carrying his physician's bag. Selena was sorely tempted to run to his warm embrace, but she stayed stock-still.

"He's passed?" Drew asked the nurse.

"Yes, Doctor. Not five minutes ago at 3:38 a.m."

"I am sorry for your loss, Your Grace."

"Thank you," Selena replied. "Mr. Mecklenberg will be arriving shortly, along with the undertaker."

"If you wish, I can escort you to your chambers," Drew offered.

Yes. Selena did not want to spend another moment in this room. Turning to depart, she saw Nurse Gretchen pulling the sheet over Barnsdale's face.

Selena took Drew's arm as he led her down the hall toward her room. "When would you like to leave?"

He knew her thoughts exactly. "As soon as the duke is removed. How long will it take?"

"I must complete the appropriate paperwork, including the death certificate. There is no need for an autopsy unless you wish there to be one."

"No. We know the cause of death."

"Then I expect this will all be taken care of within a few hours."

"I will get ready, as I am sure I will have to speak with the solicitor."

Once they reached her door, Drew took her hand and kissed

it. "I will come to escort you when that occurs. My condolences. For everything the duke was and was not in life, he was your husband."

"Thank you," Selena whispered.

She entered the room and closed the door. Selena's legs felt like jelly, and she wobbled. Penny was at her side instantly, taking her arm, and assisting her to the chair by the fire.

"That must have been difficult," Penny murmured as she laid a blanket across Selena's lap. "He's no longer in pain, I'll grant. And neither are you, Your Grace."

How true. Her marriage to Barnsdale had been, indeed, painful. But it would not discourage her from seeking happiness elsewhere. Drew Hornsby was everything Barnsdale was not.

Honorable. Generous. Kind. Passionate.

Selena was eager to move forward with her life. And Drew was a huge part of that future.

DREW LOOKED ABOUT the small chapel where the Duke of Barnsdale's funeral was taking place. Not many were in attendance, but Selena had told him that Barnsdale had no close friends. Any contemporaries were cloistered away in their country homes for the winter and would not make a trek to London for a man they did not like or respect. Not even Selena's parents had shown up, but considering what had occurred about the money, Drew was not surprised.

He and Selena, Penny, Yarrow, and a few servants were there, along with Celia, Liam, Corrine, Mitchell, and the solicitor, Mr. Mecklenberg, and his assistants. Mr. Kendall Wood, now the duke, came alone. No one would give a eulogy, not even the vicar, for what was there to say? No one mourned Barnsdale. There was no elaborate procession, only one carriage and horses with funeral plumes. There would not be a luncheon, though Drew invited mutual friends for tea afterward. It was all rather tragic—a wasted life.

As the vicar gave the departing prayer, six men came from the vestry to act as pallbearers, and they carried the coffin outside to the waiting carriage. Selena followed, dressed in the prerequisite black bombazine and matching veil. The mourners walked behind the carriage to the cemetery across the property. It was not overly chilly, but snow flurries danced in the slight breeze as the vicar gave the graveside blessing.

And finally, it was over.

Drew had borrowed the Hornsby family carriage and assisted Selena and Penny into it before climbing in himself. Once he closed the door, the carriage slowly lurched through the snow.

Selena tore off her veil and exhaled loudly. "There is such a finality to a funeral. All that is left is to attend the reading of the will the day after tomorrow. Mr. Wood looked as if the weight of the world was on his shoulders. He does not want to be the duke, does he?"

Drew shook his head. "No. I spoke to him briefly before the service. He was recently informed that he must change his family name to Woodhouse. He was not pleased at all. Giving up his position as headmaster also rankled him. It will be quite an adjustment for him and his family."

"When we were introduced, I was tempted to offer my assistance during his transition, but I could not do it. I need a clean break from the Barnsdale dukedom," Selena said solemnly.

"You owe the dukedom nothing, Your Grace," Penny replied firmly.

"There's one easy way to break from the dukedom. Penny, please stop referring to me as 'Your Grace.' Our relationship has evolved since you became my lady's maid," Selena urged.

Penny frowned, and a deep furrow appeared between her brows. "You're the dowager duchess. And although we *are* friends, I'm still in your employ. There are rules."

Drew could see Selena was exasperated when she met his gaze. He shook his head slightly to tell her she should not become upset over the conversation.

Selena patted Penny's arm. "Call me Selena when we are together or with Drew and our friends. If anyone else is in the room, you may use 'Your Grace' as society requires. Why should we care what society thinks?"

"Thank you—Selena," Penny replied.

Selena smiled in return. "Will you stay and have tea with us?"

"No, thank you. I'm exhausted. Would you mind terribly if I went to my rooms?"

"Not at all," Selena replied kindly.

"I'll come to you in a couple of hours."

They remained silent the rest of the way to Gloucester Square.

NOT TEN MINUTES later, Selena, Drew, Celia, Liam, Corrine, and Mitchell were sipping tea and eating sandwiches and other delicacies from Celia's and Liam's restaurant. It was the first time the six of them had gathered together. His feelings regarding Selena must be obvious to all, as his eyes had never left her. Drew couldn't resist attending to her every need, such as building a fire and locating a blanket when she had mentioned feeling cold. He hung on her every word. Drew was utterly smitten and deeply in love with her. To their friends' credit, they hadn't mentioned the obvious attraction between them. Besides, it would be in poor taste after just burying Selena's husband.

"I know we all lead busy lives, but I want us to get together like this more often," Selena murmured. "I have lost so many years."

Celia, sitting to Selena's left, patted her hand. "So have many of us. But we shall make up for it. In fact, you will see us so often that you will grow tired of our presence!"

Everyone smiled as a tray of frosted biscuits was passed about.

"Why don't we leave the men to their brandy? Selena, I am dying to see your flat," Corrine encouraged. "Come, Celia."

The ladies gathered their coats and headed outside to the upstairs side entrance. Drew stood and headed toward the cabinet. After pouring brandy into snifters, he handed them to Mitchell and Liam.

"So, the duke is dead," Liam stated. "What happens now with you and Selena?"

Drew snorted as he sat. "Always right to the point. We've already acknowledged our feelings. I want a future with her. Selena wants the same. It is up to her as to when."

"I guess you will be turning this place back into a single residence," Mitchell observed as he swirled his brandy. "Can you afford it? Not taking on tenants? I'm not being nosy, or I suppose I am. It's the detective in me. I worry about people I care about."

Drew gave a bemused smile. "My friend, I came into a substantial inheritance when I turned twenty-five. I haven't required tenants for the past year. In fact, I need never work again. I am quite well off."

"Jaysus," Liam whistled. "Aren't you the dark horse? You never said a bloody word."

Drew stared into the contents of his snifter. "I haven't told Selena the particulars as yet, either. I suppose I am still adjusting to the situation. I'm not used to having a healthy bank balance. Granted, I had a generous allowance through the years, but I mostly made my own way. The allowance permitted me to volunteer much of my time at the free clinics." He paused. "I want to put some of that money to good use, like expanding on the Hallahan Initiative. It is something for us to discuss in the future."

Mitchell raised his glass. "Here's to happy endings for us all. To love—and to the future."

"The future," the men said in unison.

Happily-ever-afters for the Duke's Bastards? Why not, indeed?

CHAPTER TWENTY-TWO

S ELENA SHOWED HER friends through the flat. "Penny and I are still settling in. Thankfully, it comes mostly furnished. Penny adores her living area."

"I only stayed in the small flat for a short period, but I loved the coziness," Corrine said. "You must be finding it an adjustment being alone. More or less."

"It is a welcome adjustment," Selena replied. "No, I don't have footmen and a butler at my beck and call, but I am learning to do things myself, like boil water for tea."

The ladies laughed lightly.

Selena sobered. "Actually, I welcome the quiet solitude. I want to be able to relax, read a book, have a cup of tea—one I made myself—and not think of anything if I wish. Drew is giving me time, but there are moments when-when—"

"You yearn to rush into his arms, hold him tight, and never let go?" Celia whispered.

"Yes, exactly that," Selena replied, sitting on the sofa beside Celia. Corrine sat across from her in the wing chair. "Common sense and society dictate that I should wait, but why? You both did not."

"But if you marry Drew, you will become Lady Selena, Baronetess Hornsby," Corrine said softly. "You will remain part of London society, whereas Celia and I stepped down—according to society, not by *our* standards by any means—and married into the middle class. I only bring this up to mention that you will be judged more harshly than we were."

Selena frowned. "I have already been judged by society. I know what I was called: the ice duchess, a cold fish, frigid, and any other synonym that may fit. Believe me, I do not care a fig what society thinks. Not anymore. If I did, I wouldn't have moved here."

Celia and Corrine chuckled, and Selena joined them.

"Good, I'm glad to hear it," Corrine said. "That settles that particular subject. I must say I admire that you returned to the Barnsdale residence when you did. Most women in your situation would have stayed away until after he passed."

"I had my reasons—selfish ones, I'm afraid. I wanted to ensure I had some inheritance," Selena replied gravely. "Once I arrived there, I could not allow Barnsdale to die alone, regardless of our horrendous marriage and his past behavior. Ultimately, he made amends the only way he knew how—in his will. I'm grateful for that."

Celia sighed. "I wish I had ensured my legacy years ago. I only have some money now, thanks to the new Earl of Winterwood."

"With his last few breaths, he couldn't even say, 'I'm sorry.' He bit his lip so hard to hold the words back, it bled." Selena shook her head sadly.

"Carlton asked forgiveness at the end," Celia murmured. "Before I could give it, though, he passed. My last words to him were in anger. I feel terrible about it."

"You were understandably shocked at hearing you would be left with nothing," Corrine interjected. "Do not blame yourself. The last time I spoke to Travis, we argued. I am determined that my marriage to Mitchell will not include arguments and recriminations."

"If and when I marry again, I vow to do the same," Selena said firmly. "There was no communication between Barnsdale and me. We never spoke of emotions or anything of consequence. But I will never hold anything back ever again. No secrets, either."

Corrine shifted uncomfortably in her seat. "Speaking of secrets, I have one to get off my chest, for I do not want any between us. I worked briefly for the Galway Investigative Agency. I admired the ladies who ran and worked for the agency and wanted to be part of it. I was rather bored with my life after marrying Addington. But since returning from my honeymoon, I told them I would not continue to take occasional assignments."

"How many assignments have you taken?" Celia asked.

"Just one." Corrine paused, then met Selena's gaze. "It was you, Selena."

Selena's heart tumbled in her chest. "Me?"

"I feel terrible bringing this up on the day Barnsdale was buried, but he hired the agency. I was asked to attend the Duchess of Gransford's tea party and discover what I could about you. Barnsdale believed you were cheating on him." Corrine wrung her hands. "When I was told your name, I should have refused the case then and there. I *am* sorry, Selena."

"Holy crow, Corrine," Celia whispered. "You're full of surprises. Did you invite me and Selena for tea the next day to pump us for information?"

Selena's eyes narrowed as a wave of annoyance tore through her. Barnsdale thought she cheated on him? And Corrine had spied on her?

Corrine looked horrified. "No! Never! I was genuinely pleased to see you both and glad we became reacquainted. It had nothing to do with the case, I swear it. I told the Galway sisters the next day that I wanted nothing more to do with it, and in my opinion, you were not having a clandestine affair but doing charity work. I assume they reported that to Barnsdale, and the case was closed. Can you forgive me for not mentioning it before now, Selena? Celia? I want nothing more than to be as close as we were in school. I do not want any secrets between us."

Both women looked at her. Selena could act petulant, dismiss their renewed friendship, and claim she never wanted to see Corrine again, though it would be somewhat awkward if she married Drew and refused to socialize with his half brother's wife. And she would lose her friend. And she didn't want that.

In her mind, Barnsdale's actions cut deeper. He hadn't come to her and inquired whether she was seeing another man. No, he hired a private investigator. Their communication had broken down to such an extent that her husband had hired an outside party.

Selena exhaled. "I wish you had told me before, but I understand why you did not. When you took the case, we were no longer close friends. There was no trust or bond to break. We hadn't seen or spoken to each other in nearly fifteen years, not since you left school. All is forgiven."

Corrine closed her eyes briefly, her expression one of relief. "Thank goodness. I told Mitchell, and he urged me to tell you both. I'm glad I did."

"That night after the Gransford tea party," Celia stated, "I asked Carlton about Barnsdale. He said that he never liked him. No one did. He'd heard whispers of scandalous country parties and brief affairs concerning Barnsdale. I told Corrine before you arrived the next day for tea."

Selena's mouth quirked. "And Corrine, you told the Galway Agency."

"Of course! All the more reason for the agency to drop the case," Corrine responded.

Selena shook her head. "I suspected as much. After I lost the baby, we ceased having intimate relations and grew even farther apart. I didn't care what he was up to as long as it kept him away from me. A sad state, indeed."

"All of our first marriages were horrid in their various ways and left their mark on us. But now, we all can make a fresh start. Love makes all the difference," Celia said, her expression softening. Undoubtedly, she was thinking of her new husband. "Take all the time you need, Selena. Drew will wait. I know he will. You both deserve happiness and contentment."

The ladies stood and embraced each other. A new, firm bond of friendship formed between them. This time, nothing would ever sever it.

DREW HADN'T SEEN Selena much the past three days, except when he had escorted her to the solicitor's office for the reading of the will. The new duke was in attendance and kept a solemn expression. The only time he made any reaction was shock when he heard how much money came with the dukedom. Drew and Selena spoke briefly to Kendall Wood, and she wished him well but made it plain, as politely as possible, that she wanted nothing further to do with the Barnsdale dukedom.

Ronan Wollstonecraft, Selena's solicitor, was seeing to the final arrangements. Selena would have close to fifteen thousand pounds with the safe contents, the dukedom dowager settlement, and the money remaining from the marriage payment. With proper investment, she should receive a few hundred pounds a year as an income, more than enough to live quite comfortably.

Once he tied his scarf around his neck, Drew ventured outside, carrying a covered tray up the stairs to Selena's flat. He banged the door knocker as hard as possible, hoping she would hear. The light came on in the vestibule, and the door opened.

"Drew! I am glad to see you. Come in." Selena stood aside as he crossed the threshold. "It's snowing out, judging from the snowflakes on your shoulders and hair." She smiled as she brushed the snow from his coat. When she reached up to clear the snow from his hair, he stood still, reveling in the feather touch of her fingers—every nerve ending pulsed to life.

"You're not wearing your spectacles."

"They're in my coat pocket."

"Do you need to wear them all the time?" she asked softly.

"Mostly for close-up work. It's easier to keep them on in most circumstances. Would you rather I not wear them?"

"Not at all. I rather like them." She stopped momentarily and then trailed the tips of her fingers down the side of his face and through his close-cropped beard. "Perhaps we should make an opening in the wall blocking the staircase. That way, you will not have to go outside at all," Selena teased, giving him a warm smile. It comforted him to see her so relaxed and happy.

"I could be induced to loosen a few boards," he murmured.

Selena laughed, and the joyous sound caused his heart to skip a beat. She pointed to the covered tray he held. "What do you have there?"

"Since it's teatime, I thought you might like sandwiches and biscuits."

"I already have the kettle on. Come into the parlor. I have become domestic."

Drew handed her the tray and then followed her into the room. A fire blazed in the hearth.

"I am also learning to build fires. Penny assisted me with this one before returning to her place to relax. Although we haven't admitted it to each other, we enjoy these precious moments of solitude."

Drew stopped removing his coat. "Perhaps I should leave."

"Absolutely not!' Selena replied firmly, laying the tray on the table. She came to his side and assisted him in removing his coat, scarf, and gloves. "I welcome your company—always. Sit here in the chair by the fire. I'll fetch the tea."

Drew sat, musing that he could easily get used to this. Having tea by the fire with Selena every night? Heaven on earth. Sighing contentedly, he stretched out his legs. Drew must have dozed as Selena gently shook him awake.

"You must be exhausted, considering your busy schedule," Selena observed as she sat across from him. She poured the tea, preparing it as he liked: milk and two sugars. Drew took the cup and saucer from her outstretched hand, but not before running his thumb across hers. The cup rattled precariously. "You should not do that," Selena murmured. "I nearly dropped the cup."

Drew smiled, satisfied that his touch had caused a reaction.

"What kind of sandwiches are these, I wonder?" Selena asked, turning her attention to the tray. She lifted the tea towel. "Frosted biscuits and plum tarts? Where did you get them?"

"The biscuits are left over from the tea with our friends—the plum tarts I bought at a French pâtisserie not far from here. As for the sandwiches? I made them myself. Shrimp. Your favorite."

Selena blinked rapidly. "You cut off the crusts! You made these especially for me?"

"I would do anything for you, from making shrimp sandwiches to capturing the moon and stars."

She gave him a shy smile. "Well, I won't ask for the moon and stars, though, thank you for offering. May I ask for a future with you? I cannot imagine anything I want more."

"You want to discuss this now—today?" Drew asked softly.

"Why not? It doesn't have to happen immediately, but I want to discuss it. If I learned anything from Barnsdale's death, it's that you can possess money, stature, and a dukedom and still be miserable and die more or less alone. I do not want to waste a moment." Selena paused. "But neither do I wish to rush into anything." Selena reached for a sandwich wedge and ate it.

"Right, then. Our future, it is. I have been thinking of a few things. Shall I share them with you?"

"Please do. I'm all attention."

"First, I will turn this place into a single residence again, except for Penny's flat. Penny can stay on in whatever capacity you like. Mrs. Evans informed me today that she will leave the city when her contract ends in May. She and her husband are moving to the country to be near their daughter."

Selena's eyes brightened. "This is just what I wanted to talk about. Perhaps Penny can become our live-in housekeeper. Or, if she wishes to retire from service, we can pay her a small stipend. Can a housekeeper also be my—our—friend?"

"In our house, she can," Drew replied determinedly.

Selena's expression softened. "Oh, I do love you."

The emotionally spoken words gave his heart a jolt. "And I love you, most ardently."

"Heavens," Selena breathed.

Changing the subject while he still could, he said, "I thought I might change the carriage house into a living area at some point. Recently, I thought it might be a fine place for the Critch family. Annie could be employed here as a lady's maid, seamstress, maid-of-all-work, or we can find her work nearby in a dress shop."

"What a wonderful idea! But what of Jimmy's job at Finnian's?"

"It's only three or four miles from here. Besides, by this time next year, Devil's Acre will be razed. The London Council will be building public housing on the empty lots."

"That soon? I had no idea." Her perfectly shaped brows knotted. "Drew, I hate to bring this up, but can you afford such a costly renovation? I assumed since you took in tenants that you were not impoverished exactly, but—but…"

"A struggling physician eking out a modest living?" Drew interjected, his mouth quirking with amusement.

"Not that there is anything wrong with that," Selena exclaimed. "I thought we might live in the flat below, rent out the top flat, and live well enough on what I will make from my investments. I assume that will be a few hundred pounds a year. That way, you can continue to work at the free clinics and do other charity work."

Drew set his near-empty cup on the table. "My love, I came into an inheritance when I turned twenty-five last March. The Hornsbys are wealthy, extremely so. One of the wealthiest families in the peerage, in fact, though we do not talk about it. We are not far behind the Duke of Westminster, and he is rumored to be worth over ten million pounds."

Selena started coughing. He moved to stand to come to her aid, but she waved him to sit again. "You have money?" she questioned hoarsely. Selena looked and sounded shocked.

"Scads of it. So much of it, Penny does not need to find another job, as our housekeeper or anything else. She stood by you for the past decade, as your loyal friend and companion. Now, we can reward her with a rent-free flat and pay her a generous retirement income. Penny will be part of this family, not a servant. Not ever again."

Selena's eyes misted. Then she vaulted out of her chair and into his lap, throwing her arms around his neck. "Thank you," she whispered shakily. "This is more than I could have hoped for." She hugged him tight, and Drew's heart soared. He held her close, reveling in her evocative vanilla-and-almond scent.

She sat back and cupped his cheeks, her fingers caressing his skin. "You mean it? About the Critch family? Truly?"

"Yes. After six months at Victoria Street, Annie and her children could stay at one of the family's country estates. Annie could train to be a lady's maid or a housekeeper if she wished. Then, if she wants to work for us, all the better. Or we can find other work for her either at any of the estates or with another family. I will talk to my father. I am sure he will agree. That is, if Annie is interested in such a plan."

"Estates? Plural?" Selena's eyes widened.

"We have several. There are so many that I will be given one when I marry, and so will my Hornsby brothers and sisters. The family never learned the true wealth of the Gransford dukedom until my grandfather passed. To say my father and uncles were shocked is an understatement. This town house is mine as well. I am still coming to grips with my new financial standing and becoming a baronet. Regardless, we need never worry about money. We are free to continue with all the charity work we wish."

"I am completely flabbergasted. Oh, I do want to continue with the good works. I have a couple of families I gave baskets to that I believe are worthy of the Hallahan Initiative." Selena hugged him again. "I'm so excited. And happy! What good news." She sat back and caught his gaze. "But know this. I would happily live in any financial or societal situation as long as we are together."

"I know it." Drew slipped his arms about her waist to hold her steady, then brought them both to their feet. "Let's dance."

Selena's eyes brightened. "Dance? I haven't done that for years. But there's no music."

Drew placed Selena's hand on his shoulder, then rested his at her waist. She slipped her hand in his. He began to hum Strauss's *Blue Danube* as he moved across the floor. Her first few steps faltered, but Selena soon became swept up in the rhythm. On the last beat, he stood still and spun her around before continuing. Selena laughed. Drew circled about the floor as he pulled her closer. If he was aroused before, now he was more so.

Step, slide, step. As they approached the left side of the room, Drew stopped and then moved forward until Selena's back rested against the wall. He cupped her cheeks, staring into her lovely blue eyes. "You are the only one I want. I knew it the first time I met you. From that day until the day I die, you are my lady."

Selena moaned softly. That sound broke apart any restraints, and he leaned in and captured her lips. A slow brushing, a tender touch, then she opened, and he took complete possession. The kiss grew frantic as Selena tunneled her fingers through his hair, kissing him passionately in return. Drew ground his hips against her, eliciting another sensual moan from Selena. Tunneling his hand under her gown, he lifted her leg to rest on his hip as he pressed her aching erection against her.

They became so caught up in their fiery desire that they didn't hear the pounding on the door.

"Selena? Your Grace?" a feminine voice called loudly.

They heard *that*. Selena tore her lips from his. "It's Penny, coming to check on me for supper."

Flustered, Drew released her leg and took several steps back. He was still shaking from the mutual passion unleashed between them. His entire body felt as if it were on fire. "Does she have a key?" he managed to ask.

"Yes. Quick, sit down and drink your tea as if nothing happened." Selena grabbed his hand and pulled him toward his chair. How could he sit in this condition? He was as hard as oak.

He grunted as Selena pushed him into the chair. "Your hair. I messed it quite thoroughly."

Drew smoothed his hair and hastily tied it at the nape. "You look well kissed," he murmured, his mouth quirking with amusement.

Selena felt her cheeks. "And I'm flushed. Oh, hang it all."

Drew chuckled as he reached for his teacup, wincing at the tightness of his trousers. What a predicament, but it was also amusing.

Selena smoothed her gown and hurried into the hallway. He heard the door close and the voices growing closer.

"It's Penny!" Selena announced a little too loudly.

"No need to get up," Penny said to Drew, her eyes laughing. She no doubt guessed what they were doing. What did it matter? Drew was just sorry they were interrupted. There would be more opportunities—they had all the time in the world. After their frank discussion, a future with Selena became more real. And that made him joyous beyond belief.

Nothing or no one would stand in their way.

CHAPTER TWENTY-THREE

SELENA AWOKE THE following day and lazily stretched in her bed. Feeling toasty warm under the covers, she was in no hurry to rise. Yawning, Selena turned over, pulling the quilt up to her chin, and re-lived those moments with Drew yesterday. That kiss, so passionate, and the way he had moved against her… Just thinking about it made her aroused all over again. Perhaps Drew *should* loosen a few boards in the wall blocking the stairs.

Selena giggled. When was the last time she'd giggled like a young girl? And when had she ever thought she would enjoy the touch of a man? Selena had believed she was dead inside, her heart a pile of cinders. But not with Drew. A handsome, honorable, intelligent younger man. She never would have dreamed of such an improbable scenario. And surprisingly, he was wealthy, too. Marrying Drew would go a long way to help her get over her past. Although they had never mentioned marriage, it had been certainly implied.

However, getting over her past was *not* the main reason she wanted to be with the handsome doctor. Selena was in love. There was no doubt in her mind, no more holding back. Her heart knew what it wanted. All that glorious man had to do was walk into a room, and her breath caught, and her insides tumbled with the joy of being near him. She felt no dread as she had with Barnsdale.

It was the first time she thought of her late husband in days. It was a rather sad state of affairs, but the man had made it impossible for anyone to love him, let alone like him. Selena shook her head, as if to remove him from her mind.

What to do today? Read? Relax? She had done nothing else these last few days and though she'd enjoyed it immensely, she was getting restless. Hearing Drew's plans to expand the charity work made her eager to seek out the two families she thought would benefit from the Hallahan Initiative. And once she had her mind set on something, she was determined to make it happen.

She sat upright. There was the young Folwell family: Barney, Ivy, and their young son, William. Barney had been laid off as a dock worker and was finding it difficult to obtain steady work. They had to keep moving, and each address was worse than the last. You could not sink much lower than Devil's Acre. If anyone deserved assistance, it was the Folwells. They were good people, beaten down by circumstance.

The second family had five children. The parents had experienced a run of bad luck. Nigel Bradstock had been incapacitated while working demolition for a construction company. He could have secured work with the company about to tear down Devil's Acre if he hadn't suffered injuries. How terrible that he was living in the one place he had sworn his family would never go. Hannah Bradstock took in washing and sewing, and the oldest boy of fourteen found menial work, but it wasn't enough to move from their tiny, run-down shack.

There. A good place to start.

Truthfully, she should have sought out these families before returning to the Barnsdale residence. Guilt gripped her tightly. But she had been sick and unable to make her rounds. She needed to locate them immediately and tell them of the charity plan.

Selena stood, smoothed the quilt on her bed, and quickly performed her ablutions and dressed. By the time she finished, she heard Penny calling her name. They met in the hallway.

"Ready for breakfast?" Penny asked.

"I am. Let's prepare it together. Fried this morning? Or scrambled?"

Penny smiled. "Let's be adventurous and make scrambled eggs."

They headed into the small kitchen and lit the gas stove. As they quickly fried leftover ham and prepared the eggs, Selena boiled water for tea. "I hope you are feeling adventurous," Selena said as they sat with their meals. "I want you to accompany me to Devil's Acre this afternoon."

Penny's teacup halted in midair. "What did you say?"

Selena explained her plan as she ate.

"No."

Selena raised an eyebrow. "No?"

"It's too dangerous. That criminal is looking for you!" Penny exclaimed as she poured more tea into their cups.

"Close to three weeks have passed. I highly doubt Sharpe is still interested in finding me. Besides, we are only visiting two families. We will be in and out."

"While I am pleased you've regained your confidence these past months, in this case, more caution is needed," Penny warned.

"We will be safe. As I said, we'll be in the area for less than an hour. I managed to survive for two months running the streets."

Penny's eyes widened. "By sheer luck! You had Sharpe's men chasing you, and more than once! I swear you received a thrill acting in such a careless manner."

Selena nodded as she spread jam on her toast. "I admit it. It was the first time I felt alive, felt as if I were accomplishing something worthwhile. But there's little risk now. Drew met with Sharpe, and he agreed to leave the Angel alone."

"And you believe that criminal's word?" Penny asked dubiously.

"Sharpe has a good reason to agree, although I cannot mention what it is as Drew and I have promised not to repeat what we know."

Penny sighed. "What intrigue. I suppose you'll go alone if I refuse."

"Yes, but I would prefer you accompany me. We need to stop at Annie Critch's as we left the old clothes and baskets behind. We can shop at the grocer near Annie's residence and pick up bread, cheese, and the like."

"Ask Doctor Hornsby to accompany you," Penny suggested.

"He is at the free clinic in the East End until six o'clock tonight."

"You know his schedule, then?" Penny asked, one eyebrow raised. "I had the distinct suspicion I walked in on something last night."

"Perhaps so. Things are developing nicely between us," Selena said, smiling knowingly.

"Then wait until the doctor is free to come with you. What about the police sergeant? Or Mr. Hallahan?"

"Mitchell is busy with an investigative case, and Liam is cooking at his restaurant and unavailable. Penny, I want to do this *today*. These two families are in a bad way. I cannot wait any longer. I should have seen to this before we left Victoria Street. As I said, we will be safe enough."

Penny exhaled. "Fine, I'll come with you, for I will not let you go alone. In and out, mind. I hope that in the future, all your charity works will be less hands-on. You can be plenty effective behind the scenes."

Selena frowned. "I always swore I would never be one of those society ladies who meet for tea in fancy parlors, raising a few meager pounds for starving orphans while they drink from china cups and eat from silver dishes. I *want* to be hands-on, like Drew. On the front lines, as it were." Then she smiled warmly at Penny. "Thank you for agreeing. We will venture forth after breakfast and be home before a late luncheon."

"Mrs. Beecham!" Annie cried as she opened the door. "Come in, come in!"

Selena hadn't told Annie Critch her true identity, and there was no time to explain it today. Selena and Penny crossed the threshold. "How are you feeling, Annie?"

"Good. Aye, much better than before. Sit yourselves on the sofa. I've tea on."

Selena and Penny sat. "We've no time for tea, but thank you. You remember my friend, Penny Holdsworth?"

"Aye, we met on the day of the movin'." Annie sat opposite and nodded at Penny.

Selena looked about the flat. It was certainly clean and tidy. "You seem right at home, Annie. You've had no trouble from anyone?"

"No. Nothin'. Thankfully. And we feel at home, missus. My girls are thrivin'. They're at school, the same one Jimmy goes to. We've all put on weight from eatin' better. We're doin' fine."

"I am so glad to hear it. I have two more families I need to meet with. I want to assist them as I did you through the charity. That's why I'm here. Do you still have the clothes and baskets I left behind?"

Annie's smile disappeared. "Mrs. Beecham, 'tisn't safe on the streets. Jimmy tells me there be a lot of grumblin' about Sharpe raisin' the rents. I know you mean well and all, but 'tis best you leave things be."

"Exactly what I said," Penny interjected.

"Miss Holdsworth is right. Let me send word to Jimmy. He can escort you to these two families. I know he's not exactly big enough to ward off attackers and the like, but he knows his way around and can keep you from danger," Annie urged.

"Annie, I appreciate it. But I don't want Jimmy to miss school or work. We are only stopping long enough to give these families a basket, gather information on their status, and inform them of the charity."

Annie shook her head. "You're a stubborn lady, and no mistake. Can you tell me the family names or where you're going?"

"I want to protect their identities and privacy, as they may not agree to accept further assistance. Do you still have the clothes we left behind?"

Annie exhaled. "Aye, follow me."

TEN MINUTES LATER, Selena and Penny were wearing worn wool gowns and coats, with shawls over their heads to hide their identity and, in Selena's case, her hair color.

"In there," Selena said, pointing to a collection of shacks at the end of the street.

Penny looked aghast. "That structure isn't fit for wild animals. What family lives there?"

"The Bradstocks."

"Mother, father, and five children in that lean-to? Dear heavens," Penny murmured.

Selena knocked on the door, and a woman with a tattered blanket around her shoulders opened it. She was visibly shivering. Recognition dawned on her tired face. "The angel! I never thought I'd see you again. I heard Sharpe had run you off. Come in, quickly now."

Mrs. Bradstock stepped aside, allowing them to pass. A small fire blazed in the wood stove, but it wasn't enough to heat the room. Three small children huddled under a blanket before the stove, trying to get warm.

"Is your husband around?"

"He and my two oldest boys are looking for work. He's found work as a day laborer here and there, the boys, too. But it's not enough to keep food on the table or wood in the fire. We're barely surviving, truth be told."

Selena handed the large basket to Mrs. Bradstock. "There's bread, jam, cheese, biscuits, potatoes, carrots, and onions there, as well as candles and five shillings."

"Five shillings? Oh, that will help. Thank you. I can make a soup tonight for supper."

"I will not be around as before, but I am working with a charity that takes families in unfortunate circumstances such as yours and assists them in finding steady work and a good place to live."

"That's all we want from life: a decent home, nothing fancy mind, and honest work. I'm not proud, and neither is Nigel. We'll take the help and thank you for it. Sharpe just raised the rent, and we have no idea how to pay it. These shillings will help."

"I heard about the rents. I'm glad you will accept assistance. Someone will be in contact with you in a few days. I'll send Doctor Drew Hornsby to see you. He is with the charity. The doctor is tall with blond hair and spectacles. Keep watch for him." Selena reached into her coat pocket. "Here's a few more shillings. Do not mention this to anyone. We do not want Sharpe to discover this." Even though Sharpe said he would leave her alone, there was no sense in stirring his ire. Why would he care anyway? This family did not work for Sharpe.

Mrs. Bradstock took the shillings and placed them in her pocket. "No worries there, we don't speak to anyone. We keep to ourselves."

"Very wise." Selena leaned in and whispered, "There are gumdrops in the basket for the children. A treat for later."

"How thoughtful. You ladies are kind. Ta."

With a wave, they were off. Penny and Selena stayed huddled together, keeping their heads down. "There, one family sorted," Selena said. "One to go. We will be back at Annie's in under thirty minutes. Maybe even twenty."

"I don't have a good feeling about this," Penny replied worriedly. "Where is this other family?"

"Not far, at the east end of Old Pye Street."

"I would hate to be here at night. This place is foreboding enough during the day," Penny stated, nervously scanning the street.

"Stay close and keep your head down."

"I think it's getting colder out."

"We will be relaxing before a roaring fire before you know it. Here, inside this building, on the top floor."

There was rubbish everywhere they stepped. A rat skittered about in the corner, squeaking and hissing at them. The plaster on the wall was crumbling, showing the bare wood slats underneath. No wonder the city was tearing these structures down.

"I cannot believe this place is worse than the shacks," Penny whispered.

"Hurry," Selena urged. Fractured noises filled the hallway: children crying, people shouting. Being away for a few weeks had caused her to forget just how awful this rookery was.

Selena rapped on the door, and it flung open. A grizzled older woman with rotten teeth and dirty gray hair stood before them. "Aye? What do you want?"

"Lookin' for the Folwells," Selena answered using her street voice.

"Well, they ain't here. They were tossed to the cobbles two weeks ago for not paying rent. So, sod off."

A large man hovered over the old woman. "Who 'tis it, Ma?" The young man's mouth drooped, and his eyes looked slightly crossed.

"Lookin' for the old tenants. What's in the basket? Give it here!"

The woman lunged for it, but Selena backed up several steps. Before they could turn and run, the young man grabbed them by their coats and pulled them into the grimy flat. The old woman slammed the door. Penny and Selena struggled, but it was to no avail. The man was too strong.

"I heard about some do-gooder running about the cobbles with baskets." The woman grabbed Selena's shawl and pulled it from her head. "I knew it. Chalkie, we've caught us the Golden Angel."

CHAPTER TWENTY-FOUR

S ELENA WAS MORTIFIED; worse, she felt foolish. Thinking they were safe from Sharpe, she had never entertained the idea that they could be in danger from others. So much for her supposed confidence and common sense. She had believed so entirely in her ability to stay out of harm's way that she'd arrogantly wandered into trouble. And brought along Penny to suffer the consequences.

Another large man emerged from the other room. "Whatcha got there, Chalkie?" He pointed to the basket.

"'Tis mine, Sam!" the other man cried.

The two young men started fighting, but the older woman slammed a meat mallet against the rickety table. "Enough! Get the ropes and tie these two to chairs."

"Please, let us go," Selena said as calmly as she could. "We were only lookin' for the Folwells. We mean no harm." Selena glanced at Penny. She looked terrified.

The two young men tied them to the chairs, lashing the ropes around their ankles and waist and using smaller ones to tie their hands behind their backs.

The woman emptied the contents of the basket onto the table. "Bread, cheese, candles, vegetables, bloody typical." She pushed the bread and cheese aside. "Here, lads. It's yours." The men fell on the food and devoured it like starving animals. "Hurry up and eat. I need one of you to fetch Sharpe. He's been looking for this lady, or so I heard. And I heard there's a reward."

"I'm no golden angel," Selena growled. "I was bringin' food to my friend and her family. 'Tis all I were doin'."

"We'll let Sharpe decide that. Who are you, then?"

"Who are you?" Selena shot back.

"I'm called Ma Turner. You?"

"Mrs. Beecham. Now let us go."

Turner crossed her arms. "If you're friends with Mrs. Folwell, how come you didn't know she'd been tossed to the cobbles? You're lying. The talk on the street is that the angel had golden-red hair and looked like a proper lady. And sometimes talked like one." Turner picked up the empty basket. "You think bringing crumbs to poor people will make any difference? What about tomorrow? Next week? Next month? Your bread and cheese don't make a dent. We'll all still be hungry and cold. Bloody do-gooders. You're doing this to make yourself feel better, not me or mine."

Ma Turner's severe words sliced Selena to the bone, and she felt her cheeks grow hot, for there was a harsh truth to the statement. Deep down, she knew some folks would find the meager charity offering an insult. It was why she only gave to those who accepted the help. To hear her worst fears so succinctly put caused no amount of unease.

"And you can drop the playacting and all," the woman continued, her voice filled with scorn. "One look at you with your white teeth and clean hair; it's plain you ain't one of us. Her either."

"Very well," Selena said in her own voice. "I will drop the playacting."

"There she is, the lady angel. You'll get no curtsies from me. What bloody right have you to come here? Do you like wallowing in the muck? Does it make you feel above us?"

"No, I do not feel above you or anyone in Devil's Acre. Isn't some help better than none at all?" Selena shot back.

"It's a bloody insult. People still have pride, no matter how poor. Have you ever picked rotten vegetables out of the rubbish just to have something to eat? I'll bet not. I did, to feed them two. Lads, was that food in the basket enough?"

"I'm still hungry, Ma," the one called Chalkie replied.

"See? What did I tell you? Chalkie, I want you to hie off to Finnian's and locate Sharpe. Talk to him only, not his bullyboys. Tell him that Ma Turner wants to see him. He knows me. Tell him I have something he's been looking for. And I want a reward. There was mention of one, and I aim to hold him to it." Turner waggled her finger at her son. "You bring him here. Don't return without him, or I'll give you what for. Do you understand?"

"Aye, Ma, bring back Sharpe. You've got the angel and want a reward."

"Good lad. Off with you now."

"Wait," Selena urged. "I can get more money for you than Sharpe can pay. Allow me to send word to my friends. If you agree to release us, one of them will bring you a basket of money."

Penny's whimpering grew louder, and Turner clipped Penny in the mouth. The sudden burst of violence shocked Selena.

"Another word from you," Turner said, pointing at Penny, "and I'll gag you. I think I will anyway. Sam, get me some rags off the floor."

Selena grimaced. The Folwells had managed to keep this small flat clean, but this family? There was rubbish everywhere, and the odors of rotting food filled her nostrils. She glanced at Penny, who looked angry. "Are you all right?"

"I'm fine. Don't lay a hand on me again," Penny said to Turner defiantly.

Good, Penny. Don't show fear. Selena was proud of her friend.

"What about my offer?" Selena asked as she turned her attention to Turner.

"I'll stick to the devil I know," Ma Turner replied. "It's best I stay on that devil's good side. I've known him since he was a wee nipper. Dangerous bloke. Gag them, and Chalkie, find Sharpe."

Time passed as slowly as treacle dripping from a spoon. There was one window in the place, and judging by the sun's position, it must be late afternoon—or so she surmised. Where was Sharpe? She was not in any hurry to be handed over to the horrid man, but at least she might be able to reason with him. The sooner she and Penny were away from these people, the better.

The door burst open, and Chalkie lumbered over the threshold.

"Where's Sharpe?" Turner demanded.

"He ain't been there all day. His man, Madden, wouldn't tell me where or when he'd be back. I'm hungry."

Turner's eyes narrowed. "What did I tell you, you great lummox? I said not to return here without Sharpe. Put your hand on the table."

Chalkie's face fell. "No. Ma. Please."

Penny and Selena exchanged shocked looks when Turner picked up the meat mallet.

"Place your palm on the table, spread your fingers, lad," Turner demanded.

"But I love you, Ma," the man said, his lower lip quivering as he placed his hand on the table.

The young man was obviously suffering from a low mental capacity. What a cruel woman. With a sudden mallet swing, Turner crashed it down on the man's pinkie finger. He howled in response. Selena's eyes widened. This woman was truly reprehensible.

"Stop moaning and get back to Sharpe's pub," Ma Turner barked. "Don't come back here without him, or I'll do the next finger."

The other son, Sam, stood mute. Apparently, he knew enough not to interfere. Selena stamped her feet and yelled as much as her gagged mouth would allow.

Turner pulled the rag from her mouth. "You've got something to say, lady?"

The evil woman still held the mallet menacingly. "Only that

you should wrap that finger, or it will heal crooked and be useless."

"What do you know about it?" Ma Turner spat.

"I've worked with nurses. I've seen them attend to broken bones."

"Sam, untie the lady. Do your nursing and be quick about it. Try anything, and I'll bring this mallet down on your pretty head."

"I don't doubt it," Selena murmured. Once untied, she stood and stretched; her legs felt wobbly, and her wrists hurt. She pointed to Chalkie. "Have a seat," she said kindly to the whimpering young man. "I'll need rags, as clean as you can find."

"Do it, Sam," Ma Turner spat.

A pile of rags was placed next to where she sat. Selena reached out toward Chalkie. "Let me see your hand." He put his large hand in hers. At least the bones were not completely shattered. It looked to be a clean break. "I am going to tie your little finger to the next one," Selena said gently. "It will stabilize the broken finger and allow it to heal." A doctor should look at it, but Selena would not suggest it. She gently but firmly wrapped the rags around both fingers and tied them in two places. "There. Be careful, and don't use them if you can help it. Don't take off these rags for a month."

The young man gave her a look of awe. "Ta. Thanks."

Selena felt like Androcles plucking a thorn from a lion's paw in the classic fable. "You're welcome."

"Enough niceties. Tie her up again, Sam. Chalkie, off with you."

Selena was shoved into the chair, but before they could gag her again, she said, "Can we have water? Something to drink? We've been sitting here for hours."

"Do you think I have water here?" Ma Turner laughed. "Bloody reformer. Shut her up, Sam."

Sam tied the rag around her mouth while Selena fumed. What if Sharpe declined to pay the reward and left her and Penny with Ma Turner? Would the man be so callous? She would have to remind the rookery boss of his agreement with Drew. And what about Drew? She'd told Annie Critch they would only be a half hour or less. Many hours had passed. Surely, Annie would have sent word to Drew by now, or maybe the authorities. It was a far-fetched calculation, but Selena would hang onto that hope with all her might.

Oh, Drew. Where are you?

DREW PAID THE hansom cab driver and headed toward the front door. It was well past six, and he was utterly exhausted. The clinic had been busy today, with barely time for a break. He glanced at the floors above. All was in darkness. Although Selena might be in her bedroom, that window faced the rear of the property. Someone emerged from the shadows as he slipped the key into the lock.

"Doctor Hornsby!"

"Who's there?"

"Jimmy Critch. I've been waiting for ages."

Drew pushed the door open. "Come inside, lad. You look frozen through. Come through here to my study. I'll light a fire."

"There's no time, Doctor. My mum sent me. She's that worried."

Drew motioned for Jimmy to sit on the sofa as Drew sat across from him. "Is someone sick? Did the bronchitis return?"

Jimmy shook his head. "It's the Golden Angel. She's missing."

Drew's heart froze. "What do you mean? Explain, and take your time."

"Mum told me the angel and another lady came by about eleven in the morning. They said they would visit two families and be right back. They changed into the old clothes they left behind and took two baskets. Mum asked them where they were going, the family names, and the like, but the angel said she had to protect their privacy."

That chill that had taken hold of Drew's heart now spread through his body. What in God's name had Selena done?

"They didn't come back after thirty minutes. Then an hour went by, then another. Mum was about to head to the coppers just as I got home from school. I told her Doctor Drew would know what to do, so I came here, but no one was home."

"What time was that?"

"I left our place at four."

Drew told Mrs. Evans to leave early today, blast it. Every instinct within Drew had him ready to storm Devil's Acre and tear it apart, find Sharpe, threaten bodily harm, and demand Selena's return. Oh, Sharpe would pay for this. But acting out of rage would not achieve the desired result. He had to stay calm and collected. Or try to.

The other woman with her must be Penny.

"First, we'll check upstairs. Mrs. Beecham is, in fact, the widow of a duke. Her companion lives in a small flat in the rear. Next, we'll get help from my friends, Detective Sergeant Simpson and Mr. Hallahan. Then, we'll head straight to Finnian's."

Jimmy's eyes widened. "Cor! The angel is a duchess?"

"That she is."

"I worked at the pub this morning. Sharpe wasn't there. He still wasn't there when I left for school after lunch."

"Is he usually?"

"Aye, but in the past week, he has been gone all day at least twice."

Then maybe Sharpe had nothing to do with this. That prospect filled him with dread. "Then let's go at once."

Jimmy followed Drew into the hallway. Drew opened the bottom drawer of the wood hall tree and tossed Jimmy two wool scarves and fur-lined gloves. "Use these. Wrap one scarf around your head and another around your neck to keep the chill at bay. Is your coat warm enough?"

"It'll do."

Drew changed his coat to a warmer one and bundled up with scarves and more appropriate gloves. He wished he had a revolver, but that was where Mitchell and Liam would be handy.

After checking both flats and finding them empty, Drew waved down an approaching hansom. Worry set in alongside the rage as he and Jimmy climbed inside the cab. If Sharpe had Selena and Penny, he would have sent word by now. They had an agreement, he and Sharpe. And Sharpe had better bloody well adhere to it.

Could someone else be holding her? To what end?

He'd find her. If he had to tear the streets apart, Drew would find Selena. And judging by the ferocity of the fury building within him, he would make whoever was holding her pay.

CHAPTER TWENTY-FIVE

LUCIAN ARRIVED AT Finnian's Pub at seven o'clock. After ordering his meal, he instructed the waiter to bring it upstairs to his office instead of his usual corner by the fire because he wanted to be alone. It had been a long day, spent with bankers and barristers, plotting his next steps. He still wasn't sure he would take a new identity or keep the one he had now. The way he was feeling, maybe he should leave England altogether.

He plopped into his chair, weary and sorry he hadn't asked Kit Greenwood to bring up his meal as she was working tonight. The sight of her lovely face always caused an inordinate amount of pleasure. Not that he had done anything about it. The widowed beauty remained aloof, and Lucian wasn't sure how to approach her. That wasn't exactly true—he'd had no problems with women before. But Lucian had the distinct impression that anything he started with Kit would not be casual. The last thing he wanted was something permanent. Something—serious.

His thoughts were interrupted by shouting and the sound of tables overturning and crockery smashing to the floor.

What now?

The door crashed against the wall, hanging from two hinges. Before him stood Hornsby, Hallahan, and Simpson.

His men burst in behind them. "We tried to stop them—"

"But you didn't," Lucian snapped. "Leave me with them. Go downstairs and clean the mess." Once his men left and closed the broken door as best as they could, Lucian turned toward the men. "What brings you here?"

Hornsby moved so swiftly that Lucian had no time to react. The doctor grabbed his shirt and hauled him from the chair. "Give me the pistol," Hornsby growled to Simpson.

"Wait, Drew—" Simpson urged.

Hornsby grabbed the letter opener from the desk and held it to Lucian's throat. "Where is she?"

"Who is *she*? And a letter opener? Really?" Lucian scoffed.

"Don't forget I am a physician," Hornsby hissed dangerously. "I know just where to stick this to do the most damage. And I'm speaking of the Golden Angel."

"I don't know what you're on about. I've been gone all day. Release me, or there will be hell to pay. If not now, then later. I promise you." Lucian uttered his threat with a calm malice that surprised even himself. If there was one thing he could not abide, it was being manhandled.

Hallahan stepped forward and laid his hand on Hornsby's arm. "Let him go, Drew. He means what he says. Sharpe will tell us what he knows, but not under threat. Do I have the right of it, Sharpe?"

"You do."

Hornsby exhaled and stepped back, throwing the letter opener to the floor. Lucian took his seat, keeping his gaze firm on the doctor. Of all the men Lucian expected to lose their composure, Hornsby was not one of them. This angel had to mean something to him, and that was obviously why Hornsby had made the agreement in the first place.

"I gave you my word that I would cause no harm to the angel the last time we spoke," Lucian said carefully. "I meant what I said. I have no knowledge of her whereabouts. Tell me what you know."

"She came here with her friend to pay a visit to two families she wanted to assist through the charity," Hallahan interjected. "Her name is Mrs. Beecham."

Lucian's eyebrows shot skyward. The woman who paid for the apartment for Jimmy Critch's family? The one who was with Hornsby that day? What in the hell?

"She is the Duchess of Barnsdale," Hornsby added. "If you don't have her, who does? Is someone holding her for you?"

Jesus. A duchess?

"Like it not, Sharpe, we all share a bloodline, loathsome as it is," Simpson said. "Be honest with us."

"Share a bloodline?" Lucian scoffed. "So *you* say. I reject it. I want you three to listen to me. I don't know anything about the angel. I stopped looking for her weeks ago. As. I. Pledged. If she's missing in Devil's Acre, that has nothing to do with me."

"Then you won't object if the three of us go door-to-door and check every abode?" Hallahan asked.

"Have at it," Lucian barked. "I'll put the word out you're to be left alone. But don't ever come into my place of business like this again. I don't care if you're looking for the bloody queen."

The three men exited without incident.

Moments later, Madden entered the room. "You want me to have the boys follow them?"

"No. To hell with them. But put the word out; they're not to be disturbed. I gave them permission to search every residence. They're looking for someone. The Golden Angel."

"What, the lady with the cape and the baskets, giving out bread and the like?"

"Turns out she's a duchess. Find out where my meal is."

The food arrived a few minutes later. He would say this: His bastard son, Teddy, was talented in the kitchen. The enticing odor of fried onions smothered in gravy had his mouth watering. He cut into the beefsteak with gusto. Lucian was half finished with the meal when Madden knocked and entered.

"You're not going to believe this," Madden murmured, hitching his thumb toward the door. "I have a bloke outside that says his mother has the angel and wants a reward. Do you know Ma Turner? The name sounds familiar to me."

God, that horrid woman. That was a name from his past, and one he'd rather forget. "Aye. She used to sell gin and whores on Dorne's Alley off Great Peter Street. She left Devil's Acre for a time but returned recently. She swings a meat mallet at anyone who annoys her."

"Oh, that harridan. We rented to her a couple of weeks ago."

"Right. She has two giants for her sons; one is touched in the head."

"I think he's the one outside."

"Show him in, and stay here."

The man lumbered into the room, ducking his head slightly to pass through the door frame. "You Sharpe?"

"Aye."

"Come with me. Ma wants you and no one else. She has the angel and wants a reward."

"How much of a reward?" Lucian asked casually as he sliced into his rapidly cooling steak.

"Money. Lots." The man was eyeing the plate of food with a desperate hunger that Lucian remembered all too well.

"You want the rest of this?"

Turner nodded.

"Then eat. I need to talk to my associate."

Lucian was no sooner out of his chair when Turner took it and started shoving the food into his mouth.

Lucian motioned for Madden to step outside. "I'll go with him. I have ten pounds with me. Get me seventy more from the safe. God knows how much she'll ask for."

"Do you want me to find those three blokes and tell them?"

Lucian shook his head. "Not until I'm sure it's the woman they're looking for. Have Brown come up here. I'll take him with me, along with my revolver. Ma Turner's unpredictable."

After gathering the money, pistol, and Brown, Lucian set out for Old Pye Street.

"Ma said to come alone. She won't like it," the young man kept saying repeatedly.

"What's your name?" Lucian asked as they trudged through the snow.

"Chalkie."

"Chalkie, since I'm paying, I bring who I like. If your mother wants the reward, she'll agree." Lucian pointed to the wrapped fingers. "Your mother do that?"

"Aye. I did a bad thing."

So it appeared Ma Turner hadn't changed. Lucian hoped the demented old woman hadn't harmed the duchess and her friend. He didn't need the police crawling over Devil's Acre, or to deal with Hornsby, Hallahan, and Simpson in the aftermath.

They arrived at the building. Lucian hadn't been down this end of the street in ages. It was in worse condition than he imagined. They walked through the dim halls and up the stairs until they reached the door. Ma Turner let them in.

"Before you say it or start wielding your mallet, I don't go anywhere without protection. Brown stays."

Ma Turner grumbled but stepped aside, slamming the door shut behind them. "I got the angel."

"So I heard. How do I know it's who you say it is?" Lucian glanced at the corner of the room where two women were tied and gagged. One of the women was Mrs. Beecham, the wayward duchess. "You know what? Who bloody cares. I'll take them. How much?"

"Hundred pounds."

Lucian laughed. "Not a chance. Try again."

"Seventy pounds," Ma Turner replied.

"Sixty pounds and I'll let you and your sons stay here rent-free for three years." Not that the building would be standing that long, but that wasn't his problem.

"Done! Sam, untie those do-gooders." Ma Turner greedily reached for the pound notes and quickly counted them. "I always liked doing business with you, Sharpe."

"Wish I could say it was mutual," Lucian muttered as he took the duchess's arm. Brown gripped the other woman's arm.

Lucian leaned in and whispered to the duchess, "Don't say a word. Come with me."

⟫⟫⟩✕⟨⟨⟨

SELENA WASN'T SURE if this was a rescue or a payment of services rendered. Had Sharpe ordered this abduction and offered a reward for her capture, even though he had promised Drew he'd leave her be? How foolish of her not to consider that possibility before or to think that someone had moved or been evicted since she had last seen them. How would she ever make this up to Penny?

They hurried along the darkened hallway and down the stairs. Selena stumbled.

Sharpe yanked her arm and pulled her along. "Hurry," he barked.

"Wait. My legs are not working properly. I've been tied up for hours."

"You can both rest once we get back to Finnian's. No more talking." Sharpe pulled her along, not losing a step.

It was dark and overcast, so they could move about without attracting attention. *Blast it.* Would anyone even come to her aid if she started shouting? Highly unlikely. One look at Sharpe's menacing face, and they would scurry away.

Once they reached Duck Lane, Sharpe brought them around the rear of the building. He pushed Selena through the door, and to the left, people stood around a counter, staring at them. Selena couldn't make out their faces, but judging from the enticing food odors, it must be the pub's kitchen.

"Not a word." Sharpe squeezed her arm in warning. "It's my pub staff. They won't help you."

They continued up the stairs, then down a dark, musty hallway, into a dimly lit room. Sharpe pointed to two chairs before his desk, so she and Penny sat. The other man closed the door and stood in front of it.

"Brown, stand outside the door. Let no one in until I say."

The man touched his forelock and exited the room.

Selena turned to Penny. "Are you all right? I am so sorry."

"I'm better than expected," Penny replied emotionlessly.

"Did Ma Turner hurt you?" Sharpe asked.

"They were rough. Turner slapped Penny once. They wouldn't give us food or drink."

"I'll get something for you both shortly. First, Duchess, are you the Golden Angel?"

Selena gasped. "How did you know—"

"Not one hour ago, I had Doctor Hornsby in here holding a letter opener to my throat, demanding to know where you are. He told me your true identity. Hornsby had Hallahan and Simpson with him. Answer the question."

Selena's heart soared. Drew *was* looking for her! "Yes, I am the angel. What are you going to do with us? Did you order this abduction?"

"I entered into a verbal agreement with Hornsby, pledging not to look for you in exchange for keeping quiet about an aspect of my life you, Mrs. Beecham, are well aware of. Now that pact includes *you*. So no, I was not behind this. You just knocked at the wrong door."

Selena would not wither under his intense gaze. "If you let me and Miss Holdsworth go, I will honor the pact."

"All in good time. Hornsby's tearing the streets apart, looking for you. I'll send my men out to find him and the others. They can take you home. I will also take your promise that you will never come here again."

Selena huffed. "I cannot promise that."

Penny gasped. "Your Grace—"

"And why is what?" Sharpe interrupted.

"I need to find the family that lived in that hovel before the Turners—the Folwells. You evicted them. How could you? They have a small child. Your places aren't fit for animals to live in!"

Sharpe clenched his teeth, clearly growing angry. "I refuse to be the villain in your histrionic drama, Duchess. Brown!"

The man ducked his head through the door. "Aye, guv?"

"Fetch Madden. On the double!"

The man disappeared.

"You've been nothing but a thorn in my side, Duchess, for months."

Selena ignored the statement. "Why did you promise Ma Turner three years of rent? Aren't these places being torn down starting in the spring?"

"Aye. But she doesn't know that. So she'll get a few months free. It's more than she deserves. From what I know about her, you're lucky she hadn't done worse to you. She's been known to forcibly abduct women for her simpleton sons to amuse themselves with. Did you tell her you were a duchess?"

Selena was shocked at the statement. "No."

"Smart. If you had, she might have killed you just to make a point. Many people around here have no use for the peerage, myself included."

"You could have left us there and not said a word. Yet, you came to fetch us and paid the ransom."

Sharpe snarled. His man, Madden, entered the room.

"The family that lived in Ma Turner's flat, where are they?" Sharpe asked Madden.

"They were five weeks behind on the rent. You allowed them to stay the extra two weeks, remember?"

That was a surprising bit of information, she thought. As Sharpe said, he wasn't a villain—not entirely. Why hadn't the Folwells told her they were behind on the rent? They must have been ashamed. Selena's heart ached for the young family.

"I put them out and told them to go to the Methodist mission on Tufton Street. I don't know if they're still there."

"There, Duchess. You can look for them yourself later. Madden, tell Kit to bring three mugs of tea and two bowls of stew. Then I want you and Teddy to find Hornsby and those other two.

Bring them here. Just tell them I've found the duchess and her companion, nothing else. Understand?"

"Aye, guv." Madden disappeared through the door, closing it behind him.

"You let them stay an extra two weeks?" Selena stated incredulously.

"Not only am I not the villain of your overwrought drama, Duchess, I'm also not the hero. I leave that role for Hornsby. He would have rescued you eventually. I never thought him the sort to turn feral, but he did, looking for you."

"Maybe it's in the blood," Selena replied wryly. *Wait.* One of his employees was named Kit. It had to be a coincidence. Or was it? "This Kit, can you describe her?"

"Why?"

"Please!"

"She's about your height, with dark-auburn hair and blue eyes."

"Is her last name Seaton or Greenwood?"

"Her last name is Greenwood."

Selena flew out of her chair so swiftly that she knocked it over. She flung open the door and ran straight into Brown. He grabbed her arm and pulled her back into the room.

"You don't understand!" Selena cried. "She's my sister! She left England close to fifteen years ago. I haven't seen or heard from her since. Please let me go to her!"

Sharpe rolled his eyes. "Christ, I cannot believe this—one bloody thing after another. Brown, go fetch Kit and bring her here. Sit down, Duchess. Try to stay calm. You're annoying the piss out of me."

Selena sat, her hands trembling. Kit here? How? She was about to ask Sharpe those exact questions when Madden entered the room.

"Kit's done a runner. Teddy says she ran out of the pub without a word, close to ten minutes ago."

Selena gasped. "She saw me and ran."

"Madden, give Mickey Kit's address and get him to bring her here. Now you and Teddy find Hornsby and his crew."

After Madden left, Selena brushed a tear from her cheek. "Tell me everything about her."

"Not much to tell," Sharpe replied with a shrug. "She's a widow and came from America with her son about two weeks ago. I forget the lad's name. I've never seen him. She rented the Critch's old place. I gave her a job in the pub. I don't know anything else. As I said, you are a pain in my arse."

Selena's mind spun from all the revelations. Why hadn't Kit gone to their parents? Well, she could surmise why. Her loathsome father said she hadn't written. God knows what her father had said in his letters, probably lies of all sorts. But for Kit to never answer any of Selena's letters? They had been close growing up. That bond had solidified the older they got, especially once it became plain what their parents had planned for them: marriage to dukes, whatever the cost.

There could be numerous reasons for Kit not writing. Kit might never have received Selena's letters because she'd moved away. Or perhaps her parents had never given Selena the responses. Selena's heart chilled. *Oh, how cruel!* Kit probably had no idea Selena had married Barnsdale. And Kit, a widow? What had happened to Greenwood? She remembered the footman was a tall, handsome, strong specimen. But moving to America would bring fresh dangers, especially if they hadn't any money.

Someone brought in tea and stew, but Selena was not hungry. Penny, however, ate with gusto.

"Please eat, Your Grace," Penny urged.

But she couldn't.

A man came through the door. "She's gone. The boy, too," he said to Sharpe.

Selena covered her face with her hands.

Everything had gone horribly wrong.

CHAPTER TWENTY-SIX

T HE WIND HAD picked up, tossing loose snow all around them as they trudged through the back alleys. Drew wasn't keen that the three of them were forcing themselves into people's homes, but he would do anything to locate Selena. And Penny. Grimacing inwardly, he relived his confrontation with Sharpe. Physically threatening the man? Where had that come from?

Liam patted him on the back. "Stop ruminating over Sharpe and your threats."

It was amazing how they had only known each other briefly but were already attuned to each other's inner thoughts and changing moods.

"If it were Celia missing, I would have done the same, maybe worse," Liam added.

"Do you think Sharpe was telling the truth?"

"About not knowing Selena's location? Aye, I do. I've known him for a few years. We were not exactly friends, but we shared a few conversations. We always spoke easily, which is surprising because I never used to let anyone close. Anyway, when I changed the pub into a restaurant, I made it plain that I didn't want him around any longer. I was determined to run a legitimate business. I could've handled it better. But then, I regret a lot about my life."

Drew smiled. "Including mixing up with Mitchell and me?"

Liam shook his head. "No. Maybe at first, but not now. Loving Celia changed that. Maybe someday, someone will do that for Lucian."

"When I see him again, I'll apologize."

"He'll act like he doesn't care, but deep inside, he'll remember."

Mitchell pointed to the shacks and the end of the street. "People are living in these hovels?"

"Unfortunately, yes," Drew replied grimly.

Drew knocked on the door of a small, dilapidated shack, and a woman wrapped in a tattered shawl answered. "Aye?"

Liam gently pushed the woman aside, and they stepped into the small room. Three children sat at a table eating bread and cheese. On the fire was a kettle pot, bubbling away. Drew could smell cooking vegetables.

"We're looking for someone. We mean no harm," Drew urged, since the woman looked frightened. "A friend has gone missing. A lady. You might know her as the angel." Drew's glance tore about the room and landed on a wicker basket on a shelf. "She was here, wasn't she? And brought you a basket? The Golden Angel urges people not to discuss her, but we must find her. She's been missing for hours."

The woman shook her head. "I don't know what you're on about." Her voice shook with fear.

Drew pointed at Mitchell and Liam. "This is Detective Sergeant Simpson and Mr. Hallahan. I am Doctor Hornsby."

The woman's head shot upwards and met Drew's gaze. "Doctor? It *is* you, just as she described."

"Tell us what you know," Mitchell urged.

"The angel was here late this morning. She was with a friend and brought a basket. She said Doctor Hornsby would be by in a few days to tell us more about the charity. That you would help find my husband a job and a better place to live. I'm Mrs. Bradstock."

"And I will, Mrs. Bradstock. But first, I must find the angel. Do you know where she went from here?"

Mrs. Bradstock shook her head sadly. "No, she never said. Her friend held a basket, so I think they went to another family. I wish I knew who. We keep to ourselves. I don't know many people hereabouts."

"It's all right. We'll keep looking," Mitchell replied.

"You'll tell us if you find her? I'm that worried!"

"I will," Drew said firmly.

They exited the shack. Where should they go next? It didn't matter; Drew would stay out all night if that was what it took. His determination to find Selena was unwavering. If anything happened to her—he couldn't fathom such a scenario. He was about to knock on the next door when he halted. Drew could have sworn he heard his name. He listened. There it was again. The cold, still air carried his name through the cloudy darkness. "Do you hear that?"

Liam and Mitchell listened. "Aye," Liam answered. "Here!" he yelled loudly.

From around the corner, two men appeared. Drew recognized the shorter one immediately. It was Teddy Chisholm, Sharpe's illegitimate son.

"Liam, Dr. Hornsby, Sergeant Simpson..." Teddy said, panting, clearly out of breath. "Lucian's found the Golden Angel and her friend. He has them at Finnian's. They're safe."

The three men followed Teddy and Sharpe's bullyboy to the pub.

Drew could not describe the rush of emotion that gripped him when he entered the room and saw Selena sitting in the chair. He was overwhelmed by a wave of relief and joy, knowing at that moment that he couldn't live without her. Knowing that if anything had happened to her, his life would have been over. He might still breathe the air, but his heart would have shriveled to a dry husk.

To hell with anyone else being in the room. He ran to Selena, who, in turn, ran to his open arms.

"Drew!" she cried as she laid kisses on his cheek. His heart swelled with love for her. He captured her lips and kissed her long and hard. Then he gently clasped her cheeks and looked into her shimmering-with-tears eyes. "Are you injured?"

"I am unhurt. Truly."

Drew turned toward the other chair. "Penny?"

She touched the corner of her mouth. A bruise already showed on her cheek. "I'll be fine."

Drew turned to glare at Sharpe.

Selena grasped Drew's hands and held them. "Sharpe paid the ransom. Sixty pounds."

"Now that the touching reunion is over, get the hell out of my office—all of you," Sharpe snapped, annoyed.

Drew handed Selena to Liam, and Mitchell assisted Penny. Drew stayed behind. Once the door was closed, Drew reached into his coat side pocket and pulled out his money clip. "I am indebted to you." He peeled off numerous notes and laid them on the desk. "An extra twenty for your trouble. I want to apologize."

Sharpe grabbed the notes and started counting. "For what, holding a letter opener to my throat?"

"Yes. It was not the way I was raised."

Sharpe looked upward, one eyebrow arched. "Aye, it's *precisely* the way you were brought up. When did the toffs adopt you?"

"I had just turned ten years of age."

"Then you know what I'm talking about." Sharpe folded the bills and tucked them in his coat. "Ten years you lived the life, grasping for every crumb, living in filth. That stain never washes off. It hides deep inside, festering; you never know when it will come out. Hide it all you want behind your fancy clothes and gold spectacles, and tuck your feelings away deep so no one guesses. But it's always there, lurking. Ask Hallahan, and he'll tell you the same. Simpson, maybe not so much."

"If you accept that, why won't you accept that the late Duke of Chellenham was your father?"

"Because I'm still living this life, unlike you and Hallahan, *Sir Drew*. I want no ties to anyone with the whiff of the peerage, either adopted to it or married to it. Don't come here again. And tell the others, especially that stubborn duchess."

"A baronet is not part of the peerage. And Mitchell and Liam's wives, as widows of peers, may call themselves 'lady,' but they are no longer part of the peerage, either." Drew reached into his pocket and laid his card on Sharpe's desk. "If you should ever change your mind, here is my address. You also know where to find Liam. Thank you for finding Selena and her friend."

Drew didn't wait for a reply. He turned on his heel and departed, closing the door behind him.

SELENA JOINED DREW in his study after seeing that Penny was settled in her flat. A fire blazed in the hearth, and she welcomed its warmth, for she was chilled to the bone. Her ill-advised adventure could have had a much more dire outcome.

"Would you like a drink?" Drew asked.

"Yes. A brandy, please."

He poured some into a snifter. Selena held out her trembling hand to take it. "The danger we were in has started to sink in," she murmured as she took the snifter and swirled the amber liquid.

"It's natural to feel a delayed shock," Drew said as he sat beside her. "Tell me what happened."

"I foolishly believed in my invincibility. I'd run about Devil's Acre for over two months unharmed, so I surmised a quick visit to two families would be safe. I had no idea the second family, the Folwells, had been evicted. That horrid woman, called Ma Turner, and her slack-jawed sons pulled us into the room. She guessed my Golden Angel identity right away."

Selena told Drew how they'd been tied to chairs, how Turner had swung her meat mallet at her son, slapped Penny, and charged a ransom to Sharpe. "But here's the most incredible part.

Once we arrived at Finnian's, he told his man to tell the waitress, Kit, to bring us tea and stew. Kit? What would be the odds that it would be my long-lost sister? When I asked him to describe her, Sharpe said she had blue eyes, dark-auburn hair, and was about my height. That is an *exact* description of my sister. He told me her last name was Greenwood. That is the name of the footman she ran away with. They have a son, and she told Sharpe she was a widow. Sharpe told one of his men to fetch her, but she had run away. The kitchen staff saw Sharpe bring us in through the rear entrance. Kit must have seen me and departed. She was renting the Critchs' old place. Sharpe sent a man there, but there was no sign of her and her son. Kit is gone. Again." Selena placed the snifter on the table and buried her face in her hands.

Drew immediately pulled her into his warm embrace. "My love, I'm so sorry. Why would she run from you?"

Selena laid her head against Drew's chest as he smoothed her hair. "I have no idea. She must be a widow. Why return here without a husband?"

"Unless Greenwood abandoned her and the boy."

"That is too horrible to contemplate. Why not go to our parents or grandparents? Why run when she saw me? I don't understand!"

"There could be any number of reasons. Perhaps your sister is ashamed of her reduced circumstances and wanted to have a more solid footing before approaching the family, including you. Prolonged hardship can take a toll, mentally and physically."

What Drew said made perfect sense. Selena turned slightly and grabbed his coat lapels, looking him straight in the eye. "We must find her. Promise me we will do all we can to locate her and her son."

"I will go see Mitchell in the morning. He has just wrapped up an investigative case. We will hire him. He's not returning to the police force until later this spring, so he has plenty of time to find your sister and her son. She could not have gone far. If Kit took a job with Sharpe and rented one of his rooms, she wouldn't have much money. It probably took every last penny to buy the steamship fare to England. She may even return to Sharpe if she's owed wages."

"Let's go see Mitchell now," Selena urged.

"Love, it's past ten at night. We will go first thing tomorrow morning before anything else."

"Yes, you're right."

Drew caressed her cheeks. "If you knew how terrified I was when I heard you'd gone missing. It felt as if my insides had been kicked out and stomped on. I failed you."

Selena sat back, staring at Drew. "Failed? How?"

"I tried to be Captain Hornsby and rescue you, but failed miserably. I am not the hero."

"Oh, my love," Selena whispered. "You did rescue me from a loveless, barren life and an emotionally abusive man. I never would have gathered the courage to leave if you hadn't offered me assistance the first time we met. And when we reencountered each other, you offered friendship and support and nursed me back to health when I fell ill. Your encouragement gave me the push I needed to confront the past and move forward. You're *my* hero. Forever and always."

Drew gave her such a tender kiss that a soft moan escaped her lips. "Forever and always. You are mine."

"And you are *mine*." Selena chuckled. "Even Sharpe said you're the hero. He said you would have found me eventually. I'm glad you didn't. Sharpe got us out of there without incident because he knew how to deal with that horrid woman. Who knows what would have occurred if the three of you had burst in? You, Liam, and Mitchell could have been seriously hurt. I would have never forgiven myself."

"It certainly would have been more dramatic. And more dangerous. All this drama has made things crystalline clear: I need you. I love you. I want us to get married immediately. We can have another celebration in the spring with family and friends, but I want you in my life in all ways, especially in bed, and I'd rather we were wed when that happens. What do you think?" His words were laced with emotion; his face shone with love.

"I agree. Why wait? We love each other and want to be together in all ways. Can we do it?"

"We can do anything we want. I promise I will be open and honest with you. I wish for us to make decisions together and share everything. You are my heart."

Selena hugged him tightly. "And you are mine."

Selena knew she'd never be lonely again.

CHAPTER TWENTY-SEVEN

Two days later...

P ENNY SAT IN the parlor and listened patiently as Drew and Selena explained their plans for their future together.

"My, you have it all worked out," Penny murmured.

"And what do you think of our suggestion that you stay on in the flat with a retirement income?" Selena asked hopefully.

Drew could see the hesitation and concern on Penny's face. "What is it, Penny? Do you have doubts? Please speak freely."

"I do not doubt you love each other," Penny smiled warmly. "I've grown fond of you, Doctor—sorry, Drew—but I am concerned you're rushing into this. You've only known each other for a little more than a month. Why not give it some time? So much has happened."

"I appreciate your concern; I know it comes from a place of love for Selena," Drew stated. "Why wait when we know what our hearts desire? We want to be together, be a family, and we want *you* to be part of that family."

"Me?" Penny gasped.

"Yes. Not as a loyal servant but as a cherished aunt to our children, should we be blessed to have any," Drew continued. "We want you to live your own life, join charitable organizations, make friends, and travel if you like, but know you always have a home here with us. You will be a part of our celebrations. Join us for dinner parties or any time you wish to sit at our table. Selena has much to do in the future. We've hired Mitchell Simpson to start looking for Selena's sister. We have already located the

Folwell family, and they and the Bradstocks will need assistance. Or if you choose not to be involved with Selena's charity work and want to do something else, we will support you."

Penny reached into her skirt pocket for her handkerchief and dabbed the corners of her eyes. "I'm touched. Truly. It appears you both know precisely what you want. Who am I to stand in your way?"

Selena clapped her hands together. "Thank you! And will you stay with us?"

"Yes. I accept the retirement and your generous stipend. I would love to stay in that flat; I adore it. And I adore you both. Of course, I will join the charity. And I will do all I can to assist you in finding your sister, Selena."

"I have one last request," Selena said shyly. "To be our witness. We are exchanging vows the morning after next at Bow Church."

"Aren't your friends going to be there?" Penny asked.

"No. We will invite them over the next day for a dinner party and tell them then," Selena replied. "We thought to do this ourselves. In the spring, we will do it again with everyone invited. I cannot explain it. It is just how we wish to do it."

"You do not have to explain it to me. I will be your witness. Won't you need another?"

"Reverend Wilton is supplying one," Drew replied. "All I need to do is pick up the special license this afternoon."

"Well…" Penny beamed. "You both have all this arranged to the last detail. I wish you every happiness." They all stood and embraced.

A family, indeed.

EXCHANGING WEDDING VOWS was a serious business, even within a small gathering. But after the heartfelt ceremony, Drew and

Selena found themselves alone for the rest of the afternoon and evening. As he took her hand and led Selena into his bedroom, he pointed to the table in the far corner.

"A gramophone?" Selena smiled.

"Yes, I had a phonograph with a few waxed cylinders, but I found this device with the flat discs to be superior. This is a Berliner, named after the man who owns the company and invented these discs, Emil Berliner." Drew handed her the disc.

"Gramophone Concert Record." Selena laughed lightly. "*Blue Danube* by Strauss. The very one you hummed when we first danced."

"Shall we, wife?"

"By all means, husband."

Drew placed the disc on the machine. "There is no crank with this model. A spring mechanism is used to spin the record." Once he moved the stylus on the record, the music emitted from the large brass horn. Drew gathered Selena into his arms and spun her about the room in time to the music. This continued for several minutes until they came close to his bed.

He stopped, and their gazes locked. "One part of me wants to tear our clothes to bits and fall on each other in a lustful frenzy."

Selena's eyes widened, then she smiled seductively. "And the other?"

"A slow lovemaking, where we explore and kiss every inch of skin, then join together in multiple positions."

"My," Selena murmured as she unbuttoned Drew's waistcoat. "Both scenarios have merit. I do have a medical question."

"Ask away."

"Is it true younger men have more stamina, sexually speaking?" she teased.

Drew smiled. "What a fascinating question. Yes, that can be the case. Younger men can maintain an erection longer."

Selena slipped the waistcoat from his shoulders and let it drop to the floor. "I do like it when you speak facts to me. I find it very stimulating." She started with the buttons on his shirt. "I say we conduct an experiment with scenario number two. We can try scenario one later. We have the rest of the afternoon."

"And the rest of the night."

As soon as Selena parted his shirt and ran the tips of her fingers over his bare chest, Drew was lost. "I knew from the first moment I saw you that I wanted us to be like this," Drew said roughly.

Selena pushed the shirt from his shoulders. "When you examined me last year? Truly? I felt it when I rescued you from those thugs in the alley, and we hid in the cellar. What do they call that immediate pull toward someone?"

"Chemistry?"

"Yes. How scientific. You must have studied it in university."

"Yes, but I never understood its true impact until I met you."

"Oh, well said," Selena purred as she walked around him, slowly pulling his shirt from his arms until it fell to the floor. "My... You *are* well put together." She stopped before him, reaching up, and removing his spectacles.

"Then, please continue your examination," Drew replied, swiftly removing his trousers, undergarments, socks, and shoes.

And examine, she did. Selena's hand brushed past his stiff shaft. "Yes, *very* well put together." She stopped before him, and their lips came together softly at first. Then, with an increasing hunger.

Drew pulled away and lay on the bed, propped up on one elbow with one leg bent. "Undress for me. Slowly."

She removed her various layers in the flickering firelight, leaving them in a pile at her feet. "You are entirely beautiful. Inside and out," he murmured huskily.

She was on the bed in an instant, where they commenced to explore, lick, and kiss every inch of skin. Then, he was filling her; they were joined at last. Drew slipped his fingers through hers while his other hand rested on her hip. The pace was deliberate and measured, just as he was in life. But this was Drew's new life with the woman he loved. He rolled his hips and moved faster.

Selena made a sound between a moan and a sigh. That was all he needed to hear. The pace quickened even more. Their gazes locked, adding a more profound intimacy to their lovemaking. Drew lifted his hips, and Selena met every thrust. When her nails scored his back, he held himself in check, waiting for her to reach her peak. Selena cried out. Together, they soared.

Breathless, they lay in each other's arms.

"I love you," Selena whispered.

"I love you," Drew replied. "Take a breath, my love, and we'll go again."

Her gaze trailed downward, and then she laughed. "Oh, we are going to have such fun!"

"Oh, yes. For the rest of our lives."

The following evening...

As the three couples sat around the table, Mrs. Evans brought several silver chafing dishes and laid them on the sideboard, along with a Victoria sponge cake and a three-tiered display of tarts and biscuits.

"Thank you, Mrs. Evans." Selena smiled at the cook-housekeeper. "You may go. We will serve ourselves." Selena had had quite a lengthy discussion with Mrs. Evans regarding this meal. The housekeeper had been appalled when Selena had said she would ensure the leftover food and dishes were taken to the kitchen.

"You are a dowager duchess!" Mrs. Evans had exclaimed when told of the plans. "A duchess does not clear the table or make tea!" Selena had assured her that Penny would be there to assist, and all would be well. But Selena had changed her mind and informed Penny that she would handle the hostess duties. That was another item to add to Selena's growing list: hire household staff for just such occasions.

After Mrs. Evans departed, Drew stood. "Before we dine, I want to say that as our dear friends, we wish you to attend our wedding in April."

Applause and happy exultations broke out around the table. Drew raised his hand to quiet the congratulations. "However, that will be our second wedding celebration. Selena and I were married yesterday morning at the Bow Church. Forgive us for not inviting you; it was very private, something we wanted to do together."

"You're full of wonders, both of you," Liam chuckled. "Congratulations."

Celia rose from her chair and came to kiss Drew on the cheek, then Selena. "I knew it. I am delighted at the news. You both deserve every happiness."

More handshakes, hugs, and warm wishes were exchanged, then everyone filled their plates with baked salmon, roasted chicken, and various vegetable dishes.

With the wine poured, Mitchell raised his glass. "To each of us, and all of us, may we always remain close, now and in the future."

"Hear! Hear!"

"And the next name on the list?" Corrine asked.

The men grew quiet. Drew cleared his throat. "Before we contemplate how to move forward, I believe we should focus on Lucian Sharpe. Liam was the first to notice the physical similarity. Mitchell discovered information regarding Sharpe's mother. I took that information and recently visited Damon, the current Duke of Chellenham." Drew explained in detail how he and Damon had found Sharpe's mother listed in the duke's books and her circumstances.

Everyone had varying degrees of astonishment showing on their faces.

"I believe Sharpe may be the oldest of the duke's progeny, or one of the oldest," Drew concluded. "We should not dismiss this information. Besides, I feel he will factor into Selena's sister's sudden disappearance. Mitchell started investigating today." He looked to Mitchell, who nodded. "I do not believe Sharpe is as bad as he projects. He assisted us in recovering Selena."

"Didn't he say that he wants nothing to do with us?" Liam asked. "And more than once?"

"One of my faults is that I rarely listen when people tell me to do something," Drew replied. Selena chuckled softly.

"Then, onward. To the Duke's Bastards!" Liam said, raising his glass.

Selena looked around the table. With these good and loyal friends, life would never be dull. Her loving gaze landed on Drew. And neither would it be dull with her pirate captain. She thought of the afternoon and evening they had spent together. Drew had certainly proved his stamina in all ways. Just recalling their various sessions of lovemaking caused her insides to flutter with delight. Selena couldn't wait for tonight and all the days and nights before them.

Drew was an extraordinary man. Outwardly, he projected a studious, calm demeanor, but inside was a man of great passion who felt things deeply. He was the glue that brought them all together.

And she would love him ardently and completely until the day she ceased breathing.

EPILOGUE

From the journal of Dr. Drew Hornsby, Baronet.

August 19, 1908

We have just returned home from a holiday and a picnic summer gathering of the Duke's Bastards. To say the group had grown from the initial three members is a decided understatement. I feel it only proper to put in writing how far Mitchell, Liam, and I have come in the past several years.

Mitchell Simpson: Mitchell returned to work with the Metropolitan Police in the spring of 1899 and swiftly moved up the ranks. He is now an inspector in the CID (Criminal Investigation Department) at the New Scotland Yard headquarters overlooking the Thames.

Corrine and Mitchell's daughter was born almost a year after their marriage, and they named her Rose Clara Simpson. Two years later, they welcomed a son, Charles Mitchell Simpson. With the arrival of the children, they sold the Carol Street residence and bought a larger home closer to Mitchell's workplace and not far from our house on Gloucester Square.

Corrine kept busy volunteering at the free clinics and charity work, raising money for various projects, including distributing shoes, clothes, winter coats, hats, and mittens for underprivileged children. Corrine and Mitchell experienced a near tragedy—Charlie caught pneumonia when he was two years old. Thankfully, he recovered. But as Mitchell and Corrine observed, it showed the precarious state of health and happiness, and made them embrace friends and family closely. I couldn't agree more.

Liam Hallahan: Liam and Celia made the restaurant improvements they had spoken about and took possession of the building next door for the Hallahan Initiative. It was only a small space, but large enough to run a charity kitchen, open from lunch until seven o'clock. The close-knit community family they had forged years ago with the staff is as strong as ever, a testament to the depth of their relationships. Liam has trained many apprentices over the years, always orphans from the workhouse. But the most extraordinary addition to their family? They adopted a baby girl from the Chellenham Foundling Home some years ago. Celia and Liam scaled back their duties within the restaurant, but Hope—as they named her—thrived in the busy environment.

As for me and Selena? We celebrated a large wedding with family and friends in the spring of 1899. Penny remained with us and is a devoted aunt to our two daughters, Cassandra and Brittany, and son Tremain, named for his grandfather. We located Selena's sister and her son, but I will leave that intriguing tale for another time. Selena and I are involved in our continued charity work and have found every joy we can in life, savoring and nurturing it.

We have risen above the old Duke of Chellenham's notorious legacy to be decent and honorable people. The three of us are particularly close, brothers in all ways.

The Duke's Bastards (and the Bluebells) found what they had yearned for: Family. Lifelong friends. And, most of all, never-ending and everlasting love.

<h1 style="text-align:center">Author's Note</h1>

Unwanted children have been abandoned for centuries. In Britain, it wasn't until the Adoption of Children Act of 1926 that adoption gained legal status. Before then, it was informal, if it happened at all. Most orphans found jobs in factories or apprenticeships; others wound up on the streets. An unmarried woman could not name a man as the father of her child on the birth certificate unless she gained an affiliation order against him, so most children had no idea who their fathers were.

Most widows were given a small income from their dowry or the estate from rentals or farm income. By the late Victorian age, many of these incomes had dried up. Luckily, Selena's duke husband left her something at the end. In many cases, women were often not mentioned in wills. It wasn't until the Law of Property Act of 1922 in England that a wife had equal rights to inherit.

I enjoy poring over old maps of London and researching various aspects of the Victorian era. Several streets and businesses I mention are real, but some are fictional, as are the street numbers. Devil's Acre did exist. Charles Dickens named this section of Westminster, describing that this slum "rolled its filthy wavelets up to the very walls." The demolition of Devil's Acre actually started in the mid-1880s, but I changed the dates to fit the timeline of my book.

Doctor Herbert Snow (1847–1930) developed the Brompton Cocktail, a combination of cocaine and morphine to relieve pain in cancer patients. It was used until the middle of the 20th century.

I hope you've enjoyed reading about The Duke's Bastards. And who knows? You might even see more of them in the near future.

Karyn Gerrard

About the Author

A multi-published author from the East Coast of Canada, Karyn Gerrard loves to write historical romances. Tortured heroes are an absolute must. She whiles away her spare time writing, reading romance, and drinking copious amounts of Earl Grey tea.

Karyn's been happily married for a long time to her own hero. His encouragement and loving support keep her moving forward.

Catch up with me on social media:
Website – www.karyngerrard.com
Facebook – facebook.com/karyn.gerrard
X – @KarynGerrard
BookBub – bookbub.com/profile/karyn-gerrard
Amazon – amazon.com/stores/Karyn-
Gerrard/author/B0052XUPQE
Instagram – @karyngerrard

www.ingramcontent.com/pod-product-compliance
Lightning Source LLC
Chambersburg PA
CBHW072109300726
48975CB00003B/764